D0425588

OVERNIGHT
FLOAT

overnight float

clare

munnings

W. W. Norton & Company   New York   London

For information about permission to reproduce selections from this book,
write to Permissions, W. W. Norton & Company, Inc.,
500 Fifth Avenue, New York, NY 10110

The text of this book is composed in Bembo with the
display set in Disturbance
Composition by Molly Heron
Manufacturing by Courier Companies, Inc.
Book design by Chris Welch

Library of Congress Cataloging-in-Publication Data
Munnings, Clare.
Overnight float / by Clare Munnings.
p.   cm.
ISBN 0-393-03849-1
1. College chaplains—Fiction. 2. Women—Education—Fiction.
3. Women clergy—Fiction. 4. New England—Fiction. I. Title.

PS3563.U482 094 2000
813'.6—dc21   00-031870

W. W. Norton & Company, Inc., 500 Fifth Avenue, New York, N.Y. 10110
www.wwnorton.com

W. W. Norton & Company Ltd., 10 Coptic Street, London WC1A 1PU

1 2 3 4 5 6 7 8 9 0

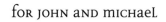

FOR JOHN AND MICHAEL

The author would like to acknowledge Debbie Federico,
Kate Baker-Carr, and Jane Uscilka.

overnight float

1

Rosemary Stubbs, when annoyed, looked like a sea squall approaching at twenty knots. In storm mode now, she left her ethics seminar, paper in hand. Tall and angular, head high and slightly cocked to listen for the New Haven traffic, she walked with the nervy energy of a thoroughbred heading for the post parade. The exchange at the end of class kept running through her head, increasing her impatience. The dean of Yale Divinity School, who taught the course, had not only cited her paper at length as a model to the other students. He'd then gone on to publicly request she stand in for him to speak about institutional ethics to a gathering of college and university business officers. Of all possible audiences, it was one she'd wish most to avoid. And it was to be on a weekend in January when she'd already promised to visit friends in Maine!

But there was nothing she could do. Feeling trapped by the plaudits of the dean and the admiration, grudging at best, of her fellow seminarians, she'd given in—weakly. Or was it graciously? How could one tell? Easy enough to put ethical labels on other people's actions . . . damned hard to discriminate among one's own intentions. Abelard, she smiled wryly to herself, had known all about that.

Perhaps if she knew her student colleagues better . . . It had been two and a half years now since she'd abandoned her life as chief financial officer at a New York computer firm and moved to New Haven to enter the divinity school, just shortly after her thirty-fifth birthday. And she *had* made some wonderful friends there—Corolla Winnants, the ex-postulant of the Sisters of Notre Dame who was now preparing for the Episcopal ministry, and Bob Tsudi, son of a long line of itinerant preachers in the Far West who'd decided in the midst of a legal career to stop making rich men richer and become a missionary himself. But like Rosemary, they were older and had never quite fit into the enthusiasms of most of the students.

She shook her head ferociously as though she meant to dislodge her thoughts from a familiar track. What difference did it make whether she "fitted in" to this setting or not? She'd come here on a pact with herself, and she would leave no nostalgia hostage to New Haven. At the moment, for whatever reason, she'd promised to do a job for the dean.

The information garnered from the dean in a subsequent phone call was not encouraging. The New England regional branch of NACUBO, the National Organization of

College and University Business Officers, had become anxious in the wake of a series of scandals involving college contracts and the disbursal of federal funds for financial aid. No longer were corruption charges bounded by the men's varsity locker room. So, according to Dean Broscow, the financial officers had decided to gird their loins and take a dose of ethics from the Yale Divinity School. "No one better than you to give it to them," he'd said in signing off, relief at his own escape curdling the edges of his teacherly solicitude.

Three weeks later, arrayed in a discreet navy suit, white silk blouse, and unaccustomed heels that made her look taller than her five feet nine inches, Rosemary turned up at Baker Hall. This outfit should make me look like a clerical type, she thought, though I certainly haven't worn anything like it since I was an assistant auditor. It's all the same, she reminded herself as she entered the lovely oval room, its incongruous rows of folding chairs only slowly filling up. This *is* my first job—in my new life.

It seemed to Rosemary that the crowd wandered in almost as reluctantly as she had herself, and it was some time before her introducer was ready to claim the podium. A fiftyish bespectacled man of military bearing, he had an unnerving habit of loudly clearing his throat. He clutched a rumpled copy of her curriculum vitae in his hands and read from it with a few misplaced efforts at lighthearted editorial comment.

"Ahem. Friends. We're lucky tonight to have the word on

business ethics fresh from Yale Divinity School. Miss Rosemary Stubbs here—mind if we call you Rosemary?—is a member of this year's graduating class. She was educated at Bryn Mawr and the Wharton School! She, ahem, worked at U.S. Computer—I don't need to tell you that's our biggest supplier of computers to colleges and universities—where she became, ahem, chief financial officer! She left that post to enter divinity school three years ago. Rosemary, even though you won't graduate until May, the dean says you're already a skilled theorist on ethical matters. Nothing like being an accountant to teach the difference between right and wrong! Things just have to add up, eh? Well . . . we're all ears."

With a staccato burst of coughing, he waved her to the podium.

This is even worse than I expected, Rosemary said to herself as she rose, smiled as graciously as she could, and looked out at the audience. It was the usual sea of gray and navy suits, interspersed with an occasional flash of color provided by the sprinkling of women in the room.

Her list of ethical dilemmas was not original, but her treatment of the way different constituencies should come into the process of calculating how to resolve them was, so that gradually the bodies slouching in the folding chairs began to straighten up, and the blank faces became attentive. "Who are you really serving in a nonprofit institution?" Rosemary asked her audience. "The clients are many, and they have conflicting interests—current students, alumni, the tax-paying public, faculty, administration, trustees."

She found herself warming to the subject as she took them through an analysis of how in each community constituencies could be affected not only by fraud but by sloppy record keeping and inappropriate, though legal, accounting treatments. Inadequate charges for deferred maintenance not only cheated future students but could mislead potential supporters by inflating the balance sheet. No system could insulate against fraud, but generally accepted accounting principles might blow away some smoke screens permitted under the old rules.

As she spoke, Rosemary caught the intense gaze of a smallish, rather stocky woman dressed in becoming red, seated at one end of the third row. Her gray hair was uncoiffed but stylishly cut, and her face, made square by broad cheekbones, was lit by striking light gray eyes. She leaned forward in her chair as though Rosemary were speaking to her personally.

Rosemary closed with a coda on the role of the business officer not only as the head of internal audit but also as the conscience of the quotidian. Every practical question ultimately would come through that office. The trick was not so much to detect fraud as to establish transparency in all dealings and to make right action natural. The applause when she returned to her place was much more lively than when she had begun.

As soon as Rosemary could escape the podium, she threaded her way to the woman in red from the third row, who rose from her seat to greet her.

"I'm Blanche Werner, the CFO at Sanderson College

and vice president of this group. I liked your talk," she said warmly. "But what about the institution itself? Isn't it also one of the stakeholders? What if blowing the whistle on some unusual financial practices would cause it to fail? We all know of such cases, and I've never been able to come to a conclusion on that question."

"To answer that," Rosemary responded, "we have to know why any institution should continue—and whether it could resume any part of its function after the trauma of exposing and curing the fraud." She stopped and looked at the smaller woman, and then continued slowly, "But why should any institution survive if a continuance of fraud is a condition of its being?"

"Just what I ask myself," said her interlocutor. "If only one could assess in advance the damage caused by a cure ... Never mind, that's not our problem tonight."

As other members, drinks in hand, approached Rosemary, Blanche offered to fetch her one too, saying that she'd be seated next to her at dinner and mustn't monopolize her for the moment.

Over the inevitable leathery chicken breast and indifferent wine, Rosemary paid perfunctory attention to the barking military man on her right, now slightly somnolent from martinis. As soon as possible, she turned to Blanche on her left.

"I'm still thinking about your question," Rosemary said, taken once again by the energy and intelligence she sensed in Blanche.

"It's a tough one, I know. I've thought about it a lot as

I've served on accrediting committees, and in these days of sudden shifts in student admissions, with all the disruption that causes in cash flow, one worries about what might happen to institutions when desperation sets in. I suppose I think the college matters more than the current generation. Wasn't the church more important than the wickedness of all those Renaissance popes?"

Under Blanche's amused gaze, Rosemary shoved her chicken to one side in exasperation and settled for a roll and butter. "Yes. Of course it was. But that doesn't change the moral predicament of anyone who connived with them, even if just by silence. But surely there's no danger of desperation setting in at Sanderson! I know it only by reputation, of course, but it's certainly noted among the women's colleges."

Blanche's eyes shone. "That it is."

"At Bryn Mawr we thought of Sanderson as a worthy rival but a distant one. What is it really like?"

"It was founded in the 1880s. It's small—we have about eighteen hundred students now. And the campus, set on the Connecticut River in Vermont, not too far above Massachusetts, is lyrical. It's a determinedly liberal arts college, of course, and still a college for women, but its real distinction is the faculty. They're absolutely first-rate. Ornery, of course, but why not?"

"Of course. The turf they're protecting is hallowed, isn't it?"

"Something like that. You should come up and visit." Blanche smiled. "But before you say yes, tell me why you're just now finishing divinity school: You were introduced as a former CFO, and you don't quite seem like the average clergywoman of uncertain age to me."

"You know the externals from my introduction. I'm not sure I trust my list of internal reasons myself." Rosemary hesitated.

"Nobody trusts their own rationalizations fully, if they're honest," answered Blanche, whose quiet tone slid under the hubbub of the room, making an island around the two women.

Rosemary began slowly, "It was two things, I suppose. When I was a child, going to church was something I did with my father. He died when I was thirteen. I'll never forget standing outside his hospital room with my mother, while they tried to revive him. Mother ran away after that. Married an Englishman and moved to England. I stayed here with an uncle. But I never could go back into a church. It was too lonely." Rosemary's voice speeded up. "After Brearley I went to Bryn Mawr. Math was easy for me, and the financial industry and accounting firms were recruiting—so I decided to become an accountant."

"Just an accountant?" Blanche's expression was quizzical.

"No, of course not. I was going to knock everybody's socks off." Rosemary smiled ruefully. "'Feminism' in my slice of the generation meant beating men in every profession they'd ever monopolized. I was damned and determined to become a CFO. And I did."

"In record time, I'd say."

Rosemary made no answer.

"You mentioned two things," Blanche said gently.

A student waiter interrupted to place before them dishes of unripe strawberries clustered around vanilla ice cream, while institutional coffee was poured swiftly but sloppily into waiting cups. Rosemary pulled the coffee toward her as she considered her response.

"I was married. A wonderful man. Jim was a lawyer, but at heart he was a sailor. And one weekend just after I'd been made CFO, we were to go sailing together. But I had work to do. So I stayed home. Jim sailed—into an unpredicted storm, it turned out. He drowned."

As Rosemary sat staring into the room, Blanche reached instinctively to touch her hand, but Rosemary took up her narrative without noticing.

"After Jim died, I began going to church again. It didn't matter. The loneliness was the same. But I couldn't go back to being a CFO. So I came here. As an experiment, I suppose."

"And now you're stuck with it?" Blanche smiled at her.

Rosemary, to her own amazement, found herself smiling in return. "I'm not sure what I'm going to do now that I've finished divinity school."

"Well, why not take our chairman up on his little gallantry and test out a college chaplaincy? It just so happens that Sanderson has an open position. Come up to Vermont and look the place over and decide whether that's the kind of work you'd like to consider."

Rosemary relaxed and turned to look directly at Blanche. "Do you always get into life-changing conversation with strangers? Maybe it's you who has the pastoral vocation."

Blanche put back her head and laughed delightedly. "No, my dear! I'm not cut out for the cloth. I do 'good work,' all right, but it's done with dollars and cents. Now, would you like to come up and visit Sanderson? I can put you up, or you could stay at the Metford Inn."

Before Rosemary could answer, a sudden scraping of chairs announced that the evening was breaking up. Rosemary and Blanche stood, produced diaries, and settled on a weekend in February.

Her introducer tapped Rosemary on the shoulder, gazing owlishly at her through a fog of alcohol. "Ms. Stubbs, Rosemary. Good of you to come. Made a real impression. Some other time, must tell me why you chucked U.S. Computer for this." He waved expansively at the emptying room. "Don't understand it. G'night."

Rosemary and Blanche stood smiling as they watched him depart.

"Never could hold his liquor," Blanche said matter-of-factly. "That probably should disqualify him from doing the books for an academic institution. Good night, Rosemary. I'll look forward to February."

Making her way across campus in the chilly evening, Rosemary felt the distinctive glow that comes from having unexpectedly encountered someone who might turn out to be a real friend. And yet she was amazed at herself. Usually she turned off questions about her own life with a few perfunctory remarks. Even now she didn't trust herself on those matters when anyone else was present. Tears were too close, and whether they came of simple loss or of guilt, she could never tell. But somehow Blanche had given her a sense of safe harbor, safe enough, at any rate, to admit the facts about her decision.

By the time she reached her own door, Blanche's invitation had taken on a real attraction. But the boisterous greeting of her aging poodle, Fannie, distracted her as she geared up for another foray into the cold to walk her. Fannie had been Jim's first Christmas present to her.

Not long after, a grateful Rosemary sank into bed. Me! Chaplain of an all-women's college, she mused, before finally giving in to sleep.

2

Four weeks later, books pushed aside, Rosemary rested her elbows on the desk that dominated the sitting room in her apartment, staring at a letter from Blanche Werner as though it might bite her. She picked it up again and reread it. Then she was on her feet pacing. What had possessed her to pour out her soul to Blanche like that? Here the woman was renewing her invitation to come up to Sanderson College, goodness knew where in Vermont. She wasn't *ready* yet to decide whether she wanted parish work or some other form of service. Rushing to divinity school had been like running for cover after Jim died. With graduation looming, that cover was thinning out, and new questions about her life were stirring up all the old ones.

The familiar surge of anger boiled up. Why had Jim gone single-handing the boat on a stormy weekend? Why hadn't she been attentive enough to stop him or generous enough to go with him? How was she going to live without him? She was a husk of a person, dead to all feeling but the many forms of her grief. She was being prodded to take up a new life. And she couldn't face it.

She stopped pacing and sank into the old sofa where Fannie lay eyeing her intently. "You've got an opinion about all this, don't you, old girl?" she asked, wrapping the dog in an affectionate hug. "Well, I daresay you'd tell me to get on with it. Or at the very least, if I'm going to pace around, to do it outside! So let's go."

Walking along the cold sunny expanse of Whitney Avenue with its capacious old houses, Rosemary began to simmer down. The question of what to do next couldn't be postponed much longer. She *had* to make some sort of a decision. And if it was wrong, well, so what. She could always regroup and try again. Why not go to visit Blanche Werner? After all, her invitation was nothing more than to visit for a long weekend and informally learn about the chaplaincy opening at Sanderson. There was no harm in putting a toe that far in the water. Maybe Metford would be enchanting. But just in case it wasn't, she would plan to go farther north to Woodstock on Saturday for some cross-country skiing. She remembered there was a B and B there that took dogs.

Satisfied that she'd hedged her bets, Rosemary looked down at the dog now trotting happily beside her. "Fannie, my girl, you're going to the groomer's tomorrow. We're heading to the country over Washington's Birthday, and you've got to look your best."

In the weak sunshine of Friday's midmorning, snow showers dusted her black Saab as she loaded her suitcase and a freshly groomed Fannie into the car. Despite her frustrating inability to decide what she wanted to do after her Yale M.Div., Rosemary's erratic spirits soared as she negotiated the weekend traffic and headed north on Route 91. It would be good to get into real countryside and spend part of a weekend with someone as savvy as Blanche had seemed. The image of a red-suited Blanche, voicing her intelligent questions, kept flashing before Rosemary's eyes. She'd allowed herself to settle too stodgily into a routine— classes, library, gymnasium, early-morning and late-afternoon walks with Fannie, an occasional movie with friends or required appearance at an evening lecture.

She and Jim had had a full social life together, entertaining his law school friends or her classmates from Wharton, going to company functions and gala dinners at the New York Yacht Club. She'd deliberately cut herself off from that life when he died, and she'd been letting her growing interest in theology and church history stand in for friendship and sociability. Her interchanges with faculty were a real pleasure, but she'd never tried to extend them beyond the library or the classroom. Her passions were intellectual but solitary, and in her current turned-off state she wasn't sure how well she could convey them to acquaintances, let alone parishioners.

An hour out of New Haven, Fannie's whimpers dictated a pause. Spotting a sign announcing a scenic outlook, Rosemary took the exit and pulled into a parking space. She walked Fannie to the edge of the outlook and stopped in her tracks. The Connecticut River Valley lay before her. The broad river glittered in the sunlight several hundred feet below, and a patchwork of snow-covered fields, barns, farmhouses, and villages rose above it, sweeping in gentle curves up to a distant line of hills. The Ice Age glaciers had smoothed the contours of the valley, leaving a wide river basin bordered by rounded hills. It was a peaceful domesticated scene, yet grand enough in scale to prompt thoughts about geological time and a different perspective on human affairs.

Settled back in the car, speeding by Northampton, Greenfield, and Brattleboro, eyeing the changing shape of the Berkshires and the recurring glimpses of the river, Rosemary was suddenly struck by something different about the day. She was registering the colors of the landscape, although since Jim's death she'd lived in a world of unchanging black and white. That's a good omen, she thought, reaching out to pat Fannie, poised for action on the seat beside her.

An hour later when the signs for Metford came into view, it became clear that Blanche had not been exaggerating when she described the beauty of the setting. The river curved in a wide arc around a town nestled beneath high, sheltering hills. The red barns and shining silos of a thriving farm community dotted the middle distance, and board fences and low stables north of the town announced horse country. The steeple of the college chapel gleamed at the far end of the town, and beside it clusters of red brick and pale granite marked the campus. The reflected light of a lake seen as a silver glimmer beyond gave the old buildings a rosy glow.

Rosemary found the Metford Inn, a rambling Colonial structure, parked, walked Fannie around the central green it faced, and then went in to find lunch. She wasn't due at Blanche's house till around four-thirty, and she wanted to explore on her own before taking on the role of weekend guest. The menu was good even by city standards. Rosemary settled for leek and potato soup, a vegetable frittata, and salad. By the time coffee arrived, strong and aromatic, the tension of a long trip on the highway had dispersed, and Rosemary began to feel the comfortable relaxation of a small community absorbed in its regular tasks.

Most of the diners had been departing as she arrived, but she enjoyed watching several lingering, animated luncheon parties, speculating about the cast of characters and their possible relationships. At one table two men and a slight blond woman were in deep conversation, punctutated by laughter. Another group seemed to revolve around a heavy-set woman dressed in stylish tweeds, who was laying down the law to her companions, a blond athletic-looking man and two younger women. They didn't look happy. Rosemary watched the dynamics of the group change when a tall, silver-haired but youthful man, in a suit of slightly exaggerated tailoring, entered the room smiling and pulled an extra chair up beside the older woman. Rosemary watched with amusement as he charmed her into a smile and the rest of the group visibly relaxed.

"Who's that who just came in?" she asked the hovering waitress presenting her check.

"That's President Eames, from Sanderson College. You ought to see Sanderson while you're here. There are some lovely buildings, and the gardens are famous. People come from all over to see them."

Despite the urging of the waitress, Rosemary skipped exploring the campus and instead drove halfway up a winding road into the hills, where she parked the car and let Fannie off her leash. The pleasure of the cold air, the gleaming snowbanks, and Fannie's excited explorations made the time race, necessitating a helter-skelter rush back to the car and a hurried drive back to the town.

Blanche's directions to her house were precise and accurate, as Rosemary had expected. But the house itself was a surprise, a spare, minimalist design of glass, wood, and stone set in what Rosemary guessed was an authentic Japanese garden. Inside, the decoration was as affirmative as the red suit Blanche had worn when they first met. The guest room showed signs of careful planning for a visitor's comfort—the upholstered chair, the well-lit writing table, a stack of recently published books on a wide range of subjects, and the bed placed just so, allowing its occupant to wake up to a panorama of hills. Blanche had provided for Fannie also, a basket and dog pillow beside the bed.

When Rosemary and Fannie appeared for tea in the living room, a welcoming fire was blazing in the fireplace. On a low table in front of the fire, flanked by two capacious armchairs, a silver tray was set with steaming pot, hot scones, and all the embellishments for Devonshire tea. A battered but elegant Duncan Phyffe sofa upholstered in faded gold velvet completed the setting. Rosemary noticed a light Japanese-style screen marking off the dining area and the Chinese rugs that covered the tiled floor.

"Now," said Blanche, expertly pouring their tea, "would you like a busman's holiday, or would you like to forget Yale and everything connected with the clergy, and just have a relaxing weekend in the country?"

"I wish I knew," Rosemary laughed. "I'd like to do both by turns if that's possible."

"Still uncertain?" Blanche asked, settling back more comfortably and propping her feet on a black leather pouffe.

"Yes. I'm more than uncertain. I'm having trouble sorting out what I feel, let alone what's sensible to do."

"Well. Let's talk about it after you've had a bath and a good dinner. I've got a bit of telephoning to do, so why don't you and Fannie just settle in, and let's have drinks around six-thirty. I haven't asked anyone for dinner tonight, because I thought you might need to unwind a bit after a long week and a long drive."

When Rosemary and Fannie arranged themselves by the fire again after Blanche's dinner—corn chowder, sole meunière, and a salad of fresh greens—the evening had settled into comfortable talk about books, music, Asian art.

With the coffee poured, Blanche sat back, patted Fannie, whose head was resting hopefully on the sofa, looked inquisitively at Rosemary, and asked the question hanging fire since teatime. "Now, Rosemary. You don't seem like a woman who doesn't know her own mind. What's bothering you about the next step?"

Rosemary smiled ruefully as she leaned forward to deposit her cup and saucer on the table. "Probably nothing more than the usual senior shivers. I've been as, well, *satisfied* as it's possible for me to be at Yale. I spent my undergraduate study in economics and math. It's only in the last couple of years at divinity school that I've discovered the whole world of church history and especially the early Christian theologians. The passion with which they drove themselves and the wonderfully complex relationship they had with the society around them fascinated me. I guess in part, I don't want to leave them."

"Then why do it? You could get a research degree and teach."

"Yes, I could. But something in me resists that." Rosemary paused. "Do you know those gorgeous old Irish manuscripts—Kells and Lindisfarne and so on?" When Blanche nodded, she went on, "Well, the monks learned to decorate them by tracing circles that had been cut into bone. Somehow I feel that in the scholarly world, I'd be forever like an apprentice monk—tracing someone else's circles. I don't have the gift to illuminate a manuscript page. My love of scholarship will never leave me, but I'm a reader, not a writer."

Blanche looked at her with approval. "Not many people know that, when tempted by an academic career. Good for you. But there are other choices."

"There are parishes. And now is the time to apply for an assistantship. But I spent six months assigned to a parish last year in Windsor, Connecticut."

"How did it go?"

"Fine. I was invited back for the summer, and I could have returned this winter."

"But?"

"But I was playing a role, not living it. I loved the hospital work and the youth group, but the daily business of the parish left me cold."

"If you mean the politics of the altar guild and the volunteers, I can understand that. Faculty politics have that effect on me here. But what do you like about clerical life? What made you choose divinity school after your husband's death?"

There was a long pause before Rosemary answered.

"Romance, I suppose. The romance of a child's dreams of security and love. I suppose I wanted to make permanent those feelings of warmth that I had in church with my father when I was a small child." She paused again, frowning, as her toe traced a pattern in the rug. "Not that I've ever admitted that to myself—before now." Her eyes were unusually bright, but there was no self-pity in the tilt of her head.

"And what was it, besides companionship and love, that Jim brought to your life?" Blanche asked gently.

Rosemary threw back her head and sank deeper in her chair, smiling. "Lightness! Jim knew instinctively how to fly before the wind. And he lived like that on land, too. Things that would frustrate me to madness made him laugh. And so did my frustration! Jim kept me from being a grind—and a bore to myself."

"And have you found any semblance of that lightness in the life you've undertaken in these last three years?" Blanche poured more coffee and stirred the fire.

Rosemary's answer came as the older woman settled back into her chair. "Yes. In advising the teen groups in Windsor. And particularly in working with the girls' club. It had a special program for girls in the old downtown, tutoring them and coaching them in basketball and volleyball. I loved it! And do you know what? The girls' grades improved that year, and not one of them dropped out of school!"

"Then you *ought* to give some thought to a chaplaincy here, or somewhere else. Its responsibilities take off from just that point. Before you leave tomorrow, you'll meet at least one of my faculty colleagues and some students, too. So you can see whether you'd like them. But remember"—Blanche's eyes sparkled at her—"you can't judge a career by your colleagues. I detest a good fifty percent of mine. Unless you decide to work on a cathedral staff, you won't see many clerics. And faculty—well, faculty are paid to live at odds with society's norms, and it gets into the blood."

They both laughed.

Glancing at her watch, Rosemary was surprised to see

how the evening hours had flown by. She and Blanche parted at the door to the guest room, where Fannie didn't hesitate to claim her basket on the floor beside the bed, and it wasn't long before Rosemary turned in, too.

"Tell me, Blanche," said Rosemary, as they walked across the campus the next morning, the slanting midwinter light refracting into little bursts of color on the snow, "why are you so settled? Have you always lived alone?"

"Me?" asked her companion, surprised. "I'm not alone in life, although it may appear so. In our case, marriage just doesn't make sense. But for fifteen years, it has given my life many more dimensions than I'd ever dreamed of as a younger woman. Autumn is so much more reliable a season than spring." Blanche smiled up at her.

"And has finance always been the right choice for you?"

"'Always' is a hard word. But I do love working behind the scenes for something I believe in. And this college is more than home to me. I graduated from it, and I still see in each generation of women who come through the gifts it gives. They grow in expertise and imagination and sympathy and, of course, self-confidence. It's a life-enhancing place, and so its financial health is—well, it's become a sort of passion with me."

"Looking around, I can see how that might happen, " Rosemary murmured.

"It *is* attractive, isn't it? Especially when the snow hides some of the horrors of our lesser architecture. But come

with me this way—I'm going to take you to one of our
quirkier relics, our nineteenth-century greenhouse, which
now doubles as an adjunct to the botany labs."

The two women turned left through a stand of larches,
their dense green needles weighed down by snow, and
descended to another distinct quadrangle at the foot of the
hill. In it Rosemary could see, cheek by jowl to a foursquare
brick building of Eisenhower-era vintage, a delicate structure of iron tracery and glass. Painted white with even its
glass panes whitewashed against the strong southern sunlight, the building curved around in extraordinary length,
putting out a bulbous two-story-high jungle room here, a
"cottage" for orchids there, and at odd angles some straightforward glass halls for growing on.

"It's wonderful!" exclaimed Rosemary.

"Wait until you get inside!" Blanche hurried ahead.

The humidity and the heat struck them full force as they
stepped in from the cold. Rosemary felt her hand grasped
and discovered a tall man, whose bald head shone with the
ubiquitous moisture and whose eyes were alight with welcome and humor, steadying her and shaking her hand at the
same time.

"Come on in. It's our formula. First we blind you, then
we dazzle you! I'm Claus Henderson. I teach botany, and
dabble in bibliography. I'm going to have my students give
you a tour of everything from phalaenopsis to *pamplemousse*.
Blanche has told me you might be curious about the college." He laughed. "In fact, she told me that if you weren't,
I'd better make you so. She seems to think Sanderson would

be good for you, and vice versa." He gave Blanche an almost imperceptible wink and steered Rosemary firmly around stacks of old terra-cotta pots and a large steamer for steriliz-ing soil.

At the entrance to the orchid house, he handed her off to three students who had disassembled a large pump con-nected to the fish pond in the center of the room and were debating the most efficient way to fix it. They cheerfully guided Rosemary through the botanical properties of the mass of blooms lining the benches and hanging from the walls.

"You're a canny old wizard," laughed Rosemary to Blanche, as they emerged into the dry cold air again. "Who could resist those students—and that setting! And Claus Henderson is a charmer."

Blanche cocked an eyebrow at her and said with a half-smile, "I've always found him seductive."

As they walked back to Rosemary's car, Blanche asked her, "Then you'll apply?"

Rosemary nodded. "This weekend has meant so much to me. It's been wonderful from start to finish, Blanche, and I'm only sorry now that I'm committed to go on farther north."

3

When the search committee met to interview chaplain candidates, Metford was alive with dogwood and spring bulbs in bloom. As she crossed the campus, Rosemary experienced a compound of examination jitters and the savage self-scrutiny that had plagued her since childhood. But no one could feel down for long in the midst of such an explosion of blue scilla, pink-edged magnolias, and rhododendrons.

The meeting room in the basement of the chapel on Cullen Street was strictly utilitarian: round oak table, metal chairs, and institutional beige carpet, the whole lot relieved only by the daffodils nodding outside the half windows high up in the brick walls.

She never caught the names of half the assembled group, because the interrogation, carefully rehearsed, began almost before she'd sat down. She guessed, wrongly, that the two men were faculty. They were trustees from the New England region with a lively sense of the challenges facing a college chapel. Two middle-aged women did look trustee-ish. The jeans and studied monotone T-shirts of the three younger women signaled students to Rosemary. One slight blond woman turned out to be a faculty member.

The trustee in a Chanel suit and wearing dark lipstick who identified herself as Madge Grant led off. "You sent in two articles you'd written on feminist questions. What does feminism bring to churches at the turn of the century? Aren't those questions really becoming *passé* now?"

So it's no holds barred from the start, Rosemary thought. But she was ready, and it might be just as well to stake out her position early. She'd do it in the driest language she could.

She looked directly at Madge Grant and spoke deliberately slowly. She was a feminist, she answered, and did not consider the question of women in the church to be merely historical. But among feminists she was probably a conservative. Early Christianity was clearly based upon the idea of women as spiritual equals of men. The institutional church had been built by progressively reducing that equality but never quite extinguishing it, since it reemerged in popular Christian belief and the cults of the female saints, and in the enclaves of freedom for women created in convents and monasteries. Protestant reformers also had tried to purge the image of the female from the understanding of transcendence, but once again many radical Protestant sects from Shakers to Christian Scientists had sprung up from popular roots to revive the idea of the transcendent female. . . .

As she droned purposefully on, Rosemary could feel the temperature in the room subsiding. She hadn't taken the bait, hadn't responded emotionally, and none of them was interested in a scholarly approach to the subject. "So," she continued with a brilliant smile at the group, "I think the record of Christian opposition to women's equality has been mixed. I see no inherent opposition between a commitment to women's equality and Christian belief. As to the current status of women in churches, well, ordination is the crucial step forward."

She paused and concluded, "But there is still the issue of

defining the churches' missions. What are churches to do, for instance, about violence against women and children in the families of their own congregations? Churches also need to face honestly the conditions of life for many women in the larger society. For Christians, feminism should include an agenda of peace and safety at home."

Gertrude Bleeker, the trustee whom Rosemary recognized as the person she'd seen berating her companions in the dining room of the Metford Inn on her last visit, wouldn't let the subject go. "It's all very well to intellectualize feminism," she persisted, "but would you permit goddess worship on the campus or over in the chapel? What language would you use about the Trinity? Change all the references to God in the liturgy to 'she' when you conduct a service?"

Something's eating her, Rosemary thought, but she's given me just the opening I need to change the subject to pastoral work. Rosemary might have been uncertain about this job if the group had wooed her, but being put on her mettle like this, ordinary contrariness made her want to win them over.

"I'm a traditionalist in liturgy, actually. The heritage of sacred music, the language of the King James Bible, the color of liturgical robes all help to evoke mystery—to move people beyond their everyday selves. But a chaplain is chaplain to the entire community, so I'd want to work with student groups from all faiths to plan worship that they would respond to. And, yes, if some wanted services using inclusive language, I'd help them do that—although I'd want to convey my own sense that we do not necessarily need to project human sexuality on something superhuman."

"What about goddess worship?" the questioner persisted doggedly.

"No. But I'd draw that line only after working with the students concerned to understand what drives them from traditional practice to a revival of primitive forms." Rosemary looked directly at the eyes under the deeply furrowed forehead until Gertrude Bleeker lowered her gaze.

Petra Hills from the faculty leaned forward, giving Rosemary the first genuine smile since she'd entered the room, but when her question came, it was the one Rosemary most wanted to dodge. "What has made you think campus ministry is your vocation? You've had another career, a very successful one. Why the change?"

Her answer, when it came, surprised Rosemary herself by its simplicity. "The students! That is, if I have a vocation for this work, it will be because they have called me to it." She turned to the three undergraduates at the table. "I don't know enough of you yet to be sure, but my sense is that working with and among you would be as rewarding as anything I can think of."

One of the students wanted to know if Rosemary could talk about spirituality with Baha'is or Muslims. "My roommate's a Muslim, and she's very lonely here," she said.

"Of course I would want to. There must be quite a number of Muslim students on campus, and if they don't have their own group for worship or discussion, they should." Apparently Rosemary's answer satisfied, for it evoked vigorous nods from the far end of the table.

Questions from the men followed the winding trail of

budgets and resource allocation, and the rest was plain sailing. Even Gertrude Bleeker relaxed, and the mood of the group, which had been reserved when she entered the room, had settled into pleasant small talk by the time of Rosemary's departure.

Not bad, she thought, as the interview ended. Now the big question is, what will I do if they invite me to come? I'll know that after I've met the students on their own ground. The few who'd been salted into the search committee were too polite to steal the conversation away from trustees. But this next interview with the students alone ought to tell me a lot about myself, if nothing else.

She knew the place well enough now to set out on her own for Stearns Hall, the building that housed the deans and the president, as well as some of the grander meeting rooms on campus.

I wonder what they'll make of me, she mused, crossing the broad expanse of green between the dormitories and the administration building. She ticked off possible first impressions. Appearance—under six feet but still tall, fairish hair brushed back off the face, hazel eyes, mouth slightly too wide for the pointed chin. Too tailored, maybe. But there was no getting around it. She couldn't look trendy if she tried.

She was inside the heavy doors of Stearns Hall almost before she noticed, her stomach beginning to churn over the possibility that she'd got it all wrong and had no vocation for the young. Following directions, she found a cherry-paneled conference room with a knot of students clustered at one end.

"Can this be all the students who care about the chapel?" she wondered to herself, as she stepped forward to ask the ten of them to sit down.

"Let's skip the introductions, shall we? You know who I am, and I'll learn who you are as we go along. Tell me about the chapel. What's it like, and what would you like it to be?" Rosemary was direct, looking at them each in turn, greeting them as equals in an important venture.

The first to speak was head of the Council of Deacons, and unhappy. "No matter what we do, we can't get people to come to chapel. We're lucky if there are twenty at a service other than Christmas vespers."

Other voices chimed in.

"They'll come for the gospel singers and the Christmas concert, and that's it.

"We've had great preachers. But no one wants to listen."

Rosemary held up a hand. "So what would you like the chapel to be?"

It should be full at Sunday services, they told her. The preaching should be brief, focused less on the troubles facing students during their college years and more on social issues. And it should be a place to celebrate life. That was why people jammed the gospel services.

But two black students disagreed. They wanted campus issues, like race, to figure in sermons. It was all very well for the crowd to come for the novelty of a gospel service, but if they went back to their dormitories with all their old stereotypes intact, the chapel wasn't doing its job. The taller and more commanding of the two went further. "I think the

chapel staff has been complicit in a lot of the racism on campus. They never tackle issues head on. Must be afraid of losing
the ten-odd regular attenders." Others felt the same way about
violence against women. They wanted the chaplain to take on
the role of educating the whole campus on problems of abuse.

As the decibel count rose, Rosemary settled in, and the
arguments intertwined. She was amazed to see that an hour
had passed without conclusion but without acrimony. She
held up a hand for silence.

"If just ten of you, the most commited to the chapel,
have these differences, imagine what the rest of the campus
is like! And we haven't begun to talk about faculty and
alumnae. I think my first task would be to get some discussion going about what the program should be and whom it
should serve." She looked around the table at the young
faces. "I wouldn't be able to do it without the ten of you
helping to rev up the discussion. I hope very much that I'll
see you all again."

As they parted on the front steps of Stearns Hall, Rosemary realized that she'd spoken as if she really wanted this
job. She watched the students go and thought she saw some
new energy in the group. And then, with a start of surprise,
she felt it there in her step, too. She set off across the quadrangle to the treasurer's office.

Her path took her past the string of dormitories on the
west side of the quad. From the windows came the thud of
rock music too recent for her to recognize. Straining to sort
out lyrics from the pounding beat, Rosemary nearly tripped
over the feet of a stalwart sunbather for whom a hesitant

sixty-five degrees had been an invitation to tan. When it reaches seventy, the lawns will be littered with bodies, she thought, smiling.

A turn in the path and she was at the steps of a granite fortress, its door protected by the traces of a portcullis over the lintel. Inside, she stopped, blinking until her eyes adjusted from the bright greens of New England in spring to the dim institutional light of an energy-conscious academic building. At the end of the hall the gloom gave way to a jumble of brilliant colors. Colorful posters lined the walls, competing offerings for Joyce in Dublin, Shakespeare at Oxford, creative writing in Iowa, Chinese in Hawaii. Students moved along the corridor and clustered at office doors. They ignored the summer blandishments of the posters and talked with the excitement that comes with the approaching end of an academic year. She passed two students engrossed in the applications of calculus to microeconomics and a larger group arguing about the place of Alice Walker in the canon of American literature. She suddenly remembered moments of intellectual pleasure at Bryn Mawr, joys crowded out by the utilitarian training of business school.

Suppressing the urge to stay and listen, Rosemary pushed open the fire door at the end of the hall and started down a set of stairs dimly lit by a series of distant fluorescent strips clinging to the high ceiling. The narrow hall below was yellow, its walls marked only by notices stating dates for submitting financial aid forms and the latest rules for repaying student loans. The third door's plaque announced, "Treasurer" and "Come In." Rosemary walked into a large rectangular room, as brightly lit as the corridor was gloomy.

"Ms. Stubbs?" A petite woman with a cheerful face and closely shorn cap of red hair rose to greet her. "Ms. Werner is looking forward to seeing you. Come this way, please."

Rosemary followed her guide, aware of the hum of voices as phones were answered and students sat with staff poring over the small print of forms. The mood of the office was as efficient as the greeting to Rosemary had been. By the time they had reached Blanche's door it was flung open, and the treasurer had Rosemary by the hand, motioning with the other to a chair opposite her desk.

Rosemary stopped, glad to see Blanche again and grateful to her for the new world that was opening up before her. Then she took in the room with a quick glance. High in the wall, just below the ceiling, mullioned windows let in strips of light. An aged refectory table was pushed against the wall beneath them, its surface almost covered with neatly labeled piles of papers. The glass-fronted bookcases covering the lower half of the two inner walls bulged with thick stacks of reports. But what set the mood of the room was its photographs, still lifes of fruit, New England wildflower fields, a single stalk of broom against a gray Atlantic seascape. The Japanese sensibility persists, thought Rosemary, as she turned to meet Blanche's quizzical gaze.

"Well?" Blanche's smile widened and her eyebrows rose. "Did they help you make up your mind?"

"The students? Yes. I almost failed to report in to you, I

was so tempted to stay upstairs and talk about American lit."

"Don't tell me you've found a vocation in a couple of hours' interviews?" The irony of Blanche's question was softened by her smile.

"No. But they made me see there's a job to be done here. I'd like to try my hand at it."

Blanche responded wryly, "Well, watch out. They're in their best spring mood at the moment, getting ready to go home. Wait till late December and early February. Students can drive you mad with complaining then, and they're remorseless. They think we're all just part of the landscape. A nice backdrop for their own emotional lives, something to project rage upon, but not real human beings susceptible to pain and disappointment ourselves."

As Rosemary started to protest, Blanche jumped up and grabbed a manila folder from the shelf behind her. "I can see you're hooked, and I'm going to take advantage of it before you change your mind. Here are the terms for the chaplain's job—salary, fringes, house, car allowance, vacation. You can negotiate about them with Nat Eames at lunch. If I were you I'd press for faculty status, even if that means you teach a course or two for very little pay. It puts you at the center of things and helps you get to know the faculty. Don't worry if Nat Eames blows hot and cold. He always does that."

Blanche stiffened for a second and then smiled. "Nat will most likely give you twenty minutes on Sanderson's one hundred and twenty years of service to women and to liberal arts education. About eighty percent of it will be true, and he's so charming he makes you think the other twenty percent doesn't matter." She paused a moment, gazing at one of the still lifes on the wall. Then she gave a shrug. "Beyond that I really can't say. You'll have to decide for yourself. In any event he keeps a good table. You'd better hurry along. I bet you'll get a soufflé for lunch."

As Rosemary was on her way out the door, Blanche called after her and added, "Feminism is a subject that makes Nat Eames uneasy, but it's a subject you'll have to discuss. Whatever you said to the search committee seems to have gone down well."

Rosemary headed off toward the student union and Cullen Street, aiming for the president's house, wondering about Blanche's unexpected ambiguity in her remarks about Eames. The thought of food and drink quickened her pace, however, and she dismissed the thought. She'd left New Haven before five in the morning. Now it was after one, and she was ravenously hungry and could do with a drink.

Nathan Eames was actually waiting for her in the driveway to the president's house. He was immaculately tailored in a bold tweed jacket and gray slacks, and his signature straight silver hair fell perfectly in a cut that was just shy of trendy. His air of welcome was irresistible. Taking his practiced handshake, Rosemary guessed that he was fiftyish, kept trim by carefully applied sport. Squash? she wondered.

"Well, Ms. Stubbs, I was afraid they had you defending Luther's ninety-five theses against all comers, and you'd never have a chance to eat! Come right through the house—we're going to dine in the sunroom so you can be seduced by the campus in springtime. Let's skip the preliminaries and have sherry at the table. That'll put you back on time."

Rosemary walked the length of a wide center hall lined with original botanical drawings to the sunporch at the back of the house, where Eames put a sherry glass in her hand. The table was set with a deep blue cloth, and a yellow tulip rested in a bud vase by each place.

She sipped her drink and wondered idly why people served cream sherry as an apéritif, while a server appeared bearing a cheese soufflé which, fortunately for Rosemary's reputation, still trembled at its full height.

"I'll bet you're starving. What time did you leave New Haven?" Eames, pressing homemade bread on her, didn't wait for an answer but continued with an easy flow of conversation. "While you get some sustenance there, let me tell you a bit about Sanderson. Then you can ask me all your questions, and I'll eat my soufflé in between answers." He smiled at Rosemary, and despite her intention to be wary, she felt herself relaxing. This man was trying to entertain her—a change from the quizzing of the morning. He wants me to like him and have a good time, even as he's sizing me up, Rosemary thought, tucking into her lunch.

"Now I know you've done your homework, Ms. Stubbs," he beamed at her, "and I don't need to tell you about the one-hundred-and-twenty-year history of Sanderson. Though, of course, you would want to know that it was founded by staunch Congregationalists. Not that there was ever a formal ecclesial connection. And not something we mention in print anymore. In fact, right around the time of the First World War, Sanderson attracted a number of faculty whom you might best call devout positivists. They built a marvelous combination of science and mathematics here. Very practically oriented. Indeed, some of our competitors—out of jealousy, I'm convinced—accuse us of being far too practical, of verging on engineering! Of course that's nonsense, although we do believe that women undergraduates, in particular, should have hands-on experience in the sciences. And what do you suppose that's gotten us?"

Rosemary recognized the rhetorical question for what it was and didn't attempt to answer.

"A *world* record!" Eames' smile was even broader. "Our graduates have taken out the highest number of patents among women graduates of any institution in the country! And that includes MIT and Cal Tech!"

Rosemary murmured in appropriate awe and wondered where Eames was leading.

"Not that it doesn't have its costs." His smile faded, and he looked into the middle distance as if inviting her to see the whole picture with him. "You see, the faculty have found their own devotion to the sciences, and the social sciences, shall we say, fully rewarding. And of course, skepticism has virtually become *the* Fine Art! So there's not much support among faculty for the chapel. And the students, well, they're deeply influenced by the faculty, of course.

"Which means that there's not much of a job here for a chaplain?" Rosemary was puzzled at the tack which a luncheon conversation that was ostensibly a recruitment tool had taken.

"There's a job, of course, and a very important one for our tiny group of believers. But it would be an uphill fight to get a larger group into the chapel. And even if that were to happen, it's not clear that the faculty would want to invest more of our resources in the chapel. Of course someone of your abilities might well succeed. But I wonder whether the task is one you'd enjoy. You've been used to a very successful life." He was pointed.

"Then, if I might ask, why are you engaged in recruiting a chaplain? And why should the chapel building still be dedicated to religious purposes? If you have the concerns you've just voiced, why go through this pretense?" Rosemary was equally pointed.

"Well, there are trustees who are still enamored of the idea of chapel. And it is an original Sanderson tradition. So, we've held the position open." Eames paused and, disengaging from the middle distance, turned to her the full force of his persuasiveness. "You know we'd love to have you take this post, Ms. Stubbs. The trustees made that very clear to me after your interview. But with your best interests at heart, I really can't advise you to take it. Unless there's an absolute revolution in the numbers attending chapel, we'll almost surely have to close the place down in a year or two, or at the very least substantially reduce the program."

Rosemary thought of the eager group of students she'd just met. Eames's cynicism put her in a cold rage.

"Is that a job offer?" Rosemary leaned slightly into the table, pressing him.

"Well, I suppose it might be, but I really don't think—"

"Then, I accept." She pushed back her chair, shaking her head at the server bearing a silver coffee pot and a plate of brandy snaps.

Eames raised his eyebrows and while accepting the coffee himself broke off her hasty departure by raising his hand. "Wait a minute—you haven't asked about salary."

"I've seen the figures. My lack of experience would undoubtedly put me at the lower end of the range."

Eames took a slow drink from his coffee cup, eyeing her appraisingly as he did so. "That can't be a tenth of what you earned at U.S. Computer, not to mention the bonuses and stock grants for a senior executive. It's none of my business of course, but I'm wondering whether you'll be able to live on a Sanderson chaplain's salary. Or if you'll want to, once you've tried it."

"You forget I've been a divinity student for three years— entirely unsalaried. It will be luxury to have monthly checks at all. And there's a chaplain's house here, a lovely place right next to the chapel. I had a tour this morning, and I'm sure it makes up for a lot of salary. It's even got space enough to cook a proper dinner and entertain students. You never can tell what home cooking might do for chapel attendance."

Eames gave her one of his most enchanting smiles. "You win, Ms. Stubbs! I've never seen anyone so anxious for a dead-end job. But far be it from me to stand against a newly minted preacher and a trustee committee at the same time. We'll look forward to having you here. I just hope you know what you're in for."

Rosemary said offhandedly, "Yes. I think I do." She paused. "I understand past chaplains have had faculty status, and I assume that goes with the job?"

Eames nodded. "You'll certainly need it."

Rosemary put out her hand for a brisk but puzzled farewell from Eames. "I'll move on then and settle the details with Blanche."

By the time Rosemary drove out of Metford around four-thirty that afternoon, she'd met with the Music Department about the organ and choir for next fall's chapel services, and confirmed her suspicions of a low starting salary with the head of human resources.

I may be crazy, she said to herself as she drove out again onto Route 91—and I'm sure Nathan Eames thinks I am—but I like the challenge of this job. All the better that the chapel is teetering on the edge of dissolution. Now there's something to focus on. By the time I've been here a year or two I'll *really* know what my calling is.

4

How could I? Rosemary thought severely. Late for the first meeting of the year with the president. Am I trying to avoid something, or is campus life making me absentminded already?

She lengthened her stride, covering the ground between

the college chapel and the administration building at double time. Eyeing the first scarlet banners among the leaves of Boston ivy that cascaded over Stearns Hall, she took the broad entry stairs two at a time. Her only other meeting with President Eames was a vivid memory. She was willing to admit that she'd revisited his question "Are you sure you want this job?" more than once since she'd graduated and made her farewells to Yale last spring. But somehow the energy the students had given her had yet to wane, and she was genuinely eager for the new fall term to begin at Sanderson.

She pushed open the heavy door of Stearns Hall and mounted the wide stairs curving past mullioned windows to the second floor. Entering the outer reception room directly opposite the stairs, Rosemary nodded cheerfully to Miss Wharton, the president's overburdened secretary.

"He's running late, as usual," Miss Wharton said, in a voice that managed to sound respectful of the demands made on the president's time and yet proprietary.

Mumblings from within and the scraping of chair legs announced the breakup of a meeting. Nathan Eames appeared, seeing a group of faculty out of the office, joking about the end of the scholarly life of summer and the impending treadmill of classes. Metford must be a shock after Paris, he teased a youngish French instructor, and the music building no match for Marlboro, he remarked to the unsmiling man Rosemary already knew as head of the Music Department.

"But we'll all adjust in a week or two." His eye picked up

Rosemary, seated on the sofa that was Miss Wharton's staging area for juggling people in and out of the office. "Speaking of adjustment, here's a terror for punishment. Miss Stubbs has just come to us from Yale Divinity School, and before that from USC. That's U. S. Computer, not University of Southern California!"

Eames laughed at his own distinction but failed to rouse an answering bonhomie from the group, whose members greeted Rosemary soberly but kindly. Abandoning any further effort at repartee, Eames glanced at his watch and ushered Rosemary into the inner office.

"Miss Stubbs, I do apologize for asking you to hurry in to see me, and then keeping you waiting, but I need your help with a—uh—delicate problem."

Rosemary, still slightly windblown from her sprint across the campus, sat down warily and prepared to listen. She crossed her long legs at the ankles and leaned forward in her chair. Eames squirmed a little in his black leather chair, looked troubled, gazed briefly at his immaculate fingertips, and then, turning to Rosemary, began to speak in a confidential tone.

"I think you've met Miss Werner, the college treasurer, haven't you?" he asked. "Of course you have," he hurried on. "She was one of the people who encouraged you to visit Sanderson in the first place. She's an alumna and interested in the chapel, as you no doubt know."

Rosemary nodded. "Yes, we had a pleasant visit. She told me a lot of the college history."

Eames nodded. "She would. She's unofficial campus historian. No one else knows as much about Sanderson as she does. Her mother and aunt were graduates." He paused and looked uncomfortable again. With the air of one mustering inner resources for a difficult task, he lowered his voice and said, "Miss Werner has been a pillar of this institution for twenty years and a very efficient treasurer. Now, however, something seems to be distracting her from her work. There are some inconsistencies in her last financial reports, but worse than that, she is"—he paused—"not herself."

Rosemary shifted forward slightly, inviting him to go on.

"That is, she's distracted and unclear in her thinking. I don't know whether she's losing her grip or whether she's . . ." Eames hesitated again and swung his chair around to look out the window. "Well, whether she's . . ." He turned around again sharply to look directly at Rosemary. ". . . been drinking, or worse."

His face showed entreaty to Rosemary. "Could you . . . could you . . . well, talk to her? See if there is something personal upsetting her?" His large hands played with a marble orb on his desk. "She needs help, Miss Stubbs, and I think you are the one to offer it."

Before Rosemary could ask the flood of questions posed by this unexpected confidence, Eames was on his feet, glancing at his watch and piling papers into his briefcase.

"Sorry, but I'm late for an appointment over at the new athletic building," he said, resuming his customary tone, "and you know that we both have to be at the old gym by seven-thirty tonight to line up for Convocation. But do see if you can help Miss Werner, and of course I shall be grateful for any advice you can give me." With that he ushered her out past Miss Wharton, nodded briskly, and almost ran down the stairs ahead of her.

Rosemary followed at a more collected pace. It was too late to go back to her chapel office and still have a moment of quiet before the ritual beginning of term. She left Stearns Hall and walked across the broad lawn that separated it from Cullen Street. The town road divided Sanderson's main campus from its more public buildings. She crossed and turned south toward the chapel and her own house beyond.

With its steeple pointing upward like a sharpened exclamation point, the old white chapel seemed to stand in exasperated challenge to the muddle of stone and brick buildings across the street.

There must be a real muddle on the other side of the road, if President Eames wants me to help sort it out, she thought. How on earth could there be anything wrong with Blanche? More than anyone Rosemary had ever met, Blanche seemed virtually inoculated against anxiety—or depression in any of its forms. Still, it was odd that in the three days since she had moved the skeleton of her possessions up from New Haven she had heard not a word from her first Sanderson friend. She stood studying the campus opposite, almost exasperated in her own right. Then she gave the slightest shrug and decided to ask Blanche herself what was up. Nothing could be easier.

The chaplain's house immediately beyond the chapel had been newly painted an antiseptic white. She made her way to it and had no sooner opened the door than all the unsettling signs of her recent migration surrounded her. Boxes, some empty, most full of books and defiantly heavy, lined the hallway, leaving only a narrow path. The living room on her left was neatly unpacked but virtually empty except for a sofa and one chair and piles of colored cushions, which she had rounded up at Yale for student sitting. Fannie, blocking the path through the hall, danced from one foot to another, anticipating an end-of-day's walk.

"Not tonight, old girl," Rosemary told her. "Performance coming up."

She made her way to the kitchen, which was hardly less cluttered than the hallway. Before starting to prepare herself an omelette, however, she picked up the kitchen phone and dialed Blanche's number. Her call was answered after only two rings.

"Hello," Blanche's clipped New England voice answered.

"Blanche, it's Rosemary! Can you come for a nightcap tonight after Convocation? I'm so looking forward to seeing you again."

"I can't." Blanche's answer was quick. "I have work to do tonight—there'll be trustees here tomorrow for the budget meeting. I must get prepared." Her voice sounded thin, bereft of the good-humored richness that had drawn Rosemary so swiftly to her last spring. Blanche sounded out of tune, oddly driven.

"Well, then," said Rosemary, persevering, "how about tomorrow evening, say about nine o'clock?"

The response was quick, almost grateful. "I'll be there, with pleasure."

As she put down the phone and put off her worry about Blanche, Rosemary remembered that tomorrow was Thursday and that she had many hours of work ahead to finish her sermon before Sunday. She would have to take Fannie out early to get in an hour's work before breakfast.

Grabbing her academic gown, still creased from shipping, and her hood, its blue-and-red velvet pouch proclaiming for all the world her new Master of Divinity degree, Rosemary set off for the old gym. The late light of early September played on the New Hampshire granite of the range of dormitories opposite her house. Their bulbous faux-Gothic visages gave an early-twentieth-century certitude to the lower end of the campus. Beyond them, the spiking yellows and occasional purple of the formal garden mirrored the last evening brightness.

Rosemary resisted the impulse to go through the garden and take the winding path along the lake's edge to the gym. This time she had better be early. After passing the first residence halls, she turned resolutely to the left and followed the wide walkway that formed the spine of the central quadrangle. Here the Gothic of the south campus was only sporadically honored. The two large classroom buildings to the east were raised up of the same granite, but ornamented in only the slightest measure by tracery at the windows. They faced a red brick language building proclaimed by its portico and columns to be neoclassical, and just to the north of it, a laboratory for the physical sciences, whose flat top and blank

glassy wastes marked it as International in style. The quadrangle was dominated at its north end by a massive library in
which the Gothic longings of previous generations had
finally become airborne. The tower over the main entrance
bore a series of generous windows, framed in ogive arches
and glazed with medieval fragments. The two great wings
flanking it marched in a series of window lozenges, each two
stories high, lifting all sense of weight from the exterior.

Rosemary paused before turning right to leave the quadrangle behind. She regarded the library with a half-smile
and murmured to herself, "You and I are going to be
friends," before plunging into the swath of larches along the
path leading to the lower campus. She cut through the circle of fine arts buildings and laboratories for the life sciences
to the far side, where a smooth expanse of grass led to the
athletic complex. The old gymnasium lay just beyond, its
original bulk crouching in a natural depression in the land,
its flamboyant addition rising like some fin-de-siècle cathedral between it and the lake.

The light was beginning to fade as she approached the
old gym. Students were streaming through its five sets of
double doors, seniors slipping awkwardly into the black
poplin robes that would set off their exalted status during
the rituals of the coming year, balancing their mortarboards
at wild angles over nose and ear. They greeted one another
with boisterous calls and hugs, welcoming each other and
the new year all at once, reveling in that singular liberation
from self-consciousness which characterizes the return of
students to a women's college after a summer's absence.

Joining the throng, Rosemary was cascaded through the doors but managed to step into the tiny faculty lounge just inside. She breathed a sigh of relief. Early. Alone for the moment. She pulled on her gown, its rich blue grosgrain rustling discreetly, and slipped the hood over her shoulders. She was almost too tall for the small mirror that hung in the far corner. Stooping slightly, she looked critically into the glass. She allowed herself a rueful smile. At least as chaplain I don't have to wear one of those dreadful mortarboards, she thought. And she ran her hands through her hair, satisfied to see that it fell back into the lines of its cut.

Having passed her own inspection, Rosemary made her way along the corridors to the training room, where the faculty, splendid in crimson, blue, and black, bearing their various universities' favors jauntily over their shoulders, gathered incongruously among machines for the enlargement of forearm and thigh. At the far end President Eames paced in his black robe in front of a long set of mirrors. Puffing slightly, the dean of the faculty, Amy Standish, arrived to complete the platform party as music sounded from the adjacent field house.

"Ready?" said Eames to Rosemary, giving her an inquiring look very different from the agitated expression he had displayed to her in his office. She nodded and fell in at the back of the faculty procession behind Dean Standish. They strode out two by two with the mix of sloppiness and grandeur by which all faculties distance their processions from those of the military.

A wall of noise met them when they entered the field

house. The excited voices of a thousand undergraduates competed with the best efforts of the orchestra, hastily assembled after the summer. On seeing their faculty, the students mingled their private hilarity with a chorus of applause and shouts of welcome. Rosemary's head spun with memories of her Bryn Mawr days.

Once on the platform, President Eames claimed the lectern and quelled the noise as if by magic. He called on Rosemary to give the invocation. Before she knew it, she was on her feet, scarcely conscious that a thousand pair of eyes were directed in cool and detached assessment at their new chaplain.

"O God, who knows the secrets of all hearts," she intoned, "open ours to one another. Teach us how to live cherishing the gifts of others. Give us grace to seek wisdom here. Give us the courage to overcome the inner fears and uncertainties which keep us from intellectual challenge. Teach us to respect the infinite diversity of Your creation, and show us Your face in the hills and streams of this countryside, so that our learning may be of the spirit as well as of the intellect."

As she turned to sit down, she noticed the faces of the audience stilled for a moment in attention. It's all right, she thought, and she felt a quiet surge of pleasure.

The program passed routinely. President Eames urged the students to understand the indissoluble relationship between a liberal education and the paideia. The dean described changes in distribution requirements. The choir sang with unexpected beauty, and the evening closed with a spirited rendition of "Gaudeamus Igitur." Watching Nathan

Eames for the sign to leave the platform, Rosemary was startled to see that even as he sang heartily, his hands were slowly shredding the program he held. Why, he's nervous, she thought. But surely he can't be worried about Convocation, she reasoned. The music signaled them up before she could catch his eye, and the platform party was forced to keep heads high and ranks closed to retrace its steps without being swamped by the enthusiasm in the field house.

As soon as the procession had made its way out, Rosemary was surrounded by faculty wishing her well and commending her brevity. Her pleasure in it all was increased when she recognized Claus Henderson in the crowd, his robe and hood caught in the crook of his elbow.

He put his hand lightly on her shoulder. "Good job!" he congratulated her. "You caught the pantheism that's common to all students, and you'll never go wrong if you build on that."

Before she could acknowledge his compliment, he was gone.

For all its boisterousness, the Convocation left Rosemary with a feeling of satisfaction in her new community, so noisily at peace with itself. That'll do for today, she thought as she eyed the packing boxes on her return home. They'll keep until tomorrow—as well as you, Fannie. You can have a real run in the morning.

The first light of morning was Fannie's excuse. She had Rosemary up and dressed for jogging long before six. Together they ran across the empty street, Fannie making arabesques between the curbstones, and cut into the south campus. Heading straight between the dormitories, Rosemary made for the gardens and lake beyond. The beds, full of empty spaces occupied by lupine and bridal wreath gone by, were still putting on a brave occasional show with bursts of heliopsis punctuated by the somber warning of aconite and the paler lavender of the first Michaelmas daisies. Rosemary had paused at a shaded corner to bend over a delicate patch of fall anemones when a sharp flurry brought her attention back to Fannie.

"Fannie, let that rabbit alone!" No good. They were gone, around the stone wall and down the embankment toward the lawn that stretched to the lake. Rosemary shrugged, picked up her run, and was not surprised to have Fannie trip her up, panting and undaunted, within two hundred yards. The air was still, and no sound came from the water that seemed at rest on the marshy ground that pillowed its edges. Rosemary and Fannie headed south, running the path between lawn and lake, and then following the shoreline as it turned into the woods that provided Sanderson's refuge from itself. They ran on, Rosemary stopping now and then to throw the stick Fannie insisted on retrieving for her. She was surprised to meet no other runners on the first day of classes, but then, remembering the excitement of the night before, she dismissed the thought.

They were turning out of the woods at the north end of the lake when the harmony of the long path gave way to signs of human disruption. Cement mixers and a backhoe had left a series of pockmarks where there had been lawn. The lakeside was smeared with oil and mud. Just beyond, the new athletics building rose, almost complete for its official opening in a few days.

Rosemary stopped, head cocked to take in the full folly of the extravagant building constructed to house a pool of specified Olympic proportions with squash and tennis courts. *Mens sana in corpore sano* . . . does that really mean equal space for the library and the gym? she thought.

She picked up her pace again and was almost past the old gym and into the lower campus when she realized that Fannie was gone. Rosemary turned, waited, and headed back toward the lake.

"Fannie! Fannie! Where are you?" she called. It was not until Rosemary had decided to plunge back into the woods that she heard a faint barking. She turned, listened, and changed direction. The sound, louder now and more insistent, seemed to be coming from the construction site. Reluctantly, she threaded her steps between the slicked puddles and over planked walkways. She could see Fannie's footprints circling in the mud. She called again, "Fannie!"

In response, Fannie's barking grew more frantic. Rosemary frowned and went on, coming to the long wall of the new building. She made her way along it until she caught sight of one of the side doors, apparently wedged open in the mud. "That must be it. Darn that dog!"

Twisting slightly, Rosemary eased in the door and found herself in a large space lighted by a rolling series of skylights. The pool was filled already, in preparation for the opening. As her eyes became accustomed to the shimmering light, she saw Fannie in the far corner, feet planted, whining now in a high keen. Clearly, she was not going to come.

Rosemary strode toward the dog at the end of the pool. Ahead she saw something gray in the water. Coming closer, she saw it was a human shape, floating facedown in the pool. Heart pounding, she knelt down and reached over the edge. She grasped the clothing on the far side of the body and pulled, but the weight of the body resisted. It rolled over slowly toward the edge of the pool, and Rosemary found herself gazing at the sightless eyes of Blanche Werner. Fannie kept up her whine. There was no other sound but the gentle sucking of the water against the edges of the pool.

Rosemary's shout for help died in her throat, silenced by panic as the bloated body brought her back to the horror of identifying Jim's body after it had been recovered from the ocean. Now she was looking at a distended, obscene version of Blanche, and her horror mounted. There must be an office open, a telephone, some way to summon help. But the telephone wires hanging from the wall told their tale. The building wasn't yet connected.

Rosemary made one more try, pulling hard at Blanche's arm and the wet material of her skirt, but her hold slipped, and Blanche's body rolled grotesquely away just beyond her reach. I've got to calm down, she told herself, trying to catch her breath. Go for help. She scooped up Fannie in her arms and ran toward the door. Her mind coursed between anger that the vibrant Blanche she'd known was dead and efforts to remember where the nearest campus security call box might be. As she pushed open the wedged door and raced into the morning light, she began silently to recite the prayers for the dead. The effort calmed her. She found her breath and began the long pull up the hill.

5

Rosemary ran toward the main campus with legs that seemed weighted by lead. Her knees and feet were suddenly clumsy, and the long stretch of the college quad gave her a nightmarish sense of running in place. Everything was wrongly, madly asleep. She turned behind the library and headed for Stearns Hall. Not until she got to the upper campus could she hope for signs of life.

Suddenly she spied a security car ahead of her. She waved frantically. The driver slowed, and Rosemary grabbed for the passenger door. In her panic she almost fell onto the front seat with Fannie.

"Blanche Werner. In the pool. The new pool. Dead."

"What?" The campus security officer's broad face was blank, weighing incredulity against belief.

"I'm the new chaplain. Rosemary Stubbs. It was the dog, she nosed in an open door, and—and when she wouldn't come, I went in and—found her." Rosemary covered her face with her hands as she struggled between shock and despair.

The officer looked at her in concern and picked up his transmitter. "Operator, Larry Bogdanowicz here. Car number one. Report of an accident at the new gym. I'm going to investigate, and I'm sending the chaplain into the office to give a statement. Have the number two car come over here to pick her up." He deposited a slightly calmer Rosemary on the edge of the quad and sped away.

A second security car appeared in minutes to pick up Rosemary. They drove out onto Cullen Street and sped past the main campus, headed for the physical plant building that lay past the south end of the lake.

"You'd better come in," he said to Rosemary as they pulled up outside the squat brick building that housed the campus police. "You look as if you could use some coffee."

She got out, clutching the dog.

The security office was a small room where the college operator did double duty as security receptionist.

"Hilda, this is Dean Stubbs. She's reported an accident. Could you get her some coffee while I go into the office to call Ted?"

The receptionist nodded reassuringly, accustomed to managing the minor crises of a closely knit academic community. Her whole manner radiated the conviction that everything would soon be all right. She walked over to the far side of the room and poured a mug of coffee from an electric percolator.

"Here you are. It won't be long now. Ted, Chief Brown, will be right in."

Rosemary forced herself back into the present moment, away from the memories that played in her mind. "Thank you. That's so kind of you. Really, I'm all right."

Before Hilda could respond, Larry Bogdanowicz reappeared. "Miss Stubbs, Ted Brown, our head of security, is going to meet me where you found Ms. Werner. He's calling the Metford police—their detective will be on his way, too. Do you feel well enough to come with me?"

Rosemary nodded.

They climbed into the car and headed north, circling the woods, to the far end of the lake. Coming in on a service road, Larry took them along the boundaries of the playing fields and right up to the new athletic facility. Rosemary was grateful to hear him suggest that they wait outside until the others arrived. Gravel crunched as a third security car sped past the playing fields toward them. Swinging his car around next to theirs, Ted Brown stepped out.

"Hello, Dean Stubbs. Sorry to meet you this way. What a terrible shock for you." Ted Brown's reserve and bearing suggested to Rosemary that he might be a retired state police officer. "Will you show us the way?"

Rosemary nodded and turned. Before heading for the new building, she leaned down and opened the car door, handing Fannie quietly back inside. "I'll lead," she said and lowered her head. She retraced the way over planks and around potholes and heaps of sand until they came to the wedged metal door. Instinctively, she turned her eyes away from the pool as they entered. She pointed. "There at the far end."

Ted Brown resolutely paced out the distance to the pathetic gray form in the water. She saw him bend over and then quickly avert his eyes. He stood and motioned Larry Bogdanowicz to join him, and the two men strained to lift Blanche Werner as gently as they could out of the water.

Rosemary's heart was sick. She heard in her mind the musicality of Blanche's voice from last spring and then how it had sounded just last night—so puzzlingly tense and short. As she turned away, she was startled to find herself looking directly into the brown eyes of a slight man just easing his way through the doorway. His hair waved back crisply from a high forehead, and he engaged her with equally crisp inquiry.

"Miss Stubbs? I believe you made the discovery. I am Raphael Ramirez. The Metford chief detective." Without waiting for a reply, he walked on with a clipped stride, his precise dark suit and polished shoes a contrast to the uniforms of the other two officers. It was evident that the Sanderson men respected him. They moved back while Ramirez crouched down to make a close inspection of the body. Then he rose and sent out a series of instructions over his pocket transmitter. He addressed the little group: "The ambulance will be here in a matter of minutes. I suggest we go outside to wait."

Gradually, a crowd formed outside the isolated building. An ambulance team arrived with a stretcher; then a doctor; then a team of photographers.

Rosemary suddenly felt faint. She looked at her watch and saw that it was just seven-twenty, but it felt as if years had passed since she'd climbed out of bed that morning. "I'd like to go home, get out of these running clothes, and leave Fannie," she told Ted Brown. "Would it be all right to do that?"

He conferred a moment with Chief Detective Ramirez. "Larry Bogdanowicz will go with you. When you're ready, please come back to the campus security office. They'll take your statement there," Brown said.

Rosemary was about to protest that she'd be happy to go alone when she realized she was under polite but firm surveillance. Walking back to the squad car, they met Nathan Eames. In his tweed jacket, he managed, despite the hurry in his steps and the deep lines in his brow, to give off an aura of propriety.

"Terrible news, terrible." He shook his head. "Such a hardworking woman. But she just wasn't herself. . . . I must get down there. Where is Ramirez? Inside?" Without waiting for an answer, he pressed on past them.

As the security car made its way back to the main road, Rosemary gazed hungrily at Cullen Street, drinking in its normality. Her modest house, back by the chapel, stood as when she'd left it. Practicality temporarily overrode her sense of horror. Fannie and the cat must be fed. Larry Bogdanowicz would probably like a cup of coffee. His calm demeanor belied her own growing sense that something profoundly evil had intruded on this idyllic rural campus.

The deposition was mercifully straightforward. Time, place, reason for run, Fannie's behavior. Afterward, Rosemary walked slowly along the edges of the campus, watching it now all alive with the bustle of classes and students on the wing. She bypassed her house and went straight to her office. Entering the chapel by a side door, she passed the simple rectangular space with its arched ceiling and plain wooden pews and went through a door at the side of the choir. A narrow corridor led to the annex beyond. Rosemary's office was straight ahead, next to a larger meeting room and its indispensable kitchen.

Here she had fully unpacked and was already at home. Her own Heriz rug was on the floor, her computer on the desk, and books ranging from Augustine's *Adversus Pelagium* to Seamus Heaney's *Collected Poems* were carefully arranged on three walls. It was a peculiar mix: a reader's library but a scholar's too in the field of her own growing passion—those God-ridden men and women of the late Roman Empire who long before had faced chaos and, more often than not, had faced it down.

Determined to face down her own feeings, Rosemary drew her chair up to the desk. Something had happened to Blanche before her death. She had Nathan Eames's testimony to that. And Blanche's own voice on the phone, so unusually rattled last night. Was there anyone else who might have known what was troubling her? She thought of Claus Henderson and immediately dialed his office. There was no answer there or at home. The Botany Department secretary hadn't seen him that morning.

Rosemary shifted in her chair and then got up to pace restlessly around the room. Her mind sifted impatiently through the few facts she did have about Blanche. They were too few. Somehow Blanche had been present for Rosemary's needs without putting forward much information about herself. Could Blanche have possibly committed *suicide*? The idea went against all sense, but how else could she have drowned in that remote pool?

Dissatisfied, she returned to her desk and absently flipped on her answering machine, an awkward relic preserved by the college's parsimony—or its poverty—in failing to invest in a campus voice-mail system. The first messages were eerily routine. The dean of students wanted her to meet with a returning student overcome by grief at her mother's illness. A tearful freshman wanted reassurance. The rabbi wanted to talk with her about an interfaith service. An unknown faculty voice, identifying itself as that of Kevin Oxley from the Classics Department, had called to congratulate her on her invocation.

But if the spread of bad news was not instantaneous on campus, it was rapid. The next message came in a voice choked with shock. "This is Gilbert Florian, English Department. Is it true about Blanche Werner? Is it true that you found her? I can't believe it. . . ." Then another, almost the same, from a student, whose voice broke.

Rosemary turned off the machine and rested her head in her hands. The blood pounded in her temples. There was no surefire antidote to grief; she saw Blanche again, helpless and gray in the water, and beyond her, an image of Jim, his body bloated by two days in the surf.

"I thought I'd find you here." A sharp but friendly voice threw out a lifeline and pulled her out of her thoughts.

Rosemary looked up to see a woman whom she recognized from the search committee last spring. Her straight blond hair was bobbed below her ears, and she was so slight she looked at first glance like an undergraduate. But the steady seriousness of her gaze was an unmistakeable sign of maturity.

"Thought you might be in a funk. I heard about Blanche." Her eyes wrinkled into tiny pouches in the corners as she smiled at Rosemary.

In spite of herself, Rosemary smiled back. "How did you know?"

"Easy. Just imagined what it'd be like in your place.. I'm Petra Hills. We met just briefly last spring. But I knew Blanche pretty well, and I know that she liked you." She paused. "Any way you look at it, this is a wretched business. It must have been unspeakable for you." Petra's face softened.

"Oh, I am glad to see you! Can you stay a minute—sit down, I mean?"

Petra sank into a voluminous chair designed to provide both comfort and confidence. "You did find her, then?"

"Yes."

"And now you can't get away from that sight. How well did you know her?" Petra pressed on.

"Better than I knew anyone else here, but not really well at all. I do know she was upset last night before Convocation. I called her to invite her over. But she was very distracted. I didn't know what to make of it—in fact, I didn't make anything of it at all at the time. Now I can't get it out of my mind. Do you know if there was something upsetting her?"

"I don't know of anything specific," Petra replied. "But Blanche had been, well, almost manic in the last few weeks. You could never get hold of her—she was always working. And if you did catch her on the phone late at night, she was very short with you. It was as if she was too busy to be disturbed, which was unlike her."

"Don't colleges end their fiscal year on June thirtieth? Could Blanche's distraction have come from trying to close the books and prepare for the auditors?"

"Unlikely. She'd been closing the books every year for twenty years now. In fact, I think she'd handed most of that off to the comptroller, Pete Zukowski."

"Had she ever been like this before?" Rosemary pressed.

Petra was adamant. "Never. Blanche was the most normal person I ever met in my life. She took everything in stride." Her eyes ranged over the top of Rosemary's bookcases. "She loved the outdoors and seemed to see human life as part of its rhythms. She was a gardener and a hiker—even an ocean kayaker. She dealt with whatever nature handed out, and about everything else she was equally unflappable."

"That was my impression, too."

There was a long pause, each of the two women absorbed in her memories of Blanche. Finally, tentatively, Rosemary asked, "Petra, is it conceivable that Blanche could have taken her own life?"

"Impossible!" Petra's answer was ferocious and unshakable.

"But then, why . . ."

"I know," Petra interjected. "Why was she in the new athletics building at all? And at night? And why did she go by herself? How on earth could she have slipped? She was as agile as a cat." Petra paused. "I don't know the answers to any of those questions, Rosemary. And I sure as hell hope the police will care enough to find out!" She looked at her watch. "Look, I have to go. I have a class in twenty minutes. But I'll catch up with you soon. You'll see—there are a lot of people who are glad you're here, not just Blanche."

Rosemary saw her out, grateful for her visit, hoping that with someone like Petra around she might think her way out of despair and concentrate on the reasons for Blanche's death. Anger being a familiar ally in her own life against the paralysis of sadness, she was grateful, too, to sense Petra's anger at Blanche's loss.

Rosemary switched her answering machine back to play and began returning calls. The student who had called about Blanche was Leslie Martineau. Rosemary reached her, unexpectedly, still in her dorm room.

"Leslie, it's Rosemary Stubbs."

"Hi, Dean Stubbs. Thanks for calling back. I, I heard about what happened to Ms. Werner. And that you found her. I sort of knew her. Not very well but maybe too well." The voice was young and troubled.

"Look, I'm here in my office. Since it's only the first day of classes, maybe you'll have time to stop in," Rosemary suggested.

"I could, but not until lunchtime."

"Right, then. See you here around noon."

Rosemary turned to her work with a will. Before clearing out the routine things, she was in touch with Miss Wharton and then Nathan Eames. Blanche had no nearby relatives. Yes, Rosemary would call Blanche's family and make plans with them about a memorial service, and she would call the funeral home. The president would be too busy with trustees in town. Miss Wharton was clearly gratified that another set of shoulders could carry these unexpected burdens. Drifts of people came by Rosemary's office as the morning wore on. Faculty and staff, looking for confirmation of the rumors that flew everywhere. Students, some of whom had known Blanche and others who came with their own concerns.

The last of the curiosity seekers had just left when Leslie Martineau appeared in the doorway. Rosemary rose to meet her and was struck by how tall and thin she was. Her prominent cheekbones and high-bridged nose would have been handsome in repose, thought Rosemary. But now deep frown lines distorted her face, and she had bitten her lips until they were puffy.

"Come on in. I'm glad you could make it." She waited as Leslie folded herself into the big chair. "Are you a senior?"

"Uh-huh. I've been here all three years, four now. I didn't take junior year away because of crew." Leslie's voice was deep, but her words were clipped, as if she had little patience with formality.

"Sanderson has a winning crew, doesn't it?"

"Yes, it has, or anyway it did. That's what I had to talk to you about, Dean Stubbs. You see, that's how I got so angry at Ms. Werner."

"She was an oarswoman too, wasn't she? I just discovered that she liked ocean kayaking."

"She might have. But she didn't really care about rowing! It was a *scandal*. Mr. Barbour, our coach, has had a team in the Nationals every year. And we've won three times! But Ms. Werner never let us have enough money for shells. Our practice boats are so old that we have to spend half of our time on repairs. And she wouldn't let us get a new racing shell for this year's season. You should see ours in comparison to some of the crews'—it's much heavier! You know, every pound means seconds in the water. It's not fair!" Leslie's voice was full of indignation.

"But I thought Ms. Werner was a supporter of the athletic program. Didn't she help find the money for the new athletic facility?" Rosemary was puzzled.

Leslie shook her head and then broke into a smile. "That's what's so strange. She did. And the college did build that pool to Olympic standards." Then her face darkened, and she shook her head violently.

"Look, Dean Stubbs, I have to tell you this. I have to tell somebody. You see, everybody thought that when the new building went up, it would mean that the college would really recognize women's athletics. Recognize what it means to be the best you can be and still live up to what your professors expect of you. Do you know what I mean?"

Rosemary nodded.

Leslie went on, "I mean running every morning until

you change the density of your bones and rowing just after the ice blocks in March until you can carry that boat over water. And standing together. Making sacrifices together. That's what we pledged to the college. And that's what we thought the college had pledged to us. That is, until yesterday. When we came out for our first practice, we were told that Ms. Werner said the money for all intercollegiate teams would be cut this year. And that the crew wouldn't be allowed to go to the Nationals or to Dad Vail—the regatta in Philadelphia—even if we qualified. Oh, Dean Stubbs! I was so angry. I'm captain of the team this year. We have a terrific stroke—she's a senior, too. And our number four is maybe the best in the country. We could have won. But she wasn't even going to let us compete! This is the terrible part, Dean Stubbs. I was so angry. In the middle of the team meeting, I just blurted out, 'I wish she were dead.' And I meant it."

"Leslie." Rosemary leaned forward, intent on capturing the attention of the young woman, who seemed about to spin off into a cycle of self-flagellation. "Leslie, you were spiteful, and you meant to hurt. *But you didn't intend that Blanche Werner die. Did you?*" Rosemary fixed the student with an unyielding look.

Leslie raised her eyes and returned the gaze unflinchingly. "No."

"Since that is the case"—Rosemary's body relaxed just the smallest degree—"you had no complicity whatsoever in her death. But I suggest you do think very hard about the way you express your anger. As for Ms. Werner, you owe her nothing but respect for the tragedy of her death."

Leslie listened with concentration. Then, with Rosemary's encouragement, she described in more detail the puzzling cancellation of the crew's intercollegiate schedule, the abrupt announcement that Sanderson "could no longer afford it," and the confused and bitter consternation of the crew members. Eventually, at Rosemary's prodding, Leslie was ready to set off again, determined to understand the reasons for yesterday's decision and, with her fellow athletes, to work constructively to reverse it.

Rosemary rose, drained, and headed out with the hope of fresh air and a walk. Just as she was locking her office door, another call forced her back. It was Penelope Wharton, the president's secretary. The trustees were assembled in the library at this moment, at least the finance committee of the board, and the president would like Rosemary to join them to give an account of what she knew about Blanche's tragic end.

"Right now?" Rosemary asked, appalled, thinking how exhausted she was and how unlikely she was to be articulate. But Penelope Wharton was adamant on the president's behalf, and Rosemary reluctantly squared her shoulders, paused to dash some water on her face at the chapel sink, ran a brush through her hair, and set out for the library.

6

Penelope Wharton met Rosemary on the library steps. "I'm sure you know your way through the collection already, but President Eames thought the route to the Cameron Room, where the trustees meet, might be confusing," she said. She turned and led Rosemary past the high stone arches of the entrance vestibule and through an oak door that might have been the entry to a medieval treasure room. On the other side was a large staging area, its grand dimensions pared to contemporary scale by a dozen office partitions, its center holding hundreds of books stacked on tables and movable trays, poised between delivery and use. Among them twined a thread of purposeful activity as cataloging librarians moved books back and forth among an array of computer terminals.

Despite her destination, Rosemary felt the magnetic tug of the unexplored as she passed the bright piles of new titles, their dust jackets not yet stripped in conformity to the sober expectations of an academic library. Miss Wharton never deviated except to nod to various members of the staff as she passed diagonally across the room to an elevator at the far side.

"There is a stairway, but this is quicker. And for people like me it saves breath on the other end."

"Ah, there you are." Nathan Eames was waiting at the elevator door on the sixth level. Looking polished in a dark gray suit, the president invited her in. His arm reached behind her, detaching her connection to Miss Wharton and the world below, as he guided her down and across the hallway to a room patterned with dancing squares of cobalt and crimson and gold. The afternoon light played through a range of stained-glass fragments. Eames paused on the threshold.

"You were good to come. The finance committee of the trustees acts as an unofficial executive committee. They're here today for a regular budget meeting, but Blanche's death seems to make all that moot. The chair of the board, Melanie Storey, asked to have you come to tell them how you found Blanche and what you might know about her death. Detective Ramirez will be here later. It shouldn't take too long." His tone was conspiratorial. He's forgotten, thought Rosemary, that I've dealt with boards of directors for a long time now. There's no mystery for me in their workings.

"Before we go in, let me give you the cast. Melanie Storey's husband is the CEO of Reoplex, the plastics firm. Mary Winchcombe is African-American, very successful in life insurance, the investment side. I think you've met Gertrude Bleeker, the alumna who gave us the new athletic center. There's Ross Easterly, chairman of the committee. He's an engineer who moved into finance—now he runs Everdale Properties, that highly successful REIT. We're lucky to have someone with his know-how."

As Nathan Eames ushered her into the boardroom, the low buzz of conversation subsided, and all eyes turned toward Rosemary.

"My dear, it's so sad that your first days at Sanderson

should be taken up with this tragedy," Melanie Storey greeted her with the voice of an accomplished hostess. "We're all in shock. Blanche was such a fine woman."

Ross Easterly extended a firm, well-tanned hand. "It's good to have you here, Ms. Stubbs," he said, his voice underscoring his careful choice of "Ms." as a form of address.

Nathan Eames pulled out a chair and motioned Rosemary to join them at the end of the long oval table. Two places were vacant, neat stacks of memoranda and financial statements awaiting late arrivals. Melanie Storey pushed back her thick mane of salt-and-pepper hair and leaned forward.

"Dean Stubbs, we're so glad to have you here. We really need someone with your training and breadth of experience. But please don't think we're neglecting all you bring to Sanderson if we ask you today about finding Blanche Werner."

Rosemary, accustomed by now to telling her shocking story, described her morning run, Fannie's excursion, and the search with its chilling end.

"Thank God it was you who found her, not some outsider who would have run straight to the press," Ross Easterly said. "Nat has done a wonderful job of keeping the reporters at bay." It was clear from his manner that the smooth management of misfortune ranked high in his catalog of virtues.

Mary Winchcombe's concerns were both personal and professional. "Did she have any close family? Or a particular friend?" Her brow furrowed with new concern. "Is there anyone who could claim we were negligent about leaving that door open?"

Nathan Eames responded quickly, "Blanche had been acting very erratically lately. She often seemed to forget herself. In the last few weeks I sometimes wondered if she even knew where she was or where she was going. I don't think anyone could claim negligence against *us*."

In the shocked silence that followed his blunt comment, Rosemary offered reassurance. "I've contacted Blanche's family. There are only two nephews and a niece. She did live alone. . . . Her closest nephew seems very distressed about her death—terribly saddened but certainly not angry or accusatory toward the college. He will be up tomorrow to talk with the police and also to meet with me about her memorial service."

Eames nodded. "I've also heard from Blanche's lawyer. Except for her household things, she left everything to Sanderson. At least she didn't try to change her will in the last few months."

Mary Winchcombe looked sharply at him, but sounds of arrival in the hallway interrupted before she could speak. The door was flung open, and a smiling woman in her thirties entered, a patch of crimson from the windows catching her in its light. Rosemary remembered her vividly from the search committee.

She greeted the others with, "The late Madge Grant! Oh, heavens—that wasn't very nice! Sorry." Her apology rippled around the table, encountering the reserve of her colleagues.

Eames came to her rescue, acknowledging the tall figure behind her. "You're in good company this time, Madge. Ben Proctor is the most punctual man on this board, as a rule. Hello, Ben. A difficult trip up from New York?"

"Traffic at La Guardia. The usual thing—we were closed up and on the runway for an hour and a half."

"Both of you, please, meet our new chaplain, Rosemary Stubbs. She's the one who found Blanche this morning. Dean Stubbs, Professor Proctor of Columbia University, and Madge Grant, one of our young alumnae entrepreneurs. Madge started a clothing store for teens on Newbury Street and now has a chain throughout the Boston area. Maybe you know them, New Berries?"

Madge leaned forward to take Rosemary's hand, undeterred by the disapproval in the room. "I think we met in the search for the chaplain. Glad you were willing to take us on."

"Now," Melanie Storey broke in, "we have a tight schedule today. We've just made Dean Stubbs tell us the ghastly story of finding Blanche, and I'm not going to ask her to repeat it. Dean Stubbs is an early-morning jogger with her poodle as company. The dog disappeared near the new gym, and when the dean caught up with her, the dog was standing by the body at the far end of the new pool." Squaring her shoulders and brushing back her errant hair, she continued, "We've been lucky about publicity so far. Just some reports of accidental death. But Nat has quite shocked us with an account of Blanche's behavior over the last few months. More than a bit ragged, apparently. Worrisome."

"Thanks for keeping us on course, Melanie," Eames interjected. "Yes, I'd been very concerned about Blanche, had even conferred with Dean Stubbs about her." He paused. "I don't know whether you were able to see her?" His broad face turned to Rosemary, a slight lift to his eyebrows.

"No. I did call her just before Convocation, but she said she would be busy later on. We had made a date to meet tonight." Rosemary looked down at her hands.

"Well, if you ask me, Nat, I think you should have seen her yourself." Gertrude Bleeker hunched forward. "You said yourself that she was erratic. I think it was a good deal more than that. She's been absolutely irresponsible recently, dismantling programs we'd just raised money to support! Suppressing intercollegiate competition when we were just funding a new athletic complex. It was worse than irresponsible, it was downright criminal. And you should have told her so yourself."

Melanie Storey turned to face her colleague. "There's nothing to be gained by that kind of talk, Gertrude. Blanche is dead, tragically dead. The entire college will mourn her as a—"

A quick tap on the door interrupted her and brought Nathan Eames to his feet. He opened the door to Raphael Ramirez, who took in the whole room as he shook hands with each trustee and nodded to Rosemary, who rose to take her leave.

"No. Please don't depart, Dean Stubbs. I want you to hear my report to the board, for you've been involved in this sad event as much as any of us."

Ramirez sat down in the chair Eames pulled out beside Melanie Storey, placed a neat manila file on the table, and rested his folded hands on it. He was dressed in a dark blue suit, his red patterned tie as securely in place as the disciplined waves in his hair.

"Mrs. Storey, President Eames, you've heard, no doubt, about Dean Stubbs's discovery of Miss Werner's body. What I have for you this afternoon is a preliminary forensic report. The medical examination suggests that the treasurer died somewhere between ten-thirty p.m. and twelve o'clock last night. Miss Werner did not drown. She had stopped breathing before she fell into the pool."

Rosemary felt her own body stiffen as if to ward off his news. Looking around, she saw the others flinch as the consequences of the detective's words played out in their minds.

"Impossible!" Eames was the first to recover. He brought his hand down flat on the tabletop for emphasis.

"Good heavens, she must have had a heart attack!" exclaimed Melanie Storey. "That would explain everything. Poor thing, if she'd had angina for months, no wonder she was short-tempered. She should have *told* us about it."

"But Melanie," Mary Winchombe interrupted, "why on earth would she have gone to the new pool in the middle of the night, especially if she was feeling ill?"

"Well, you know Blanche." Ross Easterly was clearly relieved to fasten on to reasonable explanation. "She always had to check everything herself. Probably wanted to see that the workmen had finished the punch list for that day."

Ramirez raked the group with his gaze. "I'm afraid that's unlikely, Mr. Easterly. Miss Werner would hardly have been in a condition to inspect a construction site. Her blood-stream carried a lethal dose of digitalis. We are checking her medical records today. Either she had overmedicated herself or someone else took her life."

There was a sharp intake of breath, but no one spoke. Several trustees, incredulous, nervously rustled their papers, as eyes shifted one to another.

At last, Madge Grant burst out, "I don't believe it! Your pathologist must have gotten his cases mixed up. Blanche would never make a mistake like that. And nobody would even *think* of murdering her in cold blood. She was one of those rare people who are universally useful. There wasn't anyone who could do without her!"

A tremor of hostility toward Ramirez and his conclusions seemed to roll around the table, and a murmuring broke out among the trustees. Rosemary sat numbed, unable or unwilling to move to any conclusions of her own.

"I defy you," Madge took up once more, "to find anyone who wanted Blanche Werner dead!"

Ramirez sat immobile except for his eyes, which moved without expression from one to another. He spoke to Madge in a tone low enough to force her to lean in toward him to hear. "I'm afraid, Miss Grant, that that is exactly the job before me."

An angry hubbub broke out. Eames's voice cut through it all. "This is what I've been trying to tell you all. And why I turned to Dean Stubbs here. Blanche was definitely not herself lately. I suspected she was having some personal problems, although she was far too professional to discuss them with me. Detective Ramirez will just have to find out what was going on in her private life to cause her odd behavior."

"But if Blanche was disturbed and unable to do her job, why didn't you act, Nat?" This time it was Melanie Storey.

"You should have gotten rid of her long ago!" Gertrude Bleeker, sensing an ally, pressed her attack.

"Detective Ramirez." The cool voice of Ross Easterly spoke over the group. "What are you planning to disclose outside this room? Surely this information is highly delicate. Think of Ms. Werner's family. And, of course, it would be dreadful for the students. Not to mention the college's reputation."

"I have no intention of making anything public myself at this time. The cause of death has been established, however, and that information will eventually be available to public inquiry." Before any of them could protest, the detective had gathered his sheaf of papers and was out the door, issuing a final admonishment as he departed: "In the meantime, I must ask that my report to you be considered strictly confidential."

7

As the meeting broke up in consternation, Rosemary eased her way out and down the flights of stairs at the end of the hall. Nothing made sense. Blanche a drowning victim was horrible but comprehensible. Blanche a suicide seemed impossible. She had shown none of the symptoms of despair and seemed never to have telegraphed any signals for help. Blanche a murder victim? Rosemary recoiled from the idea. And yet Ramirez himself inspired credibility.

She emerged outside and owlishly looked around to reorient herself.

"Dean Stubbs!" The voice was urgent. She turned to the tall man hurrying toward her. As he approached, running disjointedly, Rosemary could see his eyes were rimmed with red. With a start, she realized it was Claus Henderson.

His voice seemed close to breaking. "I need to talk with you. It's about Blanche." He took her arm, and Rosemary could feel the trembling in his hand. He set off across the quadrangle so quickly that Rosemary almost had to run to keep up with him. She thought back to the relationship between the two that she had sensed during her first visit to Sanderson. Now, as much as she wanted to question him about Blanche, his agitation held her in check. They hurried on without speaking for several strides.

"Where is the closest quiet place?" Rosemary broke the silence.

"The greenhouse. We won't be disturbed."

As they strode quickly down the path to the lower campus and the life sciences complex, Rosemary looked up at her companion's face. His strong features were battened down in pain, and his mouth was pressed grimly to contain his emotion. She looked away, embarrassed at how much was revealed there. As she did so, she recognized the colonnaded walkway of the little Victorian folly attached to the biology building. Claus flung open a door decorated with wrought-iron tracery.

Inside, Rosemary blinked to adjust to the sudden dimness. They passed through rooms lined with benches holding plastic pots and emerging plants, into a teaching laboratory.

Claus stopped and turned to face her.

"Blanche and I were very close, " he said. "I have to know how you found her." He stood utterly still, his eyes fixed intently on her.

Rosemary looked uneasily at the door beyond him, suddenly aware that she was in an isolated place with a very distressed and physically powerful man. "I thought she had drowned. She was facedown in the pool."

"Didn't you try to save her? To get her out?" Claus took a step toward her, not in menace but importunity.

"I tried. But I couldn't lift her."

"How did you *know* she was dead?" Again he stepped forward, very close now.

"She was facedown. And when I pulled on her clothes to draw her out, she rolled over." Rosemary turned her face away. "She was dead."

Henderson was suddenly too close for comfort. His hands gripped her shoulders in a painful vise. "What do you mean, you *thought* she had drowned?"

Rosemary hesitated, tempted to tell all that she knew but painfully aware of Ramirez's instructions to her and the college trustees. "The police say she was dead before she fell into the water."

"I knew she couldn't have gone to that pool and fallen in by accident. *I knew it.*" His voice rose, but he didn't let go of her shoulders. "What else did the police say?"

Rosemary felt his grip tighten, but she forced herself not to struggle against it. She was determined to calm Claus but say nothing more. She looked directly at him.

"You're not telling me something." His voice was desperate, and he gave her shoulders a violent shake.

They both heard brisk footsteps behind them turn into a run.

"Claus! You idiot! What are you doing? Let her go!" The voice was low but full of authority.

Claus dropped his arms, his eyes coming into focus on the figure in the doorway. Rosemary turned to see a man of medium height, with black hair brushed straight back from a high forehead. Although he was smaller than Claus, he moved with a power that gave him a physical advantage.

"What in God's name were you going to do to the chaplain? Have you lost your mind?"

"Kevin. Kevin. She was murdered. I'm sure of it. She was dead before her body hit the water! She had to have been murdered! *There was nothing wrong with her.*" The strength seemed to run out of Henderson's frame, and he lowered himself onto one of the narrow chairs by the table, head in his hands. The newcomer walked quietly over to him and put both hands on his shaking shoulders.

Rosemary stepped forward and drew up a stool opposite Claus. She explained, "I told him how I found her. And that the police now think she didn't drown."

Slowly Claus looked over at Rosemary. "I'm sorry. I hope I didn't hurt you. I think I'm going mad."

Rosemary mustered a reassuring smile and said simply, "I know how it is." Then she turned toward her rescuer. He kept his eyes on Claus but touched Rosemary's arm lightly.

"I'm Kevin Oxley, a friend of Claus's."

Claus rubbed his hands across his face like someone emerging from a trance. "I have to take all this in. I can't talk any longer. I need a walk to think things through." He got up and, shuddering slightly, drew himself to his full height, squaring his head and shoulders. "Kevin. It's a blessing you came by. Will you show Dean Stubbs the way out? I dragged her here at such a clip she may need a guide to get her back to the library."

Kevin Oxley gripped him in a quick embrace and then stepped back, never taking his eyes off Claus's grief-stricken face. " All right, Claus. I'll be back later."

There was no response from Claus. His friend motioned to Rosemary and they walked down the gallery and out the door, leaving Claus standing motionless. They walked along the way to the upper campus without speaking. As they reached the top of the hill, Kevin paused.

"Rotten, unspeakably rotten. Hideous for Blanche, and God knows what Claus is going through. And, if the police are right, it's going to be hideous for the whole campus." There were deep lines between his brows, but his eyes were clear as he looked at Rosemary. "Madam Chaplain, you waste no time. It took me two years after I came to Sanderson to sort out Blanche and Claus. You've been here not quite three days on official duty, and you have Claus baring his soul to you."

"Hardly. He was just reacting to her death and wanted desperately to know more about how it could have happened."

"Poor Claus! They were so private in their relationship. It's going to make it that much harder for him now."

"But why the secrecy?" Rosemary asked him. "It doesn't make sense."

Kevin shook his head briefly. "Claus was inextricably married. His wife suffered an early onset of Alzheimer's twenty years ago, and he either couldn't afford or didn't trust the nursing homes. So he's kept her at home and cared for her until recently. He's had help, of course. But except on the weekends and vacations, he's borne a lot of her care. Only when she needed extended medical care did he put her in a special institution. He and Blanche accommodated themselves to the situation and spent time together mostly away from campus. Not that people didn't know—you'll find that colleges are very gossipy little communities. But everybody respected the fiction, for Marie's—Claus's wife's—sake. It just seemed easier that way . . . then." Kevin's look was shot with discomfort.

Rosemary fixed her attention on the pathway before them. "Kevin?"

"Yes?"

"I wonder if Claus knew what had been bothering Blanche in the last few weeks? I wanted to ask him, but this certainly wasn't the right time."

"Isn't that a question for the police to ask?" Kevin countered.

"Yes, " Rosemary admitted, "but . . . well, having found Blanche, I feel responsible somehow. And the thought— even the remote thought—that someone might have killed her . . . well, I can't tell whether it's despair or anger that has me, but the only way I can cure it is *to find out*." She stopped to face Kevin.

"I see." He looked at her appraisingly. "I hope for all our sakes, yours not least, that this was an accident. But I'll help you this far. It will be easier for me to ask Claus about Blanche. And I promise to tell you what I find out." He smiled suddenly. "Have you eaten today?"

"I don't know," she answered, surprised. "I guess not."

"Then let's get you a bowl of soup, anyway. The student union is right over there. It'll do you good. Even if you don't like the food, the students are a tonic. Chances are they'll bring you up to the surface of life again, and that's a safer place to be for the moment."

She gave him a brief grin and nodded. "Sold me! Let's go."

The student center faced Cullen Street. Outside it was railway Gothic, replete with patterned brick and sandstone window frames, but inside it was unmistakably utilitarian. Robin's-egg-blue chairs and orange tables gave the visual shock that institutional decorators assign to youth. Settled around the cavernous main room, groups of students picked up the threads of conversations dropped there months before, while an occasional head bent over a text in a feat of concentration. Kevin threaded his way among the tables, balancing a Styrofoam cup of tomato soup for Rosemary and one of coffee for himself.

"Mr. Oxley! Hey!"

"Tara! You're a sight for sore eyes. Did you get to China? Oh, this is your new chaplain, Dean Stubbs. Rosemary, this is Tara Lavellier, a student of mine in elementary Greek a couple of years ago."

Tara, a young African-American with a dancer's economy of movement, turned to greet Rosemary.

"Glad to meet you. I was going to come to see you anyway, since I signed up last spring to help with services." Tara hardly paused before she plunged into an answer for Kevin. "We did get there. The whole ensemble from Sanderson. And we gave twelve performances. Even one to a sell-out house in Shanghai. It was awesome! The Chinese didn't know what to make of contemporary dance. And offstage they were even more curious about us! We had some great talks."

"Did the trip help you to sort out whether you want to go on in dance or stay with your premed work?"

"I'm still not sure. But right now I'm ready to concentrate on my independent project. By the way, have you seen Mr. Henderson? He's my thesis adviser, and I couldn't find him anywhere this morning. I sure would like to get my lab work scheduled at least."

"Tara, I suspect he really won't be available for a couple of days. He's had a terrible shock."

"Miss Werner's death?"

"Yes."

"Well, I guess I can work out those little details for myself. I sure am sorry about Miss Werner, though." She glanced at her watch. "Wow! I've got to get going. Nice to meet you, Dean Stubbs. See you, Mr. Oxley."

Kevin turned to Rosemary. "Have you ever noticed how students know all the essential facts about a campus without ever being told?"

"I'm beginning to see." She steered the conversation into more neutral territory. "Tara seems like a gifted student."

"Tara's a standout. She's got talent as a dancer and in the sciences. And she would have been an outstanding classics major, too, but she yearned for practicality." Kevin leaned back in his chair and gave a mock sigh.

"You must see a lot of that," Rosemary sympathized.

"Yup." Kevin nodded. "Tara decided to take Greek in her sophomore year. But as the year went on, she objected to the verbs. Had a real grudge against the Second Aorist. Not an irrational position, I must admit—I'm afraid it's an incentive for a lot of students suddenly to become 'practical' in the middle of term."

"With all due reverence for your field, I must say that I was glad enough to slide into Biblical Greek. And even then I was cheering on St. Jerome in aid of the Latin translation."

"A Latinist in Sanderson's chapel! That's mighty High

Church for the old fire-and-brimstone villages of New England!"

"Well, Jonathan Edwards I'm not." Rosemary smiled. "I don't suppose you darken the doors of chapels?"

"No, ma'am. But I'm willing to be a stage-door Johnny. I'll wait on the steps with an armful of roses."

"Wait till I knock the socks off all the reviewers, and then I'll be expecting you. And in the meantime, it looks like I'll have Tara, which is terrific," said Rosemary.

"I don't need to wait for the reviews."

Rosemary smiled ruefully. Was it only this morning that she had played back Kevin's message, congratulating her for sailing through her debut at Convocation, as he put it?

He went on, "So you can expect me outside the chapel at noon on Sunday. Afterward, I'll make up for these student rations with a proper lunch up in the hills."

"Frankly, that sounds wonderful. A Sunday outing will be very welcome." With that she rose, ready to head back to her office and the calls that were surely waiting to be returned.

8

Rosemary woke the next morning feeling anxious. Last night she'd blotted out the memories of the day with a bit too much Scotch, and now she felt a noticeable hangover as she negotiated through the packing boxes. She was moving shakily toward fresh coffee and unpacking when the trill of the phone made her jump.

"Dean Stubbs?"

"Yes."

"This is Raphael Ramirez." The soft voice brought back to Rosemary the memory of the detective she had met yesterday, attractive despite his precise and distancing manner.

"Oh. Good morning." Rosemary's eyes still hurt from her desolate crying jag of the night before—for Blanche, for Jim, for the loneliness they had left behind in her. And for her own panic at their loss, a panic she had felt in Claus's hands, too, when he had shaken her so violently. But then none of that was Raphael Ramirez's concern. "You must have been worrying all hours about this case. Can I help you?"

"In fact you can. I'm sorry to call you so early, but I wonder if you could meet me in half an hour by the pool in the old gymnasium. I'm meeting with the Athletics Department, and I think it might be a help if you were there."

"Of course. See you there."

"Well, Fannie," she said, looking down at the dog's eager face as she hung up the phone. "At least it's a good morning for you. Here comes another walk, and you don't have a sermon to prepare."

Rosemary moved back cautiously across the narrow kitchen to the stove. She turned off the flame under the aged Pyrex percolator. She fixed herself a mug of coffee and went to stand behind a rush-bottom chair at the small table by the window. The morning light was beginning to pour through it, throwing a bright sheen on the walls around her. Looking south, away from the college, the bones of an old garden, weedy from neglect, lay immediately before her. And beyond, the hills caught the glow from the east. She stood quietly, letting the mug heat her fingers, feeling the steam dissipate, taking into the air the tumbling impressions that jangled in her mind.

Blanche Werner dead. All that wry good humor and extraordinary common sense gone. A promising friendship extinguished. Rosemary shook herself out of self-pity and focused fiercely on the students. Leslie Martineau reaching out to accept guilt. How many others would do the same thing when they thought about Blanche's death? The nagging anxiety she'd woken with reasserted itself. She'd fooled herself about her too easily embraced vocation. Comfort them about Blanche? She didn't know how. She wasn't so certain herself about a divine order that encompassed that swollen gray figure in the water.

"Oh, come on, Fannie." She banged the mug down on the table and saw with annoyance that the coffee had spilled over onto the wooden surface. "Let's just mop that up and we're off."

Avoiding the dog, which alternated figure eights between her ankles and the door, she lifted a sweater from the newel post in the hall, apologized gently to the housebound cat, stepped out onto the porch, and set off for the old gymnasium with Fannie by her side.

"Dean Stubbs!" a firm, full voice carrying over distance called as she approached from the campus side.

Rosemary looked past the gym. A tall young woman, running with smooth strides, waved without breaking her pace. Behind her, four others kept pace, each with the thrust and lift of trained athletes; another waved. Rosemary recognized Leslie and guessed that the others must also be members of the varsity rowing eight. She returned their greetings and ran up the steps to the gym, snapping her fingers for Fannie. Inside, she headed quickly down the long, bright hallway, through the doors, and into the sharp, chlorinated atmosphere of the old pool room.

Walking with surefooted grace along the aisle between the diving and swimming pools came a slim woman with sharp features. "I would have thought you'd seen enough of swimming pools for one semester. I saw you outside the new pool house yesterday with the police. Didn't expect you back in this vicinity so soon." Her tone was ironic, testing.

"Evidently." Rosemary made no effort at civility.

"Don't see why Blanche had to choose the gym for her suicide, especially not our new pool. I'm Christine Fermer, by the way, the swimming coach."

"I'm Rosemary Stubbs, but you seem to know that already."

A door pushed open, and both women turned to see an

angular man in a sweat suit sweep in. Anticipating the effect of sudden humidity, he pushed his fine gray-blond hair back from his forehead.

"Hello, Christine. And you must be the new dean of the chapel. I'm Chip Barbour, coach of the crew."

Rosemary stepped forward to extend her hand. She couldn't conceal a slight wince as Cyprian Barbour gripped it.

"Sorry," he laughed. "Keep forgetting that I don't have to pull you through the water."

Rosemary winced again.

"Ugh. Damn. Didn't mean to remind . . . "

"It's okay. We can't forget Blanche for a moment, and yet we can't seem to keep her in mind, either. It just happens," Rosemary said.

"I'm not sure what we should remember her for." Christine Fermer's voice had an edge that cut through the damp air.

"You know, Christine, I really doubt that this is the time—" the coach began.

"It's certainly not the time for hypocrisy. Posing for the benefit of clergy doesn't become you, Cyprian."

"Look, Christine, discipline is a—"

"Discipline, or self-discipline, if that was to be your bloody sermon, has nothing to do with it. You know as well as I do that Blanche Werner emptied the guts out of five years of your work the day before yesterday. And you're not going to pretend now that you aren't as angry as I am," she retorted.

Chip Barbour shifted his weight back and draped his

frame against the bleachers. "I daresay, my friend, that Miss Werner of blessed memory had a helping hand from our senior colleagues in this department." He turned to Rosemary. "We're widely suspected of trying to make professional athletes out of our students, you know. Would you believe that, Miss Stubbs?"

"I met Leslie Martineau yesterday," Rosemary said.

"And? Did you find her dedication to rowing unseemly in one so young? Not to mention female?"

"I thought love of sport was the definition of an amateur," Rosemary shot back.

"*Touché*. So you haven't declared a camp. But then you haven't met the enemy yet, either." Chip turned away.

The sound of brisk steps along the hallway broke the moment. Raphael Ramirez stepped inside.

"Mr. Barbour? And?"

"Christine Fermer. Swimming."

"Yes. How do you do? And Dean Stubbs. Thank you for coming. Now, we seem to be missing a substantial number of your colleagues."

"They'll be here in a minute. They're organizing classes for the morning. We do have real jobs, you know."

"Of course, Miss Fermer. But *you* could get things in order right here, I hope? I see your predictions are correct. Here are some of the others now."

A woman in her mid-twenties, carrying a tennis racket, entered by the outside door, arguing over her shoulder with the older woman who followed her.

"Don't tell me we have to be interviewed at this hour.

Who's supposed to look out for schedules anyway, if not the chairman? I bet he's not even here yet. I have two classes this morning and not even a regular assistant. Frankly I don't see why the police should be allowed on the campus in a purely private matter."

"It may not be as private as you think, Miss . . . is it Miss Landry, tennis and squash? Well, I am Detective Raphael Ramirez, and I shall be glad to honor your rights to separation, if it proves to be possible."

"Oh, hello, Detective Ramirez." The older woman stepped forward. "I've heard so many good things about you across the road, in town. I'm Nora Blake. I coach the golf team and the skiers, and I teach aerobic and exercise classes for the general student body."

Ramirez nodded and smiled briefly as he continued to make note of the enlarging group around him. Coaches for soccer, gymnastics, track, riding, basketball, and volleyball, and the trainer. They stood awkwardly in knots of two and three along the pool's edge, waiting to be called formally into session.

"Hello, Chris! And look at Chip Barbour—not your kind of water's edge, is it?" Rosemary saw the coach wince this time, a quick shudder that hardly got as far as his shoulders, as he stiffened against the greetings of the department chair. Ned Andrews made his way to the center of the group, his bulky form wreathed in the tobacco smoke from his pipe, his florid face beaming on what appeared to be general principles. "Ah, Dean Stubbs. Splendid to have you on board. Wretched business, yesterday. But we're all on your side, of course."

Rosemary, puzzled as to what that side might be, was just as glad that Raphael Ramirez relieved her of a reply.

"You are all very kind to come here on such short notice," Ramirez said, smiling gently at the group, his eyes attentive but unthreatening. "It is true that a detective spends his life inconveniencing people, because every investigation intrudes on everyday life. Today, I must bother you with a few questions about your last meeting with Miss Werner. It may well be that you were the last people to see her before her death."

"If that's the reason you want to see us, why is she here?" Christine thrust her jaw at Rosemary.

"You were the last to see her alive, perhaps. Dean Stubbs we believe to have been the first to have seen her body. I'm looking for the bridges that can be thrown over your two sets of memories. Is there a room where we can assemble?"

"The staff room is just through here," Ned Andrews said, leading the way into the hall, past the check-in desk, and to a smaller hallway opening to locker rooms on one side and a classroom and a comfortably shabby common room on the other. As they filed along behind Ned, Rosemary's eye ran idly over the banners and trophies on display against the walls. There were the usual intramural awards, a fair number of intercollegiate championships, and in the center of the main case a large silver punch bowl, boldly engraved "Women's National Collegiate Championship, Varsity Eight.

1998." As she paused to admire it, she became aware of Ned by her elbow.

"Look here, Dean Stubbs," he said, eyeing Fannie. "Terribly sorry, but dogs are not allowed in the building. Can't make exceptions. Students would have us overrun, everything from cats to wombats, if we didn't keep a firm rule. Couldn't you put him in your car?"

"It's a she. I walked over, so I don't have a car here. But surely we can work something out." Looking out the window of the common room, she caught sight of Leslie Martineau and the rest of the crew running rhythmically up and down the stone steps that connected the old gym to the playing fields beyond. "I'll take her out and she can wait with the crew."

"Oh no you don't!" Rosemary had hardly taken two steps when Chip was in front of her. "That is a workout. Whether or not Sanderson College is going to compete at a national level, I will not have training interrupted to babysit a dog, or to do any other departmental housekeeping."

"Perhaps," Ramirez said quietly, "just this time we might relax the rules. I would like everyone present throughout the session, and we will all have to wait quite some time if Miss Stubbs must walk home with her dog and then return." Reluctantly, Ned nodded his assent, Chip turned aside, and Rosemary sank into an armchair, while Fannie, unaware of the narrow margin of her reprieve, made a quick inspection of coffee table and wastebaskets before sprawling untidily by her feet.

"Now," said Ramirez, "I would like to review the events

surrounding your meeting with Miss Werner Tuesday night. It was after Convocation, was it not?"

"Yes," Ned replied. "We met with her in her office in Stearns Hall at about eight-thirty or so."

"And what was the subject of the meeting?" Ramirez looked at each of them in turn.

"Well now," Ned began, "we were just to go back over our discussion of the afternoon. It was about some line-item cuts in the budget we had been discussing earlier."

"The hell you say!" Chip drew himself up as though he might throw a punch at his chairman. "It was a bloody dumb show. Blanche that day had coolly announced an end to our participation, for all intercollegiate teams, in national competition. Basically that meant crew and swimming, and maybe riding and lacrosse. Just to save a few thousand dollars. That's all, full stop. And that night she wanted us all to tell her how much we loved her for it. Well, she didn't get that!"

"You can say that again." Christine matched his anger. "But nothing we could say mattered because the department's position had already been given away." She glared at Ned Andrews, who turned to look out the window at the students now breaking from their drill on the steps and heading toward the locker rooms.

Nora Blake cut in on Christine Fermer precisely. "We began a little late, you know." She paused, pressing her lips together in a thin line, and looked directly at the swimming coach. "Blanche was on the telephone when we arrived and asked us to wait out in the hallway. While we were there, we got into a heated discussion."

"Can you tell me anything about the phone call? Did Miss Werner mention who it was, or what it was about?" Ramirez interrupted.

"Well, frankly, I was surprised. It was unlike Blanche to call us to an extraordinary meeting, and then to keep us waiting. She was usually so meticulous. It just set the wrong tone. Jarring, you know." Nora smiled inclusively at Ramirez, as if inviting him to join a partnership in maintaining the order of things. "She didn't go into any detail about the call. She said it was an accountant. . . . I got the impression she was still thinking about that call the whole time she was meeting with us. She was distracted, but then she'd been that way for a while."

"Why would you meet the day before the term began on a current budget matter? And why at night?"

"Well, the trustees were expected here yesterday for a meeting of the finance committee. Blanche had to get everything in order," Ned supplied. "You see, Blanche had discovered a shortfall in the budget over the summer, and you can't have that—not in a college of this size."

"Why not?" Ramirez persisted. "There must be contingency funds."

"Oh, there are! Of course there are." Ned puffed so that Rosemary thought suddenly of the little engine that could, and she struggled to suppress a smile.

"But this was rather worse than that. Quite unexpected, I think!" His pipe worked furiously.

"Does the college budget usually get settled only hours before the trustees meet?" Ramirez pressed on.

A slight shiver of restlessness passed through the room. The riding coach looked down at her hands and said softly, "I think we held the process up. We were not particularly clear about our own priorities when we realized the budget would have to be cut."

The basketball coach gave her a quizzical look. "Clear enough, I'd say—in about a dozen directions."

"Well, the fact is"—Ned leaned forward as though taking Ramirez into his confidence—"I wasn't quite up to snuff last week, and while I was out, there was quite a disagreement about our athletic policies. We have to respond to the budget crunch. All the departments will have to." He looked around the group. "And Blanche wanted us to cut programs to save some money. All depended on whether we cut the bread-and-butter work, teaching the vast majority of students, or whether we cut the varsity competition that's only for a few."

"Cutting! She was killing the crew program and swimming, not to mention an amputation or two in riding and in field sports." Chip glared at Ned until the older man shifted and tried to pick up his connection with Ramirez.

"You see, Mr. Ramirez," he said, trying to recover his authority despite the slight tremor in his hands, "some of us think we do our best by young women when we teach them the sports they'll be enjoying all their lives. Others, especially our younger members, want to train them to compete as though they had their eyes on the U.S. Olympic Team."

"And Miss Werner?" Ramirez prompted. "What side was she on?"

"She betrayed us," Christine burst out. "When I was recruited for this job, she promised us the best facilities and the best programs for women in the country. But in the last few months she'd changed. I couldn't understand it."

"How, Miss Fermer? How had she changed? What was it about her?" Ramirez's tone was gentle, but his stillness telegraphed intense concentration.

"She used to be so friendly," Christine continued. "She came to swimming meets, and we'd talk about the team afterward. This summer, when I met her on the campus, she'd never even stop to talk. She'd walk right by, as if she hadn't seen me."

Nora, every crease in her brown suit announcing disapproval, uncrossed her legs and sat up straight. "She had a lot on her mind. She had other things to do than talk about swim meets. There was a budget crisis, and she gave us a choice—whether to cut the regular class program or the intercollegiate schedule. And when the department couldn't agree, she made the decision herself. The treasurer has that right, you know, if a department won't act."

Ned nodded. "That's right. She came to me just about four weeks ago. Very down, she was. 'Ned,' she said, 'you've got to understand. We have to cut back. We just can't afford all the programs we've built up. Even though we have the new athletic building, we have to rethink our programs to concentrate on the things that benefit the most students.'" He reached absently for his pipe, cleaned it with maddening slowness, set it down on the table in front of him, and cleared his throat for emphasis. "'All right, Blanche,' I said. 'I'm your man. Tell me what it has to be,' I told her. 'I'm for Sanderson College. Athletics will do its bit.'"

"Ned, you had no right to do that," Chip said with frozen intensity. "We hadn't discussed any proposed cuts in the department. You just told us the problem and went on to cut a private deal with Blanche. You don't *own* Athletics like some little fiefdom, and she didn't *own* the college finances. Besides, why should this department suffer more than any other department? We're no frill. We're critical for women's lives and certainly for their education."

Ramirez, a still point in the midst of people obsessed with their own commitments, asked quietly, "You said Miss Werner had changed. She was less gregarious. Was there anything else different about her?"

Nora rushed to answer him. "Nothing essential had changed about Blanche. It was just that she seemed worried all the time."

"That was unusual?"

"Oh, yes! Before this summer, nothing ever seemed to faze Blanche. No matter what the problem was, she could put it to rights."

"You've been most helpful, Miss Blake."

"Oh, and another thing I almost forgot to mention. For the last few weeks, Blanche was always *busy*. That's odd, too. Usually she was in her garden by five-fifteen after work, most days anyway. But I never saw her out there in August, and I was just noticing the other day that it was looking a bit weedy."

"Thank you, Miss Blake. And did anyone else notice a change?"

Nora Blake's volubility seemed to have stunted the interest of her colleagues, and there was no response as they busied themselves looking at the ceiling, Rosemary's dog, or the inviting world outside the windows.

"You mentioned," Ramirez said absently, looking suddenly out the window himself, "that Miss Werner was on the telephone talking to her caller for long enough to delay your meeting. Did you by any chance overhear the conversation?"

Ned looked blank, Nora Blake disapproving at the thought of eavesdropping.

"I heard something," Adrienne Landry, the tennis coach, said slowly, "despite the noise we were making. . . . Guess I was closest to her door. I . . . got tired of all the arguing in the hallway. I couldn't quite hear her. But she was saying something about interest earnings." The tennis coach shrugged her shoulders. "I didn't catch anything really."

"And did she raise that topic, or anything about the college in general, at the meeting?" Ramirez's questions were brisk now.

"No." Ned pulled on his pipe and looked up at the ceiling. "She just wanted to give the department a final chance to respond to the manner of the cuts she'd laid out earlier in the day." He paused and dug a handkerchief out of his pocket to wipe both nose and mouth before beginning again. Ramirez never moved, but the restlessness of the others in the room gave away their impatience. "But since there was no agreement—"

"What *would* you call an agreement, Ned?" Chip challenged bitterly. "If you'd bothered to take a vote, you would have had ten to two for cutting *anything* other than intercollegiate athletics. You and Nora were the only holdouts."

"Now, Chip. You just couldn't do that at this time of year. The only possible savings on classes would be on salaries. And we'd already signed contracts. You know that."

"Ned, you hadn't *tried*, you'd—"

The detective broke in smoothly, "And did Miss Werner take an active part in these discussions?"

"Oh, no!" Nora was firm. "Blanche wouldn't do that. She wanted to know what suggestions we had."

"Well, I don't think she was paying any attention to us," Christine cut in. "I think it was all a charade. I saw her scribbling down numbers while we were talking. She was just going to go with Ned at the end, anyway. She didn't give a damn what any of the rest of us thought."

"How did the meeting break up?"

"How would you expect?" Christine retorted. "After one of Ned's orations, Blanche just got up and said essentially 'Thanks but no thanks' to the rest of us and showed us out."

"Did anyone stay behind?"

"We all went out together, I think." Nora spoke for the group.

"And then? What time did each of you arrive home?"

"Let's see," said Ned. "I stopped for a drink with a friend who lives just off campus, and I got there about quarter of ten."

The tennis coach shook her head. "It was later than that when we broke up. I went directly home to my suite in Englewood House, and it was ten-fifteen when I turned on the news."

Chip pinched his forehead into sharp verticals between his brows. "I went home via the boathouse. Hadn't had time to check the shells for the morning workout, what with Convocation and the extra meeting. I was too angry to go home right away anyway."

Christine thrust out her hands, "I don't know when I got home, and I didn't care—and I don't care now. We'd been betrayed. The college was backing out of every promise it made when we were recruited. And when the students had been urged to come *here* rather than some other college for a chance to compete nationally, no matter what their sport. It's not only stupid to pull the plug on all their dreams. It's *immoral.*"

Ramirez turned his attention from the department members and said suddenly to Rosemary, "Dean Stubbs, what was Miss Werner wearing when you found her?"

"I didn't look too closely," Rosemary said, reaching down to rest her hand on Fannie. "A gray suit. A streak of color, red and blue. A scarf, I think."

"And when she left your meeting," Ramirez asked the others, "what was she wearing?"

"The same gray suit and a red-and-blue silk scarf," Christine said authoritatively, "and of course she had her big black handbag on her desk. Everyone on campus knew that bag. She had everything in it. Calculator, budget papers, cough drops, makeup. We used to say she could live out of it for a week."

"Did you see that bag at the pool, Dean Stubbs, when you first arrived there?"

"No," Rosemary answered. "There was nothing."

"Well." He rose, gathered his notebook, and smiled at the group. "You have all been most helpful, and you have your own schedules to attend to, no doubt. I thank you for your time."

Under his gaze, the athletic staff wasted no time departing the room, Rosemary and Fannie with them.

9

Panic seized Rosemary when she awoke early Sunday morning. She'd spent all the previous day writing and destroying versions of a sermon and had finally stayed with the latest one in a fit of exhaustion. There was no comfort for her now in the thought of the chapel, and certainly not in the pulpit. What was she going to say to the students when all she could think about was loss and death? And how could she know what they were feeling? Although she'd been in her office the entire day Saturday, the phone had never rung, nor had a single student stopped by. She had met her group of undergraduate assistants on Friday for the first time, and she felt her palms sweat as she thought of all the ways that she might fail them.

Fannie began her usual ballet of exhortation by the bedroom door, an entreaty not to be denied. Rosemary pulled on jogging clothes, fended off the dog to tie the laces of her Nikes, and opened the front door. "All right, Fan, we'll go for a short run, but not too far. This is my morning of maximum labor."

They went up Cullen Street, circled halfway around the campus, and turned back just as the clock on Stearns Hall struck seven. Rosemary quickened her pace and raced home with Fannie careering ahead. There was a gray car outside her front door, its owner hidden behind the pages of the Sunday *New York Times*. As Fannie tore up the walk, Petra Hills lowered the newspaper and climbed out carrying two bags, brown paper in one hand and plastic in the other.

"Hi," she said cheerfully to the perspiring Rosemary. "I've brought croissants, and in here are some oranges and great coffee beans. You need some company before you climb into that pulpit?"

Rosemary's irritation at an unsolicited guest vanished. She'd needed company but hadn't known it. "How is it that you always know exactly when to be on my doorstep? Come in. Here's the percolator. You make the coffee while I shower." By seven-fifteen they were sitting in a pool of early sunshine, sipping the aromatic coffee and reducing warm croissants to piles of crisp flakes.

"How did you know I'd be in a blue funk this morning?" Rosemary asked as she took a sip of freshly squeezed orange juice.

"Well . . ." Petra hesitated. "You're not the usual chaplain type. And if you want to know the truth, you've been looking all strung out, as though Blanche Werner had been your dearest friend. I know you'd just met her, so I thought something else was bothering you."

Rosemary looked gratefully at Petra's intelligent face and decided to be frank.

"Yes," she said, "Blanche's death has been turning me inside out. My husband was killed in a boating accident three years ago, and Blanche's body, helpless there in the water, brought back the whole nightmare. I can't seem to get away from it." To her surprise Rosemary found that she was hanging on to the table like a drowning person herself.

Petra didn't look away. "Well, what a bloody awful thing to hit you here, where you probably thought you'd have a chance to put your husband's death behind you."

Rosemary's shoulders quivered involuntarily. She began to sob silently, choking back sounds, while Fannie took up a post sitting on her feet, and the marmalade cat appeared from nowhere to climb on her lap. Petra sat in silence, allowing Rosemary's grief to mount and slowly subside.

"I had thought it *was* behind me," Rosemary said, finally able to control her voice.

"I expect it never will be," Petra said gently, "but you shouldn't try to handle it all alone. How about some more coffee?"

Rosemary took some out of politeness but found it tasted surprisingly restorative. "Thanks, Petra," she said. "You've rescued me again."

"Here's the *Times*," said Petra cheerfully. "Take half an hour to read it, and then you can get ready for chapel."

"I really am ready now, Petra, thanks to you," Rosemary said truthfully, as Petra patted Fannie and let herself out the front door.

Rosemary bit into another croissant and dutifully turned the pages of the business section. There was a tombstone for the current U.S. Computer offering on the second page. Four years ago that would have been her deal, and the closing would have consumed all her waking hours. Now the challenge of her job had no time limits and no bottom lines. She saw the faces of Leslie and Tara in her mind and was surprised by the force of her growing desire to do her job well for them.

Moving with a new calm, she quickly swept away the remains of breakfast and headed for the chapel. She tiptoed around the back so as not to disturb the choir, which, without benefit of robing, presented a wild range of costume but a singleness of concentration as its members struggled toward a shared expression of Vaughan Williams. The choral director never looked around as Rosemary made her way out the side door and into her office. A knot of student lectors was waiting for her by the door.

"Oh, hi, Dean Stubbs." Ellen Tracey, a redheaded senior, spoke for them all. "We came over early because we had some second thoughts after our meeting on Friday."

"Is it about today's service?"

"Even though we decided to change the usual celebration of the new term somewhat, we're still a little worried about the way we remember Miss Werner."

"Are you concerned about the readings, or is it the music?"

"Well, it's harder than that, actually." Nan Brentner, a sophomore, casual in jeans but measured and thoughtful in manner, frowned as she searched for the right words. "The trouble is . . ." She stopped and rubbed a hand along her chin and tugged at her blond hair, caught in a wooden barrette at the nape of her neck. "You see, a lot of people in my year, well, we all heard rumors when we came back after the summer about how she was going to cut everything out of the budget. And we all sat up late after Convocation talking about how unfair it was—and how we hated her. And then, suddenly, the next morning she was dead! Now nobody knows what to feel."

Ellen was more decisive. "I think we should go ahead with a service that will let us think of Miss Werner as a person."

"Let's keep the readings as they are." Tara had come in through the door at the end of the corridor and joined them noiselessly. "Especially the one from St. Paul—'I have fought the good fight. I have finished the race.' No matter what you thought about Ms. Werner's policies, she always seemed to fight the good fight, by her standards."

"I think Blanche would have wanted that. We can remember her in prayer. That's where we can allow for all the conflicts in our memories of her," Rosemary decided.

As they were talking, members of the choir began to fill

up the hallway around them, some still singing, some off in conversations resulting from the business at hand, but all of them struggling into the maroon gowns that would finally present a visual unity to the congregation.

"I guess we'd better go," said Rosemary. "Let me open the office, and we can get our own gowns."

The sounds of the organ prelude caught them up. Rosemary felt her stomach clench, but only for a moment. She slipped quickly into the black robes of office and fell in behind the student lectors. Then all four joined the rear of the choir. Rosemary felt herself drawn in the wake of the procession into the chapel, peopled now with students and a handful of faculty and staff, awash in the plain light best suited to ecumenical Protestantism. Caught up in celebration and in grief, she found herself on the steps of the sanctuary. She felt sharply her own yearning to be part of this community. Perhaps it would be here that she finally settled the question of her vocation. She'd been on the run since Jim died, but Sanderson might be a place where she could slow down, figure out how to live life with a vacuum in her heart.

Tara and Ellen had been right. The precise tones of the organ and the voices of the choir, gaining in strength as the congregation gathered courage to join them, released the hesitations that had been palpable when they entered. Tara read with presence and in a voice that rounded each word and gave room for life to exist within it. Leaving the text of her prepared sermon aside, Rosemary preached on Psalm 119, allowing the stubborn hope of the psalmist to fill the chapel with a confidence which, even if borrowed, was contagious.

Her heart was full as she hung up her own robe and accepted theirs from the students. "Thanks, Ellen, Nan, oh, Tara, Mr. Oxley tells me you're another fugitive from Greek. Why don't we get together sometime to talk about translation, maybe even New Testament translation?"

Tara turned in the doorway, her fingers raised in a quick gesture of assent. "Okay!" And with that she was gone out the side door. Rosemary closed the window and locked her own door. Her footsteps echoed now in the chapel as she walked to the main entrance and down the broad steps.

Kevin was standing at the bottom, a brown trilby hat pulled down rakishly over his eye. "I've asked Petra to join us for lunch. But first, let me walk you over to your house. It's getting cold and you ought to have a sweater. I'll give you a report on my conversation with Claus."

As they were leaving, he turned to the lingering group of students. "How was the sermon?" he asked, tipping his head toward Rosemary.

Positive verdicts were delivered in an overlapping chorus of voices. Then they swept off, heading for brunch or the library or an afternoon's date.

As Kevin and Rosemary walked toward her house, he began, "Blanche was pretty closed-mouthed about her worries, even with Claus. She did tell him that the college has had two years in a row of unpredicted shortfalls. Both times a rise in financial aid accounted for part of it. But there was an unexpected shortfall in revenue each year from the investment side. Blanche had grilled all the investment officers who handled the Sanderson accounts, and she couldn't find anything wrong. Last year the revenue shortfall was about five hundred thousand dollars."

Rosemary listened intently, as they both slowed their pace.

Kevin went on, "Trying to find the source of it was driving Blanche crazy, Claus told me, but she didn't talk to him about any of the particulars—or what she was doing to investigate. He only knew the general situation. But he did say she was very tense and worried—increasingly so in the last couple of days before she died."

"What does he think now?" Rosemary asked.

"He's convinced someone killed her."

"Does he suspect anyone in particular?"

"Not as far as I can tell."

"But he has spoken to the police?" Rosemary was urgent.

"They spoke to him. But he didn't seem to get much comfort from that. It sounds like he had something of a standoff with that detective—Ramirez?"

Rosemary nodded. They'd arrived at her front door. She opened it and reached for a jacket hanging just inside. They headed back through a rising wind to meet Petra by the chapel.

"I see you've already met Kevin." Petra's smile warmed the windy fall day. "Did you know that, like you, he's an academic with a prior life?"

"Well, maybe a prior half-life. Before that wind blows us

away, I suggest we jump into the car," he urged good-naturedly.

"The weather seems to be sending out its first collection notice for winter," observed Petra, making a dive for the backseat of Kevin's Jeep, neat but clearly a veteran. "It's about a half-hour drive. Have you been to the Inn at Sprague Mountain yet?" she asked Rosemary.

"No. I've heard it's in a remote setting, though."

"Seems that way, anyhow," said Petra. "It's just right there, actually." She pointed to the range of hills that defined Metford's horizon to the west. "The whole mountain was made into a park by one of the local industrial families of the nineteenth century. Makes a perfect refuge from the twentieth."

Kevin, hat off now, eased the Jeep out of town with surprising speed. Very quickly the road began to curve and twist as it cut across farm country, mostly now given over to residences. In a few minutes, they left the river valley, and the road picked up the bed of a tributary that meandered down the side of the enclosing mountain. The lighter greens of maple and hickory, waiting out September to turn color, were outlined by the long reach of fir branches, almost black by contrast. Great juttings of rock, dense enough to deny foothold even to fern and moss, pushed the stream and its companion roadway into sharp bulges. As they climbed, the firs displayed their victory over the lowland trees and increasingly closed around the road. Even the broad light of midday gave way to shade as the car nosed its way farther up the mountain.

"This little wilderness may be one of the nicest things about Sanderson," Kevin observed.

"Sprague Mountain has an enormous population of woodpeckers," Petra leaned forward to tell Rosemary. "A colony of pileateds, as well as sapsuckers and red-bellied woodpeckers, which are quite rare in this part of the country. We're almost there. The woods are breaking up, and in just a minute there will be a view over the whole valley. You'll see the length of river that makes Sanderson such a pulse point for rowing."

As Kevin smoothed the car around a final curve, the mountain dipped suddenly away to their left, and the sweep of the valley opened before them, the river marking a sinuous trench in its midst.

"Look," said Petra, pointing to the south. "You see the town on this side of the river? Just there the gray tower? That's the Sanderson library. And the sharp white spiral? That's the chapel."

To her surprise, Rosemary felt a twinge of pride as she looked down.

Kevin slowed the Jeep, and all three of them surveyed their world, much reduced in scale, with satisfaction. Breaking in on their scattered thoughts, he announced they were almost at the inn.

A few minutes later they were hurrying in out of a wind that was distinctly chillier than it had been in the valley.

"Almost time for a fire," said Kevin, as he caught the entrance door half apologetically for the other two.

"Umm, but look what they've done with the fireplace!" Rosemary nodded to the far end of the lobby. A huge fireplace made of stone that suggested a neighboring quarry was filled with pale green hydrangeas flushed pink at the edges. "One would hate to move those, even for a fire."

"The inn is famous for its flowers. There's a garden in back, and the owners collaborate with the college greenhouse," Petra told her.

They were ushered from the lobby into a small dining room that looked out over lawns defined by a low stone wall edged with autumn blooms. At the far side of the room a small fire had been lit in recognition of the early cold, and its warmth completed the atmosphere of comfort. The food was plain but good, and Rosemary welcomed it.

Between them, Petra and Kevin kept the conversation to matters that carefully excised the college and any close recollection of Rosemary's own life. It was the easiest hour she'd had since the business of packing and unpacking her life had begun.

Over dessert and coffee, Kevin brought them back to Blanche. "Let me tell you what I know about Blanche and Claus. I'll start, and Petra will fill in what I don't know, or, as she says, just couldn't possibly understand. It's a bittersweet story now, although until recently I took it as an emblem that there really are second chances in life." Kevin's strong features softened.

He went on, "Claus is one of Sanderson's stars. He's a molecular biologist of distinction, one of the best historians of botany in the country, and also a connoisseur of botanical prints and drawings. Some people are jealous of him because of his public recognition and the trips abroad he takes to curate botanical art exhibitions. But his friends know that occasional trips away are a necessary relief.

"A few of us knew that he and Blanche were lovers, very quietly, mostly on those trips away. I ran into them once in Paris," Kevin recalled. "I'm something of a cynic about affairs of the heart, but I'll never forget their happiness. They were golden. All the clichés applied." He smiled at Petra. "Now you take over. I'm a man of reason, and I could never see why Claus couldn't extricate himself from a marriage to someone who didn't even know who she was anymore—and marry Blanche."

Petra shook her head violently. "Kevin, you're just being deliberately opaque. Claus is a man of strict honor, and Blanche had great moral sensitivity. Marriage just wasn't in it for either of them while Claus's wife, Marie, was still alive. Still, I know what you mean about the great thing they had going. I met them once on a gray day in London, and they seemed to be carrying their own sunshine with them."

"Tara seemed pretty much clued in the other day. How many people on the campus knew about them?" Rosemary asked intently. Her mind flickered uncomfortably over her meeting with Ramirez and the trustees. "And had anything gone wrong between them recently?"

Kevin held up a hand. "Stop. That's two major questions. Some of Claus's own students may have suspected, but I doubt if they knew anything. People who knew they loved each other were very protective of Blanche and Claus. Had anything gone wrong? Not that I know of." He raised a quizzical eyebrow at Petra. "Had it, Petra? You'd be the one to know, if anyone would."

Petra's face suddenly lost its characteristic laugh lines. "That's the problem. I don't know whether they'd quarreled. But Blanche wasn't herself this last month or so. They might have."

Kevin swept the mystery momentarily aside with a wave to the waitress. "Now you know everything we do. Who'll have more coffee?"

Rosemary gazed out into the garden, unable to shake for long the foreboding that had come so suddenly with her new job. Mentally jumping over what Kevin had related about Claus and Blanche, she found herself sharply recalling the man. "How is Claus managing?"

Kevin answered slowly, "He's going through the motions."

"Tara said she tracked him down on Friday and got her labs scheduled," Rosemary remembered.

"Claus is a real professional—he shared that with Blanche." Petra was emphatic. "He's always taken great care with his students. Most of his work on the genetic structure of corn has been done only so he can engage his honors students in the research. As a result, a lot of them graduate with a published paper, or at least a scholarly note, to their credit, and the experience is a real help to them in graduate school. He never fails them."

"He's never failed the college, either," Kevin added. "His work has generated a number of research grants, and right now he's working hard to get another, more sophisticated electron microscopy laboratory established. And that's not the end of it. He's guided the library in purchasing a number of superb early printed books on botany and attracted gifts of others. He's made it a first-rate collection."

"What's he like as a colleague? Does he ever lose control the way he did with me?" Rosemary was curious.

"Claus is always patient with students. But beyond that, he doesn't suffer fools gladly." Kevin paused. "I've seen him really angry a couple of times—and there's no question he's volcanic. That's why I broke in on you like a train the other day."

"I don't think many people have seen that side of Claus," Petra said as Kevin settled the bill and they prepared to leave the table. "For the most part, he's so generous and at the same time so fair-minded on the scholarly side that most people really do admire him. He's a good colleague there."

Back out in the chilly late afternoon, they took a last look at the inn's garden. Despite everything, Rosemary felt flushed with well-being, appreciative of the undemanding company of her two colleagues, and grateful for their confidence. As they got ready to drive off, Kevin looked over at her and cocked an eyebrow. "Too bad you haven't time for a Cook's tour. But someday I'll show you the farmer's side of these hills."

"We'll only just get you back in time for your first student tea," Petra observed, looking at her watch. "And I want to make up some transparencies for my one-hundred-level course. Productivity rates of capital investment, factored against educational attainment in the workforce.

You know, it's amazing how soft those educational figures are for the developing world. Almost non-existent for women."

"Ah, Petra, I wish you'd do a subject that scans," said Kevin, flashing her a grin in the rearview mirror. But it was lost on Petra, who had gotten an abstract cast about her eyes and was looking vaguely at the treetops.

"Now, Rosemary," he continued, acknowledging that Petra was lost to them for the moment. "Are you a gardener?"

"Better call me a gardener manqué. I have a vast collection of gardening books, and I almost make a fetish of identifying plants in other people's gardens. But up until recently, the so-called fast track didn't leave me much time for digging."

"Well, that weedy patch behind the chaplain's house ought to be a digger's delight. That'll test the Gertrude Jekyll in you."

"Do you suppose there'd be some help around? Someone who's laid out a garden before? Not to mention a friendly foot on the odd spadeful?"

"Sounds like a perfect combination for Claus and me. There's nothing he doesn't know about plants—and I'm a proven entry with a pitchfork at least."

"A maiden's dream."

"Ah, but the maiden will have to tell all to her gardeners! Is she a romantic? Is she forever formal?"

"How about a contemplative?"

"Subtle sand and rock in the Japanese style?"

"Would save a lot of spading."

"But what about all that investment in every-woman's-instant-garden books? Besides, you can't fire your subgardener that fast."

Rosemary laughed and then caught her breath slightly as the car came to the overlook at the side of the mountain. "Look!" She touched Kevin's sleeve lightly. "The valley is disappearing. Where did all that mist come from?"

"Oh, that's autumn in New England," said Petra, roused from her reverie about suitable statistics. "Usually it happens in the morning in the valleys—cold air over a warmer river can produce a real pea-soup fog. Seems the cold front that's been blowing in has set up the same cycle."

The drive down the mountain became trancelike as they moved between bands of fog and great bursts of sun in which the layered greens and occasional red of an early-turning tree made the air translucent. All three fell silent under the spell of the drama, until they were descending the last long slope toward town.

"The best trip to Sprague Mountain in years," Petra declared. "You saw it as it should be seen the first time, Rosemary. One takes it for granted after a while, until it's seen afresh through the eyes of a newcomer."

On Cullen Street, Rosemary stepped from the car into a world of mist, dampness seeping into her eyes and nostrils. "It's like a stage set for Sherlock Holmes," she laughed, waving goodbye to the disappearing taillights of Kevin's car.

There was hardly a moment to collect herself, and Fannie, before she set out, more warmly dressed, for Oakes House, the last of the three bulbous gray dormitories that ringed the circular drive across the road from the chapel.

Sunday-afternoon tea, a campus tradition, was in full swing when she entered. A few faculty members dotted the wide entrance hall and the spacious student living room, surrounded by energetically talkative students. Urns of tea, slices of lemon, mountains of brownies, and large baskets of scarlet apples gave a Dickensian mood to the room as everyone tucked in.

Fannie, always sociable, was an instant hit. She circled the room, made herself known to groups, stood proudly to be admired and patted. Rosemary let Nan, the head of the deacons, introduce her to all comers. Rosemary was astonished once again at the noise level generated by all-female gatherings. She'd spent three years at Yale never hearing a female voice raised in cheerful sociability. Now the din made conversation a matter requiring not only social skills but the stamina to shout amiably to all comers.

Nan's friends came in all shapes and sizes. There were willowy debutantes, several of whom, surprisingly, played rugby in the Sanderson Rugger Club, and others in Birkenstocks who were as likely to be painters as hockey players. There was Leslie towering over the diminutive cox of the crew, and just approaching was a group of budding journalists, intent on sizing up the new chaplain and scooping a story about Blanche's death.

"Dean Stubbs, do you think Ms. Werner was murdered?" Jane Macfarlane, a redheaded Midwesterner, asked, echoing the rumor that had swept the campus as the police continued their probe.

"What makes you ask that?" Rosemary returned soberly.

"Do you think someone could really have wished her dead?" She paused, waiting to draw them out.

"Well," Jane said briskly, "the crew and a whole bunch of other people who resented her are feeling guilty about her death. I don't see why they should, myself. Words are just words, after all. But someone must have been mad enough to push her into that pool."

Feigning detachment, Jane went on, "Do you think the police are doing a good job, Dean Stubbs?"

"Detective Ramirez is the local detective. He seems very competent."

"Well then, why would he stage a melodramatic scene like getting the Athletics Department together right after she was found? I thought that only happened in films," Jane observed in a dismissing tone.

Rosemary refused to take the bait. "It sometimes helps to jog people's memory to have them recall a situation together. And Detective Ramirez would have needed two days to take down all those observations separately."

There were some laughing references to Ned Andrews's inability ever to keep to the point and Coach Barbour's near obsession with scheduled training, and then the subject suddenly shifted.

"Dean Stubbs, would you tell us why you came to Sanderson? Why did you leave a powerful corporate job for something as sexist and backward as the church?" The questioner, called Sootie by her housemates, was slight, dark-haired, and very intense.

It was a question Rosemary had answered to herself

many times. "It has to do with an idea of a divine life force so vast it can't be limited by sexism," she said, "but come over for breakfast one day and we can really talk about it, if you like."

Nods of assent from Sootie and several others told Rosemary her work was launched. As they settled on next Monday morning, she looked around for Fannie, preparing to leave. Heading across the room to disentangle the dog from a clutch of students, Rosemary literally ran into Amy Standish, dean of the faculty.

"Ah, Dean Stubbs. Good. I was hoping to find you tonight. Do you have a moment? We can just step into the dining room here. There's something I need to ask you."

Bracing herself for yet another set of questions about Blanche's death, Rosemary reluctantly followed Dean Standish, whose utterly round figure matched a merry face that belied its owner's shrewdness. The dean closed the door behind them and began without preamble. "I need to ask you a great favor. Besides the turmoil of Blanche's loss, we're about to be overwhelmed by a terrific war over her fiscal legacy. There's a party led by Gertrude Bleeker, the trustee whom you've met, and some of the faculty, including the coaches, which is dead set on reversing her course and restoring all the budget cuts made over the summer. And others are lined up to make the budget crisis the excuse for potential changes they've wanted for a long time: elimination of the chapel and the intercollegiate athletic program, to name just a couple. They're all ready to open hostilities this week in my office at the first meeting of the budget committee." She paused for breath. "The problem is that I understand the budget as a working document for management, not as a tool for financial analysis. By no means do I have the mastery that Blanche did! And she had a pretty weak staff—she did all the conceptual work herself. I don't want to lose control over the situation because I can't command all the financial nuances. There are some pretty sharp pencils among the faculty—especially in the Economics Department." Amy looked hopefully at Rosemary.

"Can't the president stand in for Blanche? He seems like someone who is totally in command of the facts, and of their implications."

"He may be, but Nat has a genius for lifting himself above the fray. Right now he's on a trip to Cincinnati raising money. He's likely to be out of the loop just when I need him most."

"What would you like me to do?"

"I'd be grateful if you could go over the budget, and the financial materials generated for the fiscal year that's just closed, and brief me. And then if you'd come to the next faculty budget committee meeting, I'd be very grateful. I don't usually feel at sea, but we all relied on Blanche so much in these matters, and she always economized first in her own office. She had no second-in-command to just step in. Always said we couldn't afford it."

"I'm accustomed to standard GAAP accounting," Rosemary said, overcoming her reluctance, "and now that non-profits have moved away from fund accounting, I may be able to make sense of the Sanderson reports. When is the next budget meeting, by the way?"

Amy rather shamefacedly produced a thick docket from her briefcase and said, "Tuesday morning. If you could brief me at the end of the day tomorrow, it would be wonderful."

"Well! I'd better get to work, then!" Rosemary replied. And with manila folders under one arm and Fannie's leash on the other, Rosemary dashed out into a fog that seemed somewhat less romantic than it had two hours before.

10

Rosemary spent Monday plunged back into spreadsheets and budget presentations and a full run of finance committee minutes for the past two years. She cleared all the working surfaces in her office and downloaded the files Amy had given her into her computer. By the end of the day, she was confident that Blanche had maintained tight control of the college's expenditures but doubtful that budget control alone could close the income gap.

At four-thirty she left to see Amy, as promised. The dean's office, a large corner room directly below the president's, was almost entirely taken up by a large oval table and an oversize oak desk. Both were laden with paper, while on the desk a computer screen discreetly flashing gave a sense of work in progress.

Amy greeted her warmly. "Rosemary! You don't mind if we drop the formality now that we're colleagues? We don't have much time before the whole committee descends on us tomorrow. You don't need to bother about the budget. Just tell me how you read our larger financial situation."

Rosemary settled into a chair next to the dean's desk. "Well, Amy, you know that the budget is projected to be out of balance by about one point five million dollars in this fiscal year, which on the face of it need not be serious against total expenditures of eighty million. And the ultimate reason for the deficit, as you undoubtedly also know, is from a financial point of view rather admirable. President Eames, along with Blanche, seems to have raised with the finance committee the issue of the rate at which the college has been drawing on its endowment to support its operations. The finance committee minutes show that the trustees pretty quickly came to share their view—that using six percent of the endowment's market value each year for budget purposes might have been fine in the high-growth years of the mid-nineties, but it wasn't prudent over time. So, they've been edging that rate down. This year it was to have been at five and a quarter percent. But at the same time, there have been a couple of problems that have made reaching that goal almost impossible. You know all about the increase in the financial aid budget, I'm sure."

Amy nodded vigorously, signaling she already understood that issue. "We've been squeezing other costs for years to provide money for scholarships."

"Well, in addition to that really rather voracious expenditure, there's been trouble on the income side."

"How so?" Amy asked.

Rosemary leaned forward to rest a hand on the desk. "That's what I don't understand. And I don't think Blanche understood it fully either. There were revenue shortfalls from the investments. And that shouldn't happen. Revenue from the endowment shouldn't vary at all. It's set by applying the spending rate—this year's five and a quarter percent—to the average total endowment over the past three years. That's the amount of money you take out of the endowment account for spending this year. Actual income doesn't figure into it at all."

"Then how could it vary?" Amy's round face was perplexed.

"The only thing I can imagine is that there must have been some cash accounts somewhere that threw off interest. And in that case, it would be the actual realized gains that mattered."

"Do you know what those accounts were?"

"No. Not yet I don't."

"And do you think that the trustees were right, with Nat and Blanche, to cut our endowment spending rate?" Amy was clearly worried about presenting the overall financial policy at the next day's meeting.

"Yes, I do," Rosemary answered decisively. She explained, "Investment income as a percentage of market value has been declining, and that means you'd soon have to sell securities and erode your endowment totals to maintain a six-percent spending level. I can understand Blanche's and the president's concern."

She paused. "What I don't understand is why Blanche tried to make up the entire difference by expenditure cuts alone. In my experience, I always tried to work the cash that we might have on hand pretty hard. You're probably familiar with the float on corporate bank balances. The interest earned on overnight balances can be as high as five percent, and you can get banks and other financial institutions to bid for your cash with higher rates or other services. I don't see any evidence of that here, although I should think that rather large cash balances would build up in August and January, when tuition and board monies come in for the next semester. Surely that money doesn't go out again all at once but is used over the entire semester. Interest on such cash wouldn't solve the problem, of course, but it could take some of the pressure off the budget."

"Hmm. Well, I have no idea myself. But I'll raise the question. There are probably quite a few financial techniques that we haven't tried yet. It would be wonderful if this one could help. . . . Well. That gives me a start anyway, and in the meantime it's clearly important to keep some momentum in cutting the budget."

"I think so. It's going to be an awful headache for you, as it clearly was for Blanche before she died," observed Rosemary with concern. "But if I were you, I'd explore a couple of things with the president and the trustees early on. We've talked about the cash management. But I'd also ask them about asset allocation in the endowment. Were they holding pure cash? What proportion have they invested in higher-income securities, and how much are they allocating to growth in market value? The college's high spending policy, if it drove the investment advisers to chase yield, may have been costing Sanderson even more than the trustees recognized at their June meeting." With that, Rosemary rose and extended her hand. "I'll be glad to help tomorrow, if you need me, but I'd like to be as inconspicuous as possible. I'd rather not confuse my role here if I don't have to."

"Understood!" returned Amy, rising in her turn. "And thank you for this. I know you've chosen to do something else with your career, but it gives me a lot of comfort to be able to draw on your financial expertise—privately, if you like."

The next morning Rosemary reached the dean's anteroom in good time and found it about to overflow with humanity as committee members crowded between the secretary's desk and credenza beyond, where an aged coffee urn served all comers.

"Well, well. Here comes the morning's sacrifice. I suppose you're here to defend your budget." A man whose wild black hair surrounded his bald spot like some erratic form of tonsure waved his manila folder at her as she squeezed in the door. "Stay there, and I'll bring you some coffee."

His lanky body folding in a sequence of unlikely angles, he made his way through the others, two mugs of coffee and a clutch of papers held above the heads of all. In his wake came Kevin, his face brightening in a broad smile.

"Hello, Rosemary. This knight-errant with your coffee is

Phil Mason, an economist. But don't let appearances deceive you. Despite his size he is very, very micro."

"I'm the conscience of this place is what he means, Miss Stubbs. Rosemary?"

"Rosemary."

"And, as you may or may not know, God is in the details."

Rosemary let the remark pass and replied evenly, "Are you the senior member of the committee, then?"

"I'm the senior *faculty* member. You can't count the dean. As soon as you get to budgets, she lines up with the administration. Amazing, really." His voice picked up a querulous tone. "She used to be a first-rate historian. Still publishes, too."

With that, his interest faded, and he slipped back into the crowd to intercept the coach of the crew, who showed signs of moving on into the inner office. Rosemary observed the two figures. Chip, elegant, seemingly at ease, showing the slightest knot in the muscles of his jaw; Phil, kinetic, apparently garrulous, but scanning the group with a watchful eye. Behind them she could see Claus, standing by himself.

"Working on a new theory of the Trinity?"

"I'm sorry, Kevin, was I that absent-looking?"

"Just asked you twice whether you'd had an eventful tea on Sunday afternoon."

"Tea was fine. I was just trying to take the political pulse, and see if I could anticipate the fault lines."

"You do acclimatize fast. But I suggest you let it play out around the table. You'll see soon enough. Which brings me to ask, what brought you here? Your budget threatened already?"

"Probably, but that's just a cover. Amy wanted her own fiscal adviser."

"I see, so they think you're a 'two-fer.'"

"Not for long, but I'll help out if I can."

"Don't you think we'd better get started?" Amy, like any good heeler, had made her way to the far end of the ante-room and was moving everyone toward her door. "I don't think we can wait any longer for the others. They'll make their way in. We have a lot to do this morning." She passed out a short agenda. "As you can see, our order of business today is to go through the chapel budget with Dean Stubbs, review the proposed cuts in physical education, and then identify other programs in which we will recommend reductions. You remember that we need to cut another million and a half dollars in this year's operating expenses in order to bring the budget into balance."

Phil ran his hands through his hair, smiled at the group, and began what was clearly a well-rehearsed remark. "The academic program has already suffered considerable loss over the summer from the cuts that Blanche Werner instituted." As he paused for effect, the door opened noisily.

Gertrude Bleeker, severely but expensively dressed in a dark green suit, stepped inside. "Hope it's all right for me to sit in, Dean Standish?" Her voice made the question perfunctory. "With Nat engaged elsewhere and Blanche gone, I thought there should be a trustee presence here."

There was a lull as she took a seat facing Amy and accepted a folder full of background papers.

Determined not to yield the initiative, Phil made an inclusive gesture. "I'm sure Gertrude is as well aware of the deleterious effect of these cuts as any of us here. And now the dean and the administration are asking us to suffer another series of amputations." He looked around for endorsement from his faculty colleagues. Satisfied that he had his audience, he continued, "The entire purpose of this institution is academic, and it is unconscionable to reduce support for the teaching program while the administration indulges in expensive window dressing."

"For example?" Amy's voice was acidulous.

"For example, the chapel. Dean Stubbs is, I'm sure, without peer. But there is no reason whatsoever for Sanderson to run a chapel program at the start of the twenty-first century. Most of our students have never darkened the door of a church, and if the faculty here are successful in teaching anything about critical thought, the rest of them will give up the habit."

Kevin cocked an eyebrow at Rosemary, but she showed no inclination to speak. Phil hurtled on. "And the chapel isn't a drop in the bucket compared to Athletics. Blanche hadn't *begun* to get to the fundamentals. There's no use cutting *travel*"—his voice was shot with scorn—"it's *staff* that matters. Intercollegiate coaches have as few as nine and no more than thirty students a year!"

"That's a barefaced lie, Mason!" Chip's face was flushed, but the edge of his mouth showed white. "Not only do we teach a full undergradate schedule, most of us coach multiple team sports, and—"

Phil was unfazed. "Be that as it may, Chip. I am proposing that budget allocations are too important to be left to the administration. This committee has been window-dressing long enough. Blanche Werner allowed indefensible expense increases in some departments, while she cut others to the bone. Look at Biology!"

For the first time, Claus looked up. "Exactly what do you mean, Phil?"

"I don't know what kind of bargain you'd struck with Blanche, Claus, but everybody knows that work was going to start *this year* on a new laboratory for electron microscopy, and Nat hasn't *begun* to raise the outside funds for it."

"As for your 'facts,' Phil, you are hopelessly misinformed." Claus spoke slowly, his whole body deadly calm. "But beyond that, I want you to state what you are implying about Blanche."

"She made sweetheart deals, Claus. All administrators do. That's why the faculty have to take charge of their own resources," Mason insisted.

"*Whose* resources? The trustee finance committee—" Gertrude Bleeker was cut off by the unmistakable authority of Claus's voice.

"No one had a finer sense of justice than Blanche Werner, Phil. Favoritism was anathema to her. Blanche was consumed by the goal of making this college financially safe to benefit every aspect of the teaching program. She was the last person in the world who would grant a particular favor to the detriment of the whole. And if you continue making innuendos of this sort about her, you will answer to me. If you will excuse me, Dean Standish." He rose with the suggestion of a bow and left the room, rigidly erect. Kevin moved as if to follow him but stopped short.

Phil, intent on a political scene, was entirely unfazed by Claus's reproof. "And not another penny should be cut from the educational budget until it can be proved that all income streams have been maximized." He kept going. "From what I can read in the last quarter's reports, the endowment performance has been only mediocre, and I don't know that we've tried to develop other income sources."

"What makes you say that?" Gertrude Bleeker's voice rang in sharp challenge.

"Well, in fact, there's not a separate report here on the cash, and no record of what the college does or could earn by renting out its facilities in the summer. That's the trouble—the reporting is inadequate for our purposes."

"The reporting is not done for your purposes," Gertrude replied. "It is the trustees of the college who have fiduciary responsibility for its funds. And on the finance committee of the board, there is expertise enough to read these reports." The set of her chin left no doubt as to the ferocity of her conviction.

Phil's face flushed with a sudden rush of color that turned his earlobes a bright red.

But Amy, holding up a hand and leaning forward urgently, cut off any further exchange. "This is not the moment for a jurisdictional dispute. I'm sure we all have a common interest in the financial stability of the college." She turned to the squarish man in a brown plaid jacket seated on her right. She included him in the conversation with an encouraging smile. "Surely, Pete, these figures can be broken out for the committee, as they no doubt are for the trustees?"

Pete Zukowski, the assistant treasurer, ran the fingers of one hand along his eyebrow. "I'm not sure they can be. Blanche handled those reports by herself." He frowned as he shuffled through a stack of printouts pulled hastily from his briefcase. "Quite frankly, I haven't sorted out those systems yet."

"I'll show you." Phil leaned forward, ready for a chance to show up administrative incompetence. "I worked at Berkeley on software for this kind of thing. You get the codes, and we'll sort it out starting tomorrow."

Pete blanched visibly. "There's so much that has to be done right now. We've always been understaffed in the treasurer's office, but now I'm afraid I can't even look at this until we get the monthly expense reports straightened out."

"Well, Pete, we all understand the turmoil you're in." Amy's voice was reassuring and coaxing at the same time. "But I'd venture you could get to checking those systems by the middle of the week."

Pete nodded reluctantly. To Phil he said, "How about Thursday?"

"That's time enough to begin before the next meeting."

"And in the meantime," Amy pressed on with determination, "my office will coordinate the efforts begun by the treasurer to reduce the level of expenditure across the board. I asked Dean Stubbs to review our financial situation with me, and she has independently confirmed the wisdom of our current budget goals on the face of our endowment's earning power." She stopped for breath. "I know the board is in full command of our investment program. So, really, Phil, you can consider your inquiries as simply corroborative. And now, I think we'd better close for the day."

11

Rosemary hurried away from the meeting, embarrassed that Amy had referred to her help so publicly. Amy must have felt she had to take the initiative away from Phil, she reasoned, and she wondered for the first time about the intricacies of campus politics. She was hardly surprised when Phil caught up with her.

His elbows protruded sharply on each side of his body as he leaned toward her, making an uneven hexagon with his torso. Rosemary kept walking toward the main doors of Stearns Hall.

"Nothing personal in all that stuff I said about the chapel. Rhetoric! You have to get their attention. Amy has sold out entirely now that she's become dean. She doesn't think anymore. You'd think she was *scripted* by Nat and

Gertrude Bleeker and the rest of them. And believe me, Blanche Werner was even worse."

"What do you expect from the chief officers of the college?" Rosemary stopped and turned to face him straight on.

"Oh, nothing else, I suppose, from Blanche. But Amy is dean of the *faculty*." His rising tone cradled the word. "It's her *job* to represent the faculty in the councils of the college. And frankly, she hasn't been doing that. In the past year, she's let every significant budget cut come out of the academic side of the house. Mostly from faculty salaries."

Rosemary frowned. "Cutting faculty salaries or positions?"

"Both. We've lost three positions over the past two years. And salary increases have been held to the rate of inflation. Our peers have done a lot better than that. Amherst always goes up by at least inflation plus one percent, and in the past year Wellesley had a six-percent average increase for faculty. We're losing our competitive position—and pretty soon we're going to lose our best faculty to other places. The young ones. The ones who are really producing." Phil paused momentarily to gauge his effect.

"What makes you think Sanderson is capable of meeting that kind of competition? That's tough company you're running with."

"That *is* Sanderson's company. This is one of the most distinguished faculties of any liberal arts college." Phil stepped ahead and opened the heavy outside door for her. "And Nat's been raising money like he was minting it. Only none of it ever shows up where it should. Instead it goes into new buildings or rebuilt buildings or some damn extravaganza or other."

"And so the problem is priorities? The resources are there?" Rosemary had started down the stairs with Phil following at her side, his arms working as he played out his argument.

"The resources *should* be there. But the administration is always crying poor. Frankly, I don't think they know how to manage the money. I think that's why Blanche killed herself. Incompetence. She knew it, and she was afraid to face it!"

This time he got his effect. Rosemary whirled on the steps and stared at him hard. "If you're going to make an allegation like that, you'd better be ready to prove it."

"I will. That's just what I'm going to do when Pete Zukowski gives me the rest of the financial records." With that he bobbed a farewell, half salute, half bow, and was off.

"Dammit! What is that man up to?" Rosemary muttered to herself as she headed back to her office and a day now crammed with student appointments. It puts me in a rage to hear anybody talk about Blanche like that! she thought. And yet . . . oh Lord, something in me wishes he were right, that it were that simple. . . . But that wouldn't be simple for Claus. It would be worse. And I just can't think of Blanche as incompetent. Somehow I've got to put this out of my head and do my job.

She was already in the corridor heading for the line of students by her door when she pulled herself up to this other reality, and it was late afternoon before a phone call broke the pattern of conversation in her office.

"Rosemary? Kevin here. I was going to catch you after that shootout in Amy's office this morning, but I saw Phil had beaten me to it."

"I wish you'd been quicker out of the starting gate."

"Would you settle for a fast finish? How about supper at my place tomorrow night? It'll get you out of the campus pressure cooker."

"Wonderful!" Rosemary answered without hesitation. Hanging up a moment later she felt an unaccustomed flush of anticipation.

She spent the evening preparing for the next week's student gatherings, searching out texts to illuminate the anomalous effect of the early church on women's lives: the generous role for women among the Gnostics; the powerful place of Roman matrons, making conversion acceptable among aristocracy, providing patronage and labor in aid of the great scriptural translations of Jerome, and yet the mixed feelings and often downright hostility to women of the bishops and others, including Jerome himself. As she thought about the students, Saint Jerome himself became the clear vehicle for conveying the conflict between early Christian dependence on women and antifeminism. It was late when she resolved to go back to her office to pick out some of his more pertinent letters, with the treatises, to illustrate the point.

She walked automatically through the chapel, turning on only the overhead light in the narthex. She was still toying with the questions about Jerome as she walked out into the corridor to her office and turned the key in the lock. As she stepped into the room she froze, suddenly paralyzed by fear, convinced that she could hear someone else's breathing in the room.

"Who is it? Who's here?" she called loudly, fighting off panic and feeling for the light switch. There was no hint of light from the night sky beyond the window. She groped along the wall. Something she touched moved, pushed her violently with a sudden outgoing of breath, and spun her around. Hands closed on her shoulders and threw her against the opposite wall. Her head struck the corner of a bookcase, and she grabbed the shelf to keep from falling. There was a violent slamming of the door, and then footsteps echoed in the hallway. Rosemary waited for the sound of another door. She felt the hairs at the nape of her neck crawl. There were no more footsteps. Somewhere in the blackness the intruder was waiting.

Her hands searched the desk, but she found no phone. The lamp had been knocked away. Was her enemy hidden in the chapel, or outside waiting? Which way to run? Where was her umbrella, left yesterday beside the desk? Her only semblance of a weapon. Sweat began to run down her temples and her neck and soak the small of her back. She found the umbrella, grabbed it, and began to inch silently toward the door. Moments ebbed away and still no sound. Finally Rosemary could no longer bear waiting. She burst out and ran to her own house. It was some time after she'd slammed the front door until her heart stopped racing and she thought to call the security office.

The lights of a car burned through the dark street. She met Larry Bogdanowicz at the curb. Together they went back to the chapel.

"Hey, none of these lights work!" Bogdanowicz said, flicking the switches in the narthex just inside the doors. When they reached Rosemary's office, he turned on a powerful flashlight and swung its beam around the room. It brought a low cry from her. Everything had been turned upside down. Books were on the floor, drawers up-ended, pictures knocked off the wall. Larry took it all in slowly and then flicked the switch on the pager at his waist. "Call the chief," he said. "And the Metford police too. Something's wrong over at the chapel."

After Rosemary had been escorted home by a second security officer and waited patiently as he checked attic, closets, and basement, she was still sitting up in her living room, trying vainly to wrench her thoughts from the turmoil in her office to the printed page of a biography of Saint Jerome. There was a discreet knock on her door. After a moment's hesitation, she opened it slightly to see Detective Ramirez on the porch.

"Come in!" She opened the door wide, glad for a visitor.

"I saw that your lights were still on downstairs and thought you might prefer to talk now." He paused. "And I thought it would be advisable, if at all possible."

She returned his steady but troubled look and nodded slowly. "Come into the living room. Can I get you anything to drink?"

"That's a nasty gash on your head," he said while shaking his head no to her offer.

"Hurts like hell when I stand up, and I'm not going to be able to shake my head for a week."

"I'm afraid the attack on your office and on yourself was serious, Dean Stubbs."

Rosemary was almost amused by the grave demeanor of this meticulous man but still inclined to brush off his warning, since it interfered with her increasingly desperate attempts to concentrate on her job. She struggled, pretending that the terror she had felt an hour ago was only normal fear of an intruder. "Who, besides an uncle in New York, would care a jot about what I do or how I keep my office?"

"That's something I'd certainly like to know. What did you keep in that office that might have attracted attention?"

"An academic library; my computer, no files to speak of; no money; not even any bills yet—haven't been here long enough." She stopped to think. "Oh yes, Amy Standish gave me a set of the regular treasurer's reports to the trustee finance committee, and I'd made notes on them."

"Could you go through your office with me to tell me what is missing? Tomorrow morning?"

Rosemary answered, "How about tonight? Right now? Maybe it'll help with the jitters."

"All right, that may be a good idea." He rose and offered her a hand to steady her as she got up. She smiled again at his formality but at the same time felt reassured by it.

As they walked toward the chapel, she confessed, "I was

terrified that the person was still in the building and would come back again."

"I suspect you were right to be fearful. I don't think the intruder had left the building. All the electric circuits had been thrown by the time you and Bogdanowicz got back, including those in the main chapel. He, or she, must have gone to the mechanic's closet after being discovered. And I don't know what would have happened if your panic hadn't taken over and if you had stayed in your office. . . . You certainly surprised the intruder the first time. That was your best defense."

Within a few minutes, lights restored, they were working together to sort the mess, Rosemary sitting cross-legged on the floor, Ramirez shelving books at her direction, restoring scattered papers to their files. Satisfied at last, he leaned against her desk, arms folded.

"What's missing?"

"None of the books. Tape's gone out of that wretched answering machine. Chapel files all here. Finance committee documents seem to tally by months. But I can't find the notes I took from them that had my own sort of rough calculations."

"And the reason you were doing that?"

"Amy Standish asked me to give her a rough-and-ready financial briefing prior to the college budget committee meeting, and last Sunday she gave me the dossier you've got there."

"What were your conclusions?"

"Nothing much. Blanche had very tight control of expenditures, as you hear from every constituency on campus. The investment results on the endowment were okay but not terrific. I looked for returns on overnight cash invested but couldn't find any separate reports. So nothing at all, really. Certainly nothing to worry about."

"There's a great deal to worry about, I'm afraid, Dean Stubbs." Ramirez had planted his hands on the edge of her desk and was leaning back, arms stiff. Rosemary was startled by how striking he looked, his pale skin contrasting with eyes so dark they looked almost black. His high cheekbones and straight mouth added to a natural gravity.

"What makes you say that?"

"Because . . ." He paused, looking at her as though he were making some internal calculus. "Because there seems to be every indication that Blanche Werner was murdered."

"What? Are you sure?"

"She died, as you know, of a massive dose of digitalis that had been injected into her bloodstream. She had no prior history of heart-related illness and no recorded prescriptions, current or previous, for digitalis-based drugs."

"But why? Why?" Rosemary struggled ungracefully to her feet, still dizzy when she changed altitude. He reached out to help her, then looked again closely at the wound above her temple.

"You might get this checked at the health center," he said. And then brusquely, "We don't know why yet. Perhaps because of some dispute that had nothing to do with the college. Or perhaps because of some terrible chance encounter. But this attack on you and on your files implies that it might have been because she knew something.

Something that you might know, or be expected to know, also."

Rosemary felt her fingertips go cold, then numb, and then she felt the coldness seep into her whole body.

"I don't know anything that any moderately alert person with some financial awareness wouldn't know automatically on looking at the college's public records. How can you be so sure these two attacks are related? After all, this person tonight might have just been some freethinker, intent on mussing up the chaplain and scaring her out of town."

"Could be." The detective smiled at her. "And I'm sure it will be much less difficult to get through a day if you believe it. But it's my job to see that you do not just operate as usual. Until we know that this breaking and entering was inconsequential, I must ask you to exercise special care. Do not go out by yourself when it is dark—and that includes the early mornings." He was grave again, bending slightly toward her in his earnestness as he stood to leave. "I have asked campus security to escort you whenever necessary."

1 2

It took a good deal of persuading on Rosemary's part to convince Larry Bogdanowicz she didn't need his company when she started out in her own car for dinner at Kevin's the next evening. When she assured him she would arrive in daylight and have an escort home, he reluctantly let chivalry override officiousness—for the moment. Now, following Kevin's directions, she took a road out of town that became increasingly narrow as it gave way to a single lane of hard-packed, bumpy clay. It climbed steadily through second-growth timber marked out in precise angles by the remnants of stone walls. After turning sharply to the right, it rose for another quarter of a mile and then fell away in a steep dip that brought her out into open meadow and lawn. Set into the hillside on her right, a brick house commanded an extended view of the tiny valley. Below, just on the other side of the road, an old dairy barn had been converted for horses and equipment.

Rosemary looked across to see Kevin coming out of the barn. A dark brown mare was walking quietly by his side, a brindle-and-white bull terrier following some distance behind.

"Come on over while I just put this mare out, and then we can wander up to the house," he called. By the time she had joined him, the mare, released, was hightailing across the field, her hooves making a sharp tattoo on the hard ground.

"She's gorgeous," observed Rosemary appreciatively, "but what an explosion!"

"Mmm. I keep her inside during the day in early autumn. Face flies are awful up here this time of year. She can't wait to get out at nightfall."

"Is she turbocharged like that when you ride her?" asked Rosemary.

"Sometimes. But she uses that energy for liftoff. She was a great jumper in her day."

"And that was your day, too?"

"You've got it." Kevin gave Rosemary a sideways grin. "We're both has-beens now. You can tell."

"No. I've been *told* you retired from competitive riding— after the 1996 Olympics. But you've chosen such a heavenly spot to settle, no wonder you retired. I can't imagine how you even go down to the college to teach." She looked around the pocket valley, its bowl a dark green in the fast-fading light, the trees that surrounded it shaping the sunset.

"It is seductive, isn't it? You could easily misspend your middle age in a rocking chair on that porch," he said jerking his chin up toward the house. "Until about mid-October, when winter sets in!" He took her elbow to hand her up the rough granite steps leading to the house, but he stopped suddenly to stare at her forehead, where the gash was just scabbing up by her temple and the yellow streaks of bruising were spreading down her cheekbones from her left eye.

"Rigors of theology? Or do you always bang your head against the wall?"

Rosemary laughed. "Nope. Somebody else did it for me. Seems the thirst for knowledge overcame 'em, and then they overcame me."

"Wait a minute." Kevin took the step ahead of her and blocked her way. "What do you mean, 'they'? Who hit you? When?"

"Last night. I went back to my office about midnight to get some texts. Somebody was there, in the dark." Rosemary paused, feeling her skin crawl with the terror of the memory. "Anyway, the somebody didn't expect me either, and he—or she—knocked me across the room and ran off. I landed on the corner of the bookcase, and the rest you can see for yourself." She gave a dismissive smile. It had no effect.

"What did you do then? Did you get help? What about your head? Are you sure there's no damage under the surface?"

Without giving her time to answer, his fingers began to explore the edges of her wound. Rosemary was astonished at his gentleness. Her agitation at the memory of the attack subsided at his touch.

"It's okay. You *are* hard-headed." He looked at her without smiling, taking in her wide-set hazel eyes and her smooth complexion, flushed now enough to raise the color in her cheeks. "Too hard-headed for your own good. Why didn't you call me? Did you get any help?"

Laughing, she stepped around him and started up the steps. "I'm going to be helped right into a straitjacket if I don't look out. The campus police came and have insisted on 'watching' me after dark. I had to promise to arrive here on my own *before* dark. And you, kind host, will have to escort me back!"

"Before the witching hour? Now that *is* too bad. I was hoping you'd stay way beyond chaplain's hours. We've got a lot to talk about. Far too much for an early evening."

She gave him her most devastating smile. "Perhaps I'll just dodge the police then."

"I'll try to make it well worth your while." He bent over to halt the dog, who was determined to come into the house with them.

"Don't stop her on my account."

"Mona? She has to stay out. Otherwise she'll drink up your bourbon and branch. And we can't have that. What's the point of dodging your escort if you stay sober?"

She laughed at his comic expression, gave Mona a pat, and stepped into the small, square kitchen, painted white, that took up the center of the house.

"Come this way. No kitchen duties tonight for you, my friend. You're to be waited on hand and foot."

They turned right and stepped into a large, rectangular room that reached up a full story and a half to a cathedral ceiling. At the far end a series of double windows opened to a stone wall and the sharply climbing hills beyond it. To the left, a pair of French doors led to a meadow that swept down from the house and its borders and around one side of the pocket valley. About fifty yards from the house, a broken line of sugar maples marked off the lawn from the field beyond.

Kevin watched as Rosemary took in the view. "Now I will take your drinks order."

"I need a stiff one. I still get bent out of shape when I think of Blanche."

A moment later he was back, generous doses of bourbon in hand. As he gave her hers, he murmured, "οὐ γὰρ θέμις ἐν μοισοπόλων † οἰκία † θρῆνον ἔμμεν· οὔ κ' ἄμμι πρέποι τάδε."

"Will you give a poor preacher a hand?" She smiled at him.

"'It is not right that there should be lamentation in the house of those who serve the Muses. That would not be fitting for us.' Sappho, embellished by Socrates on a fateful night. And fitting for us. No death tonight. No attacks. Just a little wine and, if you're lucky, some food."

"You're right. What a gift this evening is." Rosemary paused for a moment to listen to the night sounds of early autumn before the first killing frost silences the insects. Then she turned from the French doors to the lit fireplace at the other side of the room.

They settled comfortably into the oversized easy chairs drawn up before the fire. On the table between them was a fresh pâté de foie gras, amply laced with port.

"Now tell me about those Greek lyric poets. They wrote popular songs, didn't they? Designed to be sung to the lyre?" Rosemary began.

"I see you know it all. But yes, that's where 'lyric' comes from. And Sappho was surely the best of them all." He tilted his head back against the chair and spoke to the ceiling. "Sappho would have said to you tonight, 'As the sweet apple reddens on the bough-top, on the top of the topmost bough, . . . the apple-gatherers could not reach it.'" His gaze was more direct than she'd expected, and she felt herself redden. The silence in the room deepened until he began to fuss happily with the fire and to freshen their drinks.

"How did you end up here?" Rosemary asked at last, stirring lazily in her chair.

Kevin stood up, his back to the fire, and looked down at her. "The secret of life, as far as I'm concerned, is to know when to quit . . . I'm not a Yank, you know—it was Canada I rode for in the '96 Olympics. We did very well as a team overall. And old Absinthe out there did even better lugging me around the cross-country course. Together we had the second-highest individual score. But that was it for me. I could have gone on and on pushing the envelope, busting my gut to be number one and probably breaking down Abby and a bunch of other horses in the process—or I could just quit cleanly. And I've read far too much Homer for obsession to have any appeal for me. So, quit it was."

"And Sanderson?" she asked.

"Oh, that was the easy part," he laughed. "I'd filled in here a couple of semesters when the previous Greek professor was on leave. And as my luck would have it, he retired in the summer of '96. It was made to order. Especially when I found this farm."

"But how did you manage to ride competively at those levels and still have an academic career? I thought training for the Olympics was pretty much a full-time job." Rosemary was genuinely puzzled.

"Well, it is, or at least it was for me, in the year immediately prior to the Games. But other than that, I'd get up and work the horses very early in the day and then go off. I never wanted to be a professional at riding." He laughed. "Or at anything else for that matter. I never was a full-time scholar either, until maybe now, at Sanderson. I'm not a Ph.D., you know. Just an 'M.A., Oxon.'"

"I see it all now. You're one of those people who read 'Greats' as an undergraduate at Oxford and knows everything in the world from that time on!"

"Yup." He spread some pâté on a slice of bread and, smiling, handed it to Rosemary. "Makes the rest of life so simple."

"All right then, what made you choose Greek in the first place?"

"Laziness, probably. Greek wasn't all that hard for me. Except for the verbs." He bowed his head to her. "And when I went to Oxford after the University of Toronto, I got into the old academic habit of writing poetry in antique forms. Spoiled me for an honest day's work and made an amateur poet of me ever after. Which reminds me, if I don't give up poetry for the moment and rescue our supper from the fire, you'll remember me as a man who couldn't even put dinner on the table."

Kevin refused all offers of help from Rosemary, and in a few minutes they were seated at a small table lit by a scattering of candles against the sudden darkness of New England autumn visible outside the French doors. Salmon with tarragon, roasted on the grill outside, was accompanied by a gratin of potato and leeks, followed by mesclun and toasted walnuts. Rosemary noted that Kevin was opening a second bottle of Stonestreet Chardonnay before she was even aware of how many times he'd filled her glass. She felt exhilarated in the company of a kindred spirit, someone who loved learning as a way of life, not a scholarly field to be grittily worked upon.

When it was time to leave, Kevin pulled back Rosemary's chair, steadied her as she rose, and kissed her, cradling her face very gently in his hands. She felt a sudden surge of physical attraction, something she'd thought a thing of the past. She settled happily against his body, looked up, and said, "How would Sappho say, 'I find you very attractive'?"

"Will you stay then?" he asked, his hands lightly caressing her shoulders.

She straightened her back and pulled gently away. "It's too soon for me, Kevin. But you're getting me there faster than you'd think."

"I guess I'm in the same place as Sappho's apple-gatherers tonight. Never mind. I'd better be taking you home, or the police will want to know where you are. I'll just borrow your car for the night, if you don't mind."

She nodded silently, and they made their way back down the granite steps. The ride back to the college was quiet, each of them absorbed in thought. When they reached her house and she turned to go, Rosemary was dismayed by how distant he'd become.

"Kevin. I hope you'll forgive my contradictions. I'm a lot more mixed up than I look, you know."

"It seems that way," he said. "Now let me get you safely in the door, or I'll be cited for contempt of police orders or something."

With a formal bow at her threshold, he was off.

Rosemary closed the door tightly and looked down at the waiting Fannie. "Fan, old girl, *why* was I such an idiot?"

13

It was still dark at five o'clock when Rosemary, unable to sleep, gave it up and pulled on her sweats to go to the office before running. The tumult of the last week, overlaid now by Detective Ramirez's virtual certainty that Blanche had been murdered, raced constantly through her mind. Without notifying campus security or indulging in a twinge of fear for herself, she crossed the lawn between her house and the chapel in the dark. As she settled at her desk, pulling out the liturgical texts for the coming Sunday and turning on her computer to begin writing a new sermon, she admitted to herself that she was distracted.

The memory of Kevin's voice last night as he leaned toward her, her sudden surprise at the delight of his touch, his withdrawal—or was it anger?—after her sudden disengagement; the recollections wouldn't let her sink into a work routine. He was a very attractive man; she wondered why she hadn't noticed before. Why didn't I stay? she asked herself. Was it because Kevin seemed so damned practiced? The evening had been too smooth, as though seduction were just another of the learned arts with him. Because she'd like some sense that his affection was *real*? And then she was off, debating with herself whether the wish to have tenderness last was not just some form of greed extended over time. The sermon languished on her desk as the day broke, gray with a light rain.

Suddenly her quiet was interrupted by the arrival of the entire crew team.

"Dean Stubbs! Why are you here at this time of day? You'd better come with us!"

A crowd of young women, all bathed in varying degrees of perspiration, spilled into the office. They were identifiable by their collective aroma of gym and by their Sanderson sweats with crossed oars over the heart.

A diminutive Asian student pushed through the group to the edge of Rosemary's desk. "I'm Martha Kim, cox of the varsity eight. We were running and saw the light in your window, and we thought you might be lonely. So we came to get you." Her smile was kindness itself. "You can work out with us."

Rosemary surveyed them. "And what if Coach Barbour were to catch us? You know what he's like about workouts."

"Oh. That's okay. This isn't official or anything. We've finished that part, with our final lap to the river and back. Now we're on our own time."

"Have you ever worked out on the machines?" The questioner rested her elbow on Martha's shoulder and leaned forward to inspect Rosemary.

"Not rowing machines. In fact, not even Nautilus."

"Come on down to the old gym with us and we'll introduce you to the rowing machines. It won't take long. I'm Melanie Nuccio, by the way, number seven oar."

Rosemary gave in, happy that she had dressed for a morning run. "Okay. Set a pace to the gym that I've got some hope of keeping to."

As they streamed out of the back door of the chapel, she took her place between Martha and Melanie. Leslie and the others in the first four ran abreast ahead of them, keeping to what was, for them, a measured gait. To Rosemary it seemed blistering, reducing her conversation to an occasional nod or smile. When they reached the gym she was red-faced and winded.

"This way!"

The crew kept jogging matter-of-factly, peeling off to the left, heading downstairs into a basement that had never seen the light of day and was weakly illuminated by some defeated bulbs of low wattage.

"Whew!" Rosemary reacted to the low ceilings and close atmosphere.

"Yeah," said Melanie. "This is definitely not on the prospective-student tour. And no tank for the crew in the new building either. Guess we should have known." But neither the gloom of the place nor the dashing of their intercollegiate prospects could dampen Melanie's spirits for more than an instant.

The group broke up as they came into a small anteroom strewn with foam mats covered in royal-blue plastic. Weights in varying sizes and shapes lined the perimeter.

Leslie pointed out to Rosemary, "The rowing room's just through here. When I first saw it I thought it was straight out of the fun house in some amusement park."

"You mean I can't help but watch myself," Rosemary laughed as she came into a workout room lined with mirrors on all four walls and filled by a double rank of machines, each of which hitched a bicycle wheel with movable handle bars to a rowing seat, constructed to slide between two long steel rails. Foot pedals were fixed at the head of the rails.

"Just climb on and put your feet here, just on the pedals. Now take hold of the handlebars, and as you pedal, let the seat carry you back. You pull the handlebars with you. Then the handles will carry you forward again."

"And don't laugh. You won't be able to spare the breath."

In spite of the warning, Rosemary could hardly keep from laughing at herself as her seat scooted awkwardly back and she tipped crazily rearward when the whole mechanism slid forward. Nowhere but the ceiling was there mercy from the multiple reflections of her own flailing. In an instant, Leslie was laughing with her, and then the whole eight applauded as she began to get her own rhythm.

"Enough! The one thing I did learn in business was to stop when I was ahead." Rosemary uncoiled herself as deftly as she could and stood up.

As she headed up the stairs a moment later, the students' voices followed her. "Pretty good!"

"Almost ready for the novice boat."

The most satisfying benediction came from Martha. "Hey, Leslie was right. You may be the chaplain, but you're not weird!"

Rosemary emerged into a rain that was now heavy and set out through the lower campus on the shortest route home, literally floating with a sense of inner liberation. Her sweatsuit hung shapelessly, limp with rain and perspiration; her hair was plastered to forehead and eyelids; she had never felt better.

"Rosemary! Dean Stubbs—hey!"

Rosemary hunched up her shoulders at the thought of meeting anyone in this condition.

"You're looking *très sportive*. I had a hard time figuring out it was you!" Phil Mason came up beside her, a spymaster's raincoat bunched up around him, his head protected by an ancient ski cap. "You're just the person I wanted to find."

Rosemary greeted him without warmth. "Oh, really? Well. Let's talk as we go. I need to get home and get out of these things."

He seemed puzzled by what he took to be her negativity. "I hope you're not holding some kind of a grudge from Tuesday's meeting? I mean, that sort of thing doesn't matter. It's just part of the give and take that gets the debate down to real essentials."

Rosemary was aware now of an ever-increasing rivulet of rain coming from her wet hair down the inside of her sweatshirt. She wriggled her shoulders as she turned toward him. "If the chapel budget wasn't the point on Monday morning, should I assume that Dean Standish was?"

"Well, I wouldn't be so personal, really. I'd say the whole administration was." Phil was fully in earnest, as though her good opinion was crucial to him.

"What do you mean, the administration? When it's only Nat and Amy—and was Blanche as well—it's got to be personal!"

"No, no, you don't understand! It's not the people. What matters is that we don't have our priorities right at the college at the moment. We're going off after will-o'-the-wisps. You have to understand that there are hard times coming for private colleges in this country . . ."

Rosemary felt that had she been wearing lapels, he would have grasped them.

"And we have to conserve our resources for the educational program." The rain had gathered in beads all over the wool of his ski cap, and they fell, one by one, making little splashes onto his nose as he spoke.

"Faculty salaries?" Rosemary recalled their earlier conversation and hoped it would not have to be repeated in the pouring rain.

"Only salary enough to keep us competitive with the very best. And then the library and the academic support staff. We absolutely have to have more staff for academic computing. It's not right that faculty should be left on their own to do the software for their courses."

"And, I suppose, laboratory equipment?" Rosemary interjected.

Phil rubbed the sleeve of his raincoat over his forehead and nose and shook the water from his cap. "I wouldn't worry about that at Sanderson," he said. "The Biology Department always got its favors from Blanche. And Claus always seemed to get things for his colleagues as well as himself." He laughed shortly. "The Chemistry Department has had three of its labs completely rebuilt in the last couple of years."

"Well, then, Sanderson is lucky," said Rosemary coolly. "I bet there are many colleges that would give a lot to have well-provisioned laboratories."

They had come to Cullen Street, and Rosemary was making her way resolutely toward home. Phil, who had followed her as far as his sense of propriety would allow, put out a hand. "You know about these things, Rosemary. Just try to see it now from the faculty point of view."

In spite of herself, as she shook hands with him, Rosemary felt a certain sympathy toward the man

"Okay," she said. "At least I'll take a stab at considering things from your point of view. But don't count on winning a convert in me." With that she ducked across the street and headed for home, noting on the way that Kevin had returned her car. I hope he stuck the key through the mail slot, she thought as she opened the front door.

He had. She picked up the bulky envelope lying on the floor and opened it as she stripped off her sweatshirt. With the keys was a note that opened in Greek and finished in a brief translation: "The moon has set and the Pleiades; it is midnight, and time goes by, and I lie alone."

At least he's not angry with me, she thought as she spread the soaking pullover out to dry in the kitchen. She noted her own relief wryly and then paused again at the south-facing window, the rain making the garden drearier, if anything, than it had been. Today the sight of it did nothing to diminish her spirits. The voices of the students, their generosity in hunting her down and folding her momentarily into their group, the sense of laughter and exhilaration at her "workout" had lightened her spirit. This is it, she thought. This is where I want to be, among these students. Useful, if I can be, in the college. She looked out at the garden more closely and imagined she could make it grow. Remembering the invitation pressed on her by the crew, she was determined to join them next week on the river to watch their workout from the motor launch.

Getting ready to shower and face the day, she knew she had come for good. I'll strip out that apartment in New York, she thought. There's no use living in what looks like a campsite here when there are rooms full of furniture ready to be moved from the city. She kicked at the book boxes that remained in the hallway and decided to pack things up in New York on Saturday.

She smiled to herself as she took the stairs in twos and thought, When I do get all unpacked I'll find that tag from Horace. How does it go—"Put aside all this Greek and speak to me in Latin." For Kevin Oxley!

14

As Rosemary went through the rest of the day, seeing students, meeting with the organist, taking her turn on the campus committee for community outreach, she felt a growing confidence. Even the crucial meeting with Blanche's two nephews in preparation for tomorrow's memorial service did not seem quite as painful as she'd feared. They were Episcopalians, as Blanche had been, and asked that the service contain passages from the now disused 1928 Book of Common Prayer. Rosemary was glad to comply, to fit that elevated language into the plainness of the nondenominational memorial.

She worked now through her own, much-thumbed copy of the old prayer book, selecting texts. The music had been settled. The full Sanderson choir had been practicing Pachelbel's Canon for some days. Nathan Eames had agreed to give the eulogy, followed by Petra, who would offer a more personal remembrance. It fell to Rosemary to lead the prayers and to give a brief sermon. As she struggled with the problem of how to capture ordinary life in extraordinary language so that the heart might be stopped for reflection, she came back time and again to the Elizabethans and their immediate successors. There was always the comfort of George Herbert, of course, who had known something about the uncertainties of casting a sermon. "Judge not the preacher . . . /Do not grudge /to pick out treasures from an earthen pot."

Well, I'm an earthen pot, for sure, she thought. Somehow the violence of the Tudors and the follies of the Stuarts seem to be close to this dreadful time in Metford. I can't *say* murder. The police themselves haven't said it publicly. But still there's a smell of violence in the air. Shakespeare would have recognized it—so would Donne.

She swept everything from her desk, pushed the computer to the farthest corner, and spread her favorite seventeenth-century texts around her. As night fell, the anguish of loss ceased to be personal; it became the dominant mountain range in the human topography, overarched only by the anguish of hope. She worked until she literally fell asleep at her desk.

As Rosemary waited for the other participants in Blanche's service to gather at her office the next morning, she watched a long line of cars discharge passengers along Cullen Street. The chapel was already full of faculty, staff, and a large scattering of students who had put aside any resentments they might have earlier felt toward Blanche. Among the strangers now crowding up the steps, she thought she recognized faces from last winter's gathering of college treasurers in New Haven, as well as unknown friends of Blanche's in astonishing number. The buildings and grounds crew, many of whom had come only to attend the service, were now hurrying to fill the side aisles and even the narthex with folding chairs. It's a good thing we had no plan to have a procession, she thought to herself as she went out to greet Nat Eames on the steps. Petra met them at the office door; they slipped into plain black grosgrain robes and entered the chancel by a side door.

Waiting for the congregation to settle, Rosemary looked for familiar faces in the crowd. She saw Tara and Nan in the crowd, and then was touched to see the whole of the crew's varsity eight lined up in a pew close to the front. Farther back, she made out Claus's significant height and bald head, and next to him Kevin. With that, she looked away and prayed passionately that this service might bring some comfort to Claus.

The prelude over, the congregation joined in the hymn "For All the Saints" with a sound too subdued for its number.

Rosemary rose: "The Lord is my light and my salvation; whom then shall I fear? The Lord is the strength of my life; of whom then shall I be afraid? . . . For in the time of trouble he shall hide me in his tabernacle. . . ."

Nathan Eames gave a fulsome account of Blanche's career and of her many ties to the college. It was as lavish in its praise as it was detached in delivery. But whatever it lacked, or suppressed, in emotion was supplied by Petra's reminiscences, which managed to be funny and respectful and loving by turns. Rosemary took as her text Psalm 39, "Lord, let me know mine end, and the number of my days," and contrasted John Donne's long and elaborate preparations for his death with Blanche's sudden demise. She found violence enough in that very suddenness and asked how the community and friends Blanche had left behind were to find peace in the shadow of her passing. She would turn them from the violence of resentment and remind them of the universal prayer of the psalmist: "And now, Lord, what is my hope? Truly my hope is even in thee. . . . Hear my prayer, O Lord . . . for I am a stranger with thee, and a sojourner. . . ."

At the end, the congregation found its voice, and the final hymn filled the chapel with a resurgent spirit. That alone was enough to quicken an ephemeral sense of community, and Nat and Rosemary were able to greet guests and college members alike with some semblance of good feeling. Out of the corner of her eye, Rosemary saw Claus avoid them and the crowd and make his way alone up the street.

Kevin waited until the end of the line at the chapel doors. He took Rosemary's hand and held it a moment. "Well, you are a chaplain indeed! For the first time in my life you've made me less than a cheerful pagan! No less pagan, perhaps, but certainly less cheerful about it." The tone of his voice became less playful, and he simply said, "Rosemary, I know your sermon was a great help to Claus."

Seeing Nat Eames approach, Kevin turned to greet the president, after calling over his shoulder to her, "Oh, Rosemary, when you're finished here, would you have a minute to see me in your office? There's something I'd like to check with you."

Rosemary nodded briefly before speaking to the last stragglers and heading to the chancel to see that everything was in place. Aware of her obligation to be present fairly promptly at the campus reception for Blanche's family, she hurried to her office. Kevin had let himself in and was pacing the tiny area between bookcases and desk.

He left no time for pleasantry. "What do you know about digitalis?" he asked.

"In particular?"

"In the case of Blanche's death," Kevin retorted.

"Why do you ask?" Against her every inclination, Ramirez's warning to confidentiality echoed in her memory.

"Because the police searched Claus's laboratory and supply closets this morning and removed a container of digitalis from one of them."

Rosemary sank onto the arm of the big chair. "I can't not tell you now. Detective Ramirez told the trustees when I was present that Blanche died of a massive dose of digitalis.

Because it wasn't known whether she had any prescription for its use, he asked us not to tell anyone else. But Tuesday night, after the intruder broke in here, Ramirez told me that Blanche had no medical history of heart disease and no prescription for the drug. He didn't, however, free me to say anything about it." She sighed.

"So he believes Blanche was murdered," Kevin stated flatly. He stood for a moment, hands in pockets, staring out the window. When he turned back to Rosemary, his face was severe. "And does he think it was the murderer who attacked you in here?"

"He didn't say that. He just said he'd take precautions."

"He might have some brains after all," Kevin admitted reluctantly. "But I don't like it—not any of it. It's only one police-jump from seizing that digitalis to seizing on the idea that Claus is a murderer. And meanwhile, a likely *real* murderer is breaking in here and God knows where else on campus."

"I don't like it either, Kevin. But I do think Detective Ramirez exaggerated the significance of the attack on me. And surely the presence of a chemical in a laboratory supply room is no indication that it was used for . . ." Rosemary's voice trailed off.

Kevin shook his head. "You're more optimistic than I am about police work, Rosemary," he said, reaching to open the door for her. "But use those security guards, will you?"

"All right. I will. But I *won't* stop trying to find out who killed Blanche."

15

When Rosemary arrived at the dean's office the next morning for a hastily called meeting of the budget committee, there was an air of hectic excitement about the group in the outer office. Searching the crowd, she saw that Kevin was not yet there. Amy greeted each new arrival with studied normality, but she was clearly anxious. She counted heads as Rosemary came in the door.

Claus entered behind her, his shoulders drawn up, his mouth pinched. He moved to the coffee urn without speaking to anyone.

Before she had time to decide whether or not to approach Claus, Rosemary became aware of Kevin by her side. She was surprised once again by her pleasure at his presence, but she noticed that he, too, looked particularly grim.

"Something's up, Rosemary."

"Claus looks worse."

"It's not that, though you're right there. It's Phil. Amy called me first thing this morning to say that Pete Zukowski couldn't get the documentation for him yesterday. But he did give Phil the monthly expenditure records dating from July first. Not just the printouts. Phil was so insistent, Zukowski handed him the entire bunch of files. Phil must have been working on them all night, because now there are rumors that he's discovered something,

something that involves Blanche. He's the one who insisted on this meeting."

"I think we'd better get started." Amy was herding again. They moved at her behest into the office.

Rosemary settled at the end of the table between two of the senior women on the committee, the three of them facing Amy. Phil took the seat at the dean's left, while Chip Barbour and Kevin filled in.

Phil began as if he were the chair of the meeting. "Because I had to wait for Pete Zukowski to get his house in order, I got from his office a printout of departmental expenditures since the beginning of the fiscal year and the related files." His eyes swept the group aggressively, daring anyone to challenge his action.

Kevin took him up. "You know, Phil, line-by-line accountability has never been the charge of this committee. That's the business of the treasurer. We're here to give advice on policy matters."

"That's exactly it. Blanche Werner's dead. Maybe by her own hand. What did she want to hide? What couldn't she account for? *That's* what I want to know."

Rosemary watched Claus shift in his chair, then lean forward to face Mason. "Shut up, Phil!" His voice rose. "Don't you ever speak about Blanche in that way again—whether I'm present or not! Because if you do . . ."

Kevin reached out and grabbed Henderson's shoulder. His voice, low but tense, cut between the two men. "Phil, you're way out of line! You can't go rooting through departmental accounts. You don't have the background or the authority. And you've got no right to throw innuendos around about Blanche or anyone else."

"Listen, Kevin. I don't know what's made you so namby-pamby all of a sudden. I can read records as well as anyone. And I don't care about innuendos; I'm after the facts."

"Now wait a minute." Kevin leaned forward.

"I'm not waiting at all. You can speak when I've finished my report. A total of fifteen thousand dollars has been spent since April on repairs to various boats used by the crew. And, in addition, an entirely new launch was purchased just to tag after that flotilla on the river every morning, and *that* cost forty-two thousand dollars."

"That launch replaced one that was twenty years old and beyond repair." Chip sat bolt upright.

"Why should it have been repaired at all, Chip? That's the question. What business does Sanderson have with a crew that soaks up money like a sponge? And especially why does it need one now, when our income is down?"

"*Because* it is the mission of this college to educate the whole human being."

"Bullshit. We've heard all that *mens sana* piety before. I'm talking about educational priorities now. In real money. And just those few items come to fifty-seven thousand dollars. But that's just the beginning. I found in Blanche Werner's handwriting"—Phil paused to look around the group again, his eyes glittering with excitement—"an authorization for the expenditure of five hundred and sixty-two thousand dollars for a new electron microscope for the botany laboratory. An expenditure which had been discussed with no one and which was to be a direct charge to this year's operating budget." He leaned back in his chair to watch the effect of his bombshell on the group.

"What are you implying, Mason?" Claus slammed his open palm on the table furiously.

"That Blanche Werner had clearly made a sweetheart deal with you to buy a single piece of equipment at an astronomical cost for your own use and, in effect, to take it out of the paychecks of every member of this faculty."

"This is outrageous." Claus began to rise from his chair. "I won't stand for it. Yes, there is an electron microscope on order—for the Biology Department, not for me. I have discussed the purchase personally with the president, and so did Blanche. He was absolutely sure he could find a donor for the instrument. He had someone in mind. There was no question, ever, of it being a charge to the operating budget of the college." His face was white with rage. He leaned toward Mason. "I deeply resent, on Blanche's behalf, even more than on my own, your totally unfounded accusation."

"What made you so sure, Phil, that this was to be a charge to the operating budget?" The faculty member on Rosemary's right, Beryl Pettit, raised her eyes from her papers to fix Mason with an intense gaze.

"Because there's no provision for that sum, or anything approaching it, in any capital budget. In fact, as far as I can tell, we don't even *have* a detailed capital budget, except for building repairs. And authorization for the electron microscope is for delivery in December, with payment beginning in January."

"There is nothing in that schedule which is inconsistent with Nat's usual way of fund-raising. It's just what one would expect if there is a donor already interested and planning an end-of-the-year gift." Beryl spoke slowly and exactly, turning from Phil to Amy.

"Look, Phil," Kevin said, his voice low. "There is absolutely no point in making a public spectacle of this note of Blanche's. Nat Eames knows all about it, I'm sure. As Beryl says, it's consistent with his way of doing things." Kevin was speaking now less to Phil than to the rest of the group. "If he likes an idea, Nat usually goes off to raise the money for it. What you're alleging about some special favors has absolutely no basis in evidence. I suggest that we leave it alone until Amy has had a chance to discuss it with the president."

As he sat back the majority of the group, acutely embarrassed by the confrontation and by Claus's outburst, began a low murmur of assent. Amy rode the wave decisively.

"Nat's tied up today, but I'll brief him as soon as I can. And, Phil, you might want to talk with him yourself."

"All right, Amy," Phil conceded. "And by the next time we meet I will have reviewed in detail the investment returns. Pete Zukowski's going to turn the system over to me. I have all the necessary codes." He was jubilant, oblivious to the unhappiness his report had caused. He went on, "Then, I suggest we'll find either two million dollars in a combination of unwarranted expenditures, or investment underreturns, or both, which can be remedied with improved management."

"Phil." Amy spoke with authority but without anger. "Nobody would be happier than I would if you could find us two million dollars for the operating budget this year. I'd even take some of it to strike you a medal! But I suspect that the savings you are counting on just aren't there. I don't know about the electron microscope, but I imagine Kevin is right. Nat never has talked about things much until he's got the money in hand. Damned inconvenient from time to time, if I may say so."

"Amy." Claus rose and stood towering above the table, now only the slight shaking of his hand showing the extent of his anger. "I've had all I can stand of this. You and I have been talking about that damned electron microscope for eighteen months now, and not only that but a whole raft of computers for the advanced lab in the cellular structures."

"Of course we have, Claus. And I support the department fully on this. It's just that I didn't know Nat had found a donor."

"It should be enough that I say so!" He slammed his papers onto the table and was gone, leaving waves of dismay throughout the room. Kevin followed him out.

Amy was quick to react. "I think, my friends, that I had better end the meeting here. Next week, somehow, we are simply going to have to get down to approving cuts—or I'll have to go ahead with them without your approval. We can't postpone it forever."

Rosemary rose to leave with the rest of them. As she filed out, she found herself shoulder to shoulder with Chip Bar-

bour. "Leslie and the crew invited me to watch them practice on the river. Is that okay with you?"

"Sure, you can come out in our infamous launch! Want
to come tomorrow?"

"Thanks. But I'll be in New York tomorrow morning.
Monday would be fine."

"Right, then! See you at the dock."

1 6

Rosemary had planned to use Columbus Day weekend
to close her old New York apartment. The prospect
of a relatively free schedule for the rest of Friday and a free
Saturday tempted her instead to contemplate spending it
settling into the house on Cullen Street, unpacking more of
her books, and enjoying the luxury of an unhurried Sunday
afternoon. But there was no dodging another inevitable
parting from her former self, and she wasn't going to allow
any avoidance strategies to delay the break. She decided to
close up the New York apartment right away. The puddle-
jumper from Keene Airport was on time for once, and it
dropped her unexpectedly quickly into the past.

As her cab turned onto 79th Street, inching through
the Friday-afternoon traffic toward Lexington Avenue,
she felt her body stiffen, bracing against memory. There

was 128, its facade of limestone enlivened by rustication for the first three of its twenty-six floors. At the street level, polished brass plates announced the suites of psychiatrists and physicians, discreet presences behind windows decorously swathed in brocades. By the door, two small conifers in battered wooden tubs battled gamely for life beneath a fading green canvas awning. Inside the black marble foyer, she was greeted warmly by the doorman. "Welcome, stranger. It does my eyes good to see you walk in. When I heard you'd be coming, I could hardly believe it."

"Thanks, Pete. I'm here for just a day. A Mr. O'Malley from Allied Van Lines will be coming by at the first of the week to move some things to Vermont and others to storage."

"It's true then? You're leaving us?"

"Yes, Pete. It was a hard decision to make. While my niece needed the place I just let things be. But I don't live in New York now, and it just doesn't make sense to keep the apartment."

She hesitated in front of the elevator, postponing the moment when she had to open the door to her life with Jim, its loss surprising her once again by its sudden power to overwhelm all other moods.

Pete made a gesture toward the lobby phone. "Shall I call Andy and get him to go up with you, just to check on things? He was in there after Miss Jennings left and did a bit of tidying up." Pete rolled his eyes expressively.

Rosemary laughed. "These days, college students have so

much electronic equipment, the place probably was turned upside down."

"It was," Pete said, "but Andy put it all back the way he remembered, after the cleaners were in."

"Thanks, Pete, I'll be all right," Rosemary said briskly, stepping into the elevator and pressing the button for the fifteenth floor. She'd been saved by the absurdity of life. Secretly, she'd been hoping that Jim's niece, Wendy, *had* made the place unrecognizable, but Andy, doubtless with Pete helping after hours, had restored it.

When the door to 15C swung open, the parquet floor of the foyer was still redolent with the lemon wax that had recently been applied. The bow-windowed living room opening onto the back of the building was bathed in late-afternoon sunlight, its chintz sofa cushions plumped, its lamps set squarely in the center of tables, the eighteenth-century prints she and Jim had collected each just slightly awry after being dusted. After three years of being away, first in New Haven and then at Sanderson, Rosemary was amazed that at first glance the apartment hadn't changed.

She walked into the bedroom and flung open the windows to the autumn air. In the brilliant light the striped damask curtains and bedcover looked faded, their jewel colors dimmed by three more years of New York grime. Signs of the passage of time stiffened her resolve. It was no use clinging to this piece of her past. It was better to have it pristine in her memory than visibly fading with the passage of time.

The study had clearly been Wendy's hangout. There were

lighter squares on the pale yellow walls where her niece's posters had hung, and signs of the recent removal of a computer in the scratches left on the leather-topped desk. A note was taped to the back of the big green leather desk chair, where Rosemary couldn't miss it.

How can I thank you for the last three years here in this wonderful apartment? It's been the dream life for a student. No one else I knew could relax in all this space in a safe building. I know it has been the key to my success at Barnard. I hope you'll be as happy as I am that I'm off to law school. I like to think that when I'm there I'll be following in Uncle Jim's footsteps. I used to think a lot about the two of you while I was living here. You have both been the most important influence in my life. I'd never have gotten it together without you.

All my love and more gratitude than I can say,

Wendy

The telephone rang suddenly, interrupting Rosemary's thoughts of her niece.

Picking up the phone, she smiled at her uncle's familiar voice.

"So you're real? Not a ghost? Down here from those frozen woods of yours? Would you be willing to discuss predestination over a drink and dinner?"

Rosemary abandoned all thought of her carefully planned evening of sorting through the past. "Uncle Warren! Where shall we meet? Name the time. My only condition is that we can't go to one of your clubs where every half-sentence is interrupted by one of your clients, and the smell of cigars lets a woman know she's there on sufferance."

"Well then, Périgord at eight-fifteen. I bet you need a sinfully good meal."

"Eight-fifteen it is. You'll know me by the straw in my hair."

Setting down the phone, Rosemary smiled, her mind traveling happily back through thirty-odd years of her uncle's treats. He had a gift for finding the perfect indulgence to ease one's path through the challenges of the moment. He'd taught her, when she was an awkward fifteen-year-old, to see the humor in her mother's remarriage to an Englishman whose life revolved around the horse trials at Badminton.

"Think of her perpetually in Wellington boots, my dear, and be thankful you can stay in school over here, away from those awful drafty houses."

She remembered the luncheon at the Four Seasons during which she'd told him of her plan to resign from U. S. Computer and enroll at Yale Divinity School. An unbeliever himself, he had listened companionably, hearing her out in silence. She knew that her sudden change of direction was as incomprehensible to him as if she'd chosen to become a circus performer or a seal trainer. As she spoke, no flicker of surprise had altered the expression of his intent gray eyes, and his stylishly tailored body remained as attentively inclined toward her as if she'd been discussing the business world in which she'd been a cherished protégé.

"Well, Meg," he'd said back then, using his pet name for her since childhood, "what sort of party does one throw for an ordination? You mustn't expect me to understand what you're doing. But you've got a good head on those elegant shoulders, and I'm sure you know what's best for you. I haven't been to Yale since the Game in 1967, and it troubles an old Harvard man to think of your wearing that wishy-washy blue. But I'll get used to it."

And he had. He'd come faithfully to visit her in New Haven, meeting her divinity school classmates with the same lively curiosity he gave to his corporate law practice. On occasions, he'd even read theological works she had praised.

A sudden burst of the door buzzer put an end to Rosemary's memories. She opened the door to find Andy standing in the hallway balancing a pile of clean laundry and an enormous bouquet of autumn flowers.

"Welcome home, Ms. Stubbs. We've all missed you. That niece of yours was nice enough, but the place hasn't been the same without you." He moved assuredly to pile the laundry beside the linen closet and thrust the flowers into Rosemary's arms.

"Thanks, Andy. The apartment has never looked better. I'm sure Wendy left it quite a mess. I'm very grateful to you and the cleaners for putting it all back in such good order."

At the door Andy paused. "What's this I hear about you selling? Surely you're coming back to Manhattan one day."

"It's the sensible thing to do. I like my new life in Vermont, and I really do live there now."

Andy showed a New Yorker's incomprehension of any possible life outside the city. "You're bound to be back in a few years. But for now, how can I help you?"

After a quick, decisive discussion of how best to plan the packers' work, Rosemary pressed the overlarge bouquet from Wendy back into his hands and watched Andy disappear into the elevator, her heart filled with gratitude for his solicitude. Glancing at her watch, she calculated that there was just time to find a suitable New York dinner dress in the hall closet, shower, and call Metford to see how Tara was getting along house-sitting with Fannie and Amaryllis. She stepped into the closet and gazed in astonishment at what now seemed like a plutocratically rich array of dresses, suits, and coats. Life at Sanderson College was a matter of tweeds, slacks, sweaters, and one or two silk dresses for formal occasions.

She selected a timeless black dress, rummaged for the right scarf, and came upon a forgotten red cashmere cloak. These laid out at the foot of the bed, she curled up to dial the number of her house at what seemed a very distant Sanderson. Fannie could be heard barking in the background as Tara answered.

"Dean Stubbs. Hi! How was your trip? Everything's okay here. Fannie had me out running already this afternoon. She doesn't give up, does she? Say—Cheryl Marquetry—you know her? In the boat with Leslie? Well, she and Leslie are coming over tonight. Do you care if we cook out? It's real warm again."

Rosemary approved the cookout but issued a reminder

to her housesitters about being careful to lock up the house early and to call Kevin Oxley or the Metford police at the first hint of an intruder. Reassured by the call, she found herself actually enjoying being in New York. After her plunge into life in Metford she was positively looking forward to dinner in a good restaurant.

Warren Walters had characteristically found the best corner table, and he was joshing the headwaiter about his diet when Rosemary arrived. She felt as intensely happy as she had in her girlhood, seeing the familiar gray-headed figure, flawlessly tailored. She could have described his navy suit with its slightly daring chalk stripe with her eyes closed. The crimson tie and exaggeratedly bouffant matching handkerchief were her uncle's trademarks.

After a lengthy and high-spirited discussion of the possibilities of oysters or caviar, the choice was made in favor of caviar and champagne. Rosemary was firm about her selection of red snapper, even though her uncle pursed his lips and ordered roast pheasant, but she agreed without the slightest qualm when he ordered ripe peaches and Château d'Yquem for dessert. When the first glass of Dom Pérignon had been poured and their reunion toasted, her uncle raised a quizzical eyebrow.

"Tell me, Madam Dean, what is life like at Sanderson College? Do you like your charges? Are you really contented in all that rural tranquility?"

"Uncle Warren, far from being tranquil, Metford shows all the signs of original sin. In my first week there one of my colleagues was found dead, possibly murdered, it turns out. And since I found the body, I'm still not off the suspect list." She paused to sip her champagne. "One of my most interesting acquaintances is the local chief detective, a very savvy Hispanic gentleman. And someone there wants me to leave, because there was an intruder in my office last Monday night, who took flight when I came in unexpectedly. I'm not jumping a plane to Washington or flying off somewhere to try and close a deal, but I've had enough excitement per diem to last me awhile."

"What? Was your departed friend male or female? Once you tell me that I may be able to guess at why someone wants you to leave town."

"It's not some sordid *crime passionnel*, if that's what you're thinking," protested Rosemary. "Blanche Werner was a very respectable middle-aged woman who was treasurer of the college, chief financial officer, that is, in nonacademic language. It's clear that she had a lover, but I don't know of any lover's tiff, and she was too straitlaced and well off to have been involved in embezzlement or fiddling the books."

As their main course arrived, accompanied by Corton Charlemagne, 1984, for Rosemary, and a Château Mouton Rothschild of equally impeccable year for her uncle, he smiled warmly at her description but insisted on a more worldly view of the subject.

"My dear, the oddest people have violent quarrels with their lovers though all looks calm on the surface. And you'd be surprised how many relatively affluent people with the best credentials feel positively deprived of money. Mark my

words, I know from fifty years of legal practice that everyone has a lover somewhere, and most violence has something to do with money or sex, or both. But tell me, if
you're not being run out of town because you've inadver-
tently thwarted some deep passion, why do you think
someone would take the risk of breaking and entering to
frighten you?"

Underneath the question her uncle's legal mind was hard
at work.

"That's the problem. It must be that I've seen something
or heard something significant and just don't recognize it.
Or maybe it has nothing to do with the murder. Maybe it
was someone who hates chaplains and religion or who
objects to the ordination of women."

"Those are somewhat extreme steps to take just to gratify
a prejudice. But, joking apart, do you have good legal
advice? Who is looking out for your interests?"

"Even though I'm a newcomer, there are several faculty
and some wonderful students who take very good care of
me, and there's also the chief detective, Raphael Ramirez.
He isn't your usual bumbling cop. He has a way of making
one feel confident that evil-doers will be brought to justice."

"That's all very well. But I'm understandably prejudiced
about the value of the legal profession. You mentioned that
you've been a suspect, incredible as that sounds to me. You
need a good lawyer."

"I may need one to negotiate all the committees of the
faculty and the trustees. Every time I appear at one it's clear
I'm walking straight into a minefield. But I'm confident

Ramirez is too intelligent for us to waste a cent on legal fees for my protection. He's clearly looking out for me, and so are two very likable faculty members."

Egged on by her uncle, Rosemary gave a colorful account of her encounters with the governance system of Sanderson College. When she came to the trustees, her uncle stopped her at the name of Gertrude Bleeker.

"Tall woman, is she? Heavyset? Very serious, and obsessed with the value of competition? I knew her father. He was the same. The money came from lumber. Old Fred Bleeker wasn't that good a businessman. But his father got the title to a lot of Maine woods and was compensated handsomely by the state when the railroads and roads were put in. The family company also owned a big parcel of land adjoining Augusta, and two sites which later became ski resorts, so there's real estate money there, too.

"As I recall, the daughter had ambitions to be a world-class skier, but the old man wouldn't allow it. Since she inherited the money she's been a big financer of political causes all over New England. I'd watch out for her—she's something of a fanatic."

Rosemary wasn't surprised that Uncle Warren's acumen confirmed her own impressions of Gertrude Bleeker. But she purposely turned the rest of the evening's conversation to less troubling subjects, and their time together ended all too soon.

In the cab on the way home, Rosemary realized that she had crossed an important psychological frontier. She had spent an entire New York evening without once mentioning the past. Moreover, by telling her story to her uncle, she had confirmed for herself how much she liked life at Sanderson College despite the horrific event of Blanche's death. In the face of Uncle Warren's evident concern, she had promised to make regular reports on the murder investigation, but her main theme that evening had been not the murder but her pleasure in her new job.

She was up by five the next morning sorting her belongings with brisk efficiency. One pile, in the living room, was for storage. In the corner of the bedroom the pile to be given to the nearest charity thrift shop mounted steadily. In the hall a more modest pile was reserved for transportation to Metford.

By late afternoon, the apartment looked bare. The only thing left to do was to pack the clothes that could be used at Sanderson, pile the books to be added to her study into cartons, take a bath to ease her sorely tested muscles, and snatch a quick dinner before picking up the rental van and hitting the road for the long drive to Vermont.

After she had fallen into a bath, her mood suddenly collapsed. She had been inwardly elated that the much-dreaded encounter with her other life was going so smoothly. But now the dismantled flat, the piles of clothes, all the impedimenta of life with Jim, were there to haunt her. For the thousandth time she began reliving her last moments with Jim, his hurt feelings that she wouldn't sail with him that weekend, the shock of the police notification of his drowning, the horror of identifying the body. And, as always, she began to berate herself for not having acted differently.

So she hadn't put it behind her. She'd been fooling herself. She felt the familiar and dreaded emptiness in the stomach, the sense of life being unreal, emptiness of mind and spirit accompanied by grief that broke over her like a strong surf. She found a half-full bottle of Scotch in the kitchen, poured a generous measure into the cracked glass left on the counter, added a hint of tap water, and between large gulps began to consider what to do next. He's gone, and I'm here, and I've got to get on with it, she told herself.

She tossed out the half-finished Scotch, pulled on slacks and a sweater in a frenzied hurry, and began loading the Sanderson pile in the elevator. She had had a rental van delivered, and the doorman had thoughtfully allowed it to be parked right at the entrance. When it was loaded to the rooftop, she stopped to thank Pete.

"I think everything's ready for the movers. Thanks, Pete, for all you've done to help. No one else will ever take such good care of me."

"You're going now? Just like that? Aren't you stopping for dinner before you take that long drive north?"

"No. I'm going to get going and stop to sleep somewhere along the way. Then I can arrive fresh and rested tomorrow." She waved to him as she pulled out onto the street, her eyes blurred with tears. I'm headed for the blandest motel I can find, she told herself. Somewhere as empty and colorless as I feel.

Once on the familiar bustle of the highway, she kept her mind deliberately averted from anything but the lights of the vehicles ahead and behind her. It was nine o'clock when she pulled off the highway and settled into a comfortingly impersonal Treadway Inn. In her room, faced with the prospect of a sleepless night, she picked up the phone on an impulse. She'd call Petra and get a good dose of her breezy, compassionate common sense.

Petra's voice at the other end of the phone was as reassuring as her clear blue eyes were in person. "Rosemary! Where are you? You sound bushed."

"I'm somewhere west of New Haven. I spent the day in New York packing up my old apartment, closing down my old life permanently. I'm—" Rosemary's voice crumpled round the edges.

"Why did you try to do it alone? I'm too far away to cosset you with coffee and croissants! What happened?"

Rosemary felt the knot in her stomach relax. "I've been doing so well, Petra. Not allowing a moment for being alone. I've really loved beginning to settle into Sanderson, despite Blanche's horrible death. I haven't had a moment to look back. I'd really believed I'd escaped those dreadful regrets about the way Jim died, and the way we parted. I chose Metford in part to live far away from the ocean."

Petra said gently, "You've got to talk about these things. No one can handle them alone."

Petra's presence at the other end of the telephone made it possible to review the whole sad story. The budding marriage, interwined with joy, companionship, peaceful acceptance; the sudden battles over mutually resented career demands; Rosemary's wild grief and guilt; her struggle to get her feet back on stable emotional ground.

Petra's brisk voice broke a companionable silence. "So now you're there alone, facing up to the real ending of things."

"Yes," Rosemary said exhaustedly. "And I can't bear it."

"Remember, endings are just that—endings. You've made some strong beginnings here at Sanderson, so when you let yourself live through your loss, you'll find most of your life is still ahead of you. Not the old life by any means, but another that's a worthy vocation. But, I must say," Petra added with exasperation, "for someone who's chosen pastoral care as her career, you are downright *incompetent* about yourself. What possessed you to go and close that apartment on your own?"

Rosemary actually laughed.

"I guess it's a case of the shoemaker's children. I'll remember in the future."

"I'll be at the house to meet you about seven-thirty tomorrow morning, shall I?" asked Petra. "You're not ready for martyrdom yet, my friend. You're alive and well, and tomorrow is another day."

The Treadway Inn gave Rosemary five hours of exhausted sleep but not enough to alter how tired she was when the alarm went off at four in the morning. She switched on the light and made some coffee in the room's low-tech percolator, dressed quickly, and stepped out into the brisk, faintly frosty darkness. Sliding behind the van's wheel, she squared her shoulders, turned on the ignition, and headed for the highway.

I won't give in to grief any longer, she promised herself. I *will* be grateful to be alive, grateful for the time Jim and I spent together, not forever brooding over my loss.

Edging the car out into the fast lane, she flew past the tractor-trailers in the early-morning light. As the speedometer settled on 75 she settled herself back to resume her inner conversation.

In her mind's eye, Leslie and her teammates came quickly into view, their athletic grace and youthful vigor triggering an involuntary smile at the memory of her sweat-sodden workout in their company. Her inner world had already begun to lighten long before the sun rose over the horizon to dispel the mists in the Connecticut Valley. Her old pleasure at the landscape of Route 91 weaving its way north beside the long glittering sweep of the Connecticut River reasserted itself, and she began to think longingly about Petra and their breakfast, and then about the Sunday service to follow.

17

Rosemary pulled into the parking lot at the marina in the dark of Monday morning. Only a few stars poked through the curtain of the sky. She could hear the river softly nuzzling at the dock, but there was no sign yet of crew or coach. She had thought it prudent to be early when she came to watch the crew and, she hoped, take the olive branch proffered by Chip Barbour. His goodwill might not tolerate even a two-minute delay. She could see light under the boathouse door and thought she could hear an occasional voice inside. Rather than disturb them in what the coach probably considered to be the sanctum sanctorum, Rosemary hunched down behind the wheel and waited.

It could hardly have been five minutes later when an overhead door began to rumble and what seemed a far-larger-than-life armadillo was outlined in the rectangle of flooding light. Rosemary blinked and then laughed out loud to see that the creature was, in fact, an overturned shell carried on the shoulders of the women who were soon to row it. They came out at a smart walk, sure of themselves in the dark, and made their way straight for the dock. Behind them, the crews of four other shells, some with eight, some with four oarswomen, emerged at carefully spaced intervals. Rosemary got out of the car and made her way to the dock. She stood to the side, waiting, until at a signal the last shell was lifted high overhead, rolled over, and lowered gently into the water. Even in the dark she recognized Leslie's tall frame and Martha's tiny, buoyant figure.

"Hi, Dean Stubbs. Coach said you might be here. Now you can see the real thing!" Leslie greeted her.

"As long as I don't have to provide my own power!" Rosemary called back.

"You don't. The launch is over here." Chip had a windbreaker turned up against the predawn air, but his head was bare and his hair blown slightly up from his brow. He unwound the launch's bowline from the pier and leaped onto its long prow with easy balance. Then he made his way aft and held out a hand to Rosemary. "Catch that other line, would you. That's it—now just bring it up with you."

She clambered in, and in a moment Chip had the launch reversed, pushed away from the dock, and turned nose upstream to follow the crews pulling against the river.

The five lozenges moved smoothly against the current, their outlines gradually becoming more distinct as light began to break in the sky. Rosemary watched the steady tip, rise, and feather of the oars, mesmerized by the rhythm and grace of movement so completely in unison. Chip said nothing but leaned far forward, one hand on the wheel as his eyes checked each boat in turn. The river made a sweep to the left and seemed to flatten out as they reached the broad low-lying meadowland to the north.

"They're paddling now," Chip called over to her. "Going against the current. They'll do their pyramids after they've turned downstream."

"Pyramids?" Rosemary felt that she was poking a wall of concentration, but her question got through.

"Ziggurats." Barbour's eyes crinkled as though he would smile if he had time.

"Tigris and Euphrates stuff?"

"Yep. The kind of ziggurats that rise up for a certain distance and then level off, then rise up again. Come down the same way on the other side. Model to rate speed. A crew will start at the rate—say twenty strokes a minute. Then the cox will move them up, say to twenty-five. They change the rate on the strokes and hold it for one minute, maybe two—cox sets the duration. Then they might go up again to thirty or thirty-five. They come down the same way. In steps. Can't just taper off and still stay together."

"How *do* they stay together in the ziggurat?"

"Count. You'll hear 'em."

The shells had rounded the river bend and feathered their oars. Rosemary could see the rowers alert, suspended, as they waited for any last-minute instructions from the launch.

"Eights first. Varsity. Then one minute between boats. Regular order. Martha, remember, get to thirty-five, hold one minute, down to thirty, and back up one minute," Chip called through his megaphone.

Rosemary saw Martha nod sharply.

"Novice, begin at fifteen, but then pick up to twenty and hold it steady. Fours, start upstream one hundred yards—at the oak tree. Wait two minutes after the novice start. All right, line up."

As the shells turned in the water, pearl-gray light played over the river, the cherry-red jerseys of the crew the only color between it and the sky. The voices of the coxes called out like the occasional notes of birds about to migrate for the winter. They hunched forward, their hands just above the water as they held the twin lines that guided the shells. Quickly they moved their thin projectiles into line, the novice boat turning more widely than the others.

When the last boat had turned, the varsity eight, closest to the Metford side of the river, picked up oars. Martha leaned forward, arms by the keel as she fixed the course ahead of them. Cheryl Marquetry was at number eight, facing the cox directly. As Martha let out her cry for the start, Cheryl picked up the stroke with a surge of back and legs, and Melanie, at seven, set the rhythm for her side. The shell shot forward.

"Good heavens! They're flying! You don't mean they can go faster than that?" Rosemary exclaimed.

"Up to thirty-five miles an hour." Chip slowly let out the throttle and moved at a cautious distance behind the varsity. His eyes swept the river as the junior boat shot off in its turn.

"Plenty of momentum in these things. Figure the weight of the oarswomen and the speed. Always put the strongest crew in front. If any boat struck the shell ahead at speed, it could cut the cox in half—as well as split the shell."

Rosemary shivered and thought that was probably not the only hazard on the river. The September water looked calm enough, but what about March? Meltoff from winter snow was bound to bring branches and who knew what other flotsam rushing down the river. What if a shell in full flight hit an obstacle like that?

She turned to Chip to ask how they did manage the spring water, but he was caught up in the effort on the river. All the eights were in flight. He checked the launch, turning it crosswise to the current, and looked down at his watch. A veritable wrist-sized instrument panel, Rosemary thought, as she observed him wait for the seconds to flash and then look upriver to see the varsity four take off on time.

When the next two shells had negotiated the bend, Chip turned the launch downstream, moving on the Metford side of the river in the lane sketched out by the varsity eight. The river lay before them, alight now with the near yellow of horizontal sunlight. Each shell flew its course straight as a die, framed by the uninterrupted green of the wooded shoreline. The wind blew through her hair, and Rosemary was conscious that she, like Chip, was leaning forward to keep each boat in her gaze.

They picked up speed, leaving the fours and passing the novice eight and then the JV ahead of them. With the boathouse dock just coming into view, the varsity was picking up the final stages of its pyramid. Rosemary could hear Martha's sharp cry.

"Call thirty-five!"

"One, two, three . . ." the whole crew counted their strokes as their oars flashed together through the air and cut the water as one.

"It *is* a champion crew!" Rosemary found herself shouting at Chip.

"Damn right it is, and it will be! We're going to the Nationals—no matter what!"

Martha's crew shot its last sprint now, and she called them down to twenty-five and then to twenty, as the marina came up on their left. The boat slowed and turned to shore.

"Martineau's caught a crab. God damn!" Chip thrust down the accelerator, and the launch burst forward with a roar. Ahead they could see the body of number three crumpled forward across her oar while the others, quite still with oars struck, waited tensely. As the launch pulled alongside, Leslie straightened up.

"Get a cramp?" her coach asked impatiently.

"No." She tried to catch her breath. "Something in there—on the oar."

They looked across the shell and saw that the blade had not come out of the water. Its handle, which had struck Leslie in the diaphragm, was now angled up, lock pulled out; only the instinctive grasp of her hands kept it from tearing away completely.

Chip threw the launch in reverse and then slowly backed behind the shell and nosed cautiously toward Leslie's oar. Rosemary leaned over the side. Anchoring one hand on the side of the launch, she reached her other hand along the submerged blade.

"I have it—wait." She gave what tug her precarious position would allow, and the oar floated up in Leslie's hand. With it came a dark square and then, bent away at an angle, a balding head and the shape of a man's shoulders.

1 8

"Oh, my God!" Rosemary pulled her hand away and fell back into the launch.

"Here, take this." Chip pushed her across him. "Let me over there. Just hold it steady." She grabbed the wheel.

"Good God. It *is* somebody. Phil Mason?" He caught himself and reached for the megaphone. "All shells to dock. Shelve them and wait in the boathouse."

"Don't you have a phone to shore?" Rosemary pointed to the launch's instrument panel. She made the brief awful calls to campus security and the town police, and watched the crews bring the shells into dock, jump out, lift them, and set off to the boathouse without a word. The coach held grimly on to the body floating off the launch's starboard side.

Within a few minutes two police cars pulled into the marina, and Raphael Ramirez climbed from the first one. Still speaking to Rosemary by the launch phone, he asked if they could bring the body to shore. Chip fastened a boathook through the sodden sweater that had caught on Leslie's oar and fought to keep the body from becoming entangled under the launch as Rosemary guided them to the dock. Ramirez and Ted Brown reached over when they came alongside the dock and grabbed the body, while two others jumped into the water to help lift it out. All four strained to the work until one of the officers groped below the surface and found a weight tied to one leg of the body.

"Philip Mason." Raphael Ramirez stood back, his feet planted apart, and stared down at the body. He turned to Ted Brown.

"Ted, could you call the president for me? And the dean and, yes, Peter Zukowski, the comptroller. Ask them all to meet me here as soon as they are able."

Ramirez hurried on in the wake of Rosemary and Chip,

who had tied up the launch and were on their way to the students. They stepped inside the boathouse, barren except for the tiers of fiberglass shells that lined the walls and two heavier wooden practice shells hanging overhead. On the far wall, racks held rank upon rank of oars, each blade painted the cherry red and white of Sanderson College, each labeled with the name of the oarswoman to whom it was assigned.

Thirty-two young women stood at the near end of the room, the silence among them eerie. In the far corner, Leslie Martineau was bent over a table, one hand across her mouth. She was turned away from them.

"Ladies." Ramirez's form of address would have been an anachronism, or an insult, from anyone else. "It is your professor Philip Mason who has just been found, dead, in the river."

Cries interrupted him. Martha burst into tears. "Mr. Mason! He was my adviser. He was *wonderful*." Amid the rising clamor of voices, other students could be heard. Only Leslie and the group immediately around her were silent, still stunned. Rosemary walked over to them.

"We have no information at present as to the reason for Professor Mason's death," Ramirez went on, his voice cutting through the noise. "Nor do we have any idea when he died. My colleagues and I will begin now to look into Professor Mason's death, and it may be that we shall have questions, but in the meantime, well, there is very little to be said about this tragedy." He looked over at Rosemary. "I think that is all."

"Just a moment." Rosemary came back to the center of the group to stand beside him. She motioned to Chip, who was standing to one side, immobile, and then she extended a hand for Leslie. "I'd like all of us just for a moment to bow our heads in prayer for Professor Mason." She forced her voice to be steady as she spoke from memory. "'May the Lord bless him and keep him, may the Lord make His face to shine upon him and give him peace for ever more.'" She took a breath and went on, "And in this life, may the love with which he burned for this college enlighten all our hearts, so that we act now to preserve it and protect its members. Amen."

Silence hung over the group of young athletes. Rosemary broke it to caution gently, "Now you all should get on with the day. You needn't be silent about this—it will soon be public knowledge anyway. But remember what Detective Ramirez has advised. There's very little to be said."

Rosemary accompanied Leslie out the door, and as she watched the students wind in a serpentine out of the parking lot and up the road toward Sanderson, she saw a stream of cars pulling in. The first belonged to Nathan Eames, who drove right up to the dock and got out just a few feet from the knot of policemen and medics who were gathered around the body. Eames hurried over to them, his heavy shoulders hunched up, his head thrust forward. Rosemary set out to join him. Then Pete Zukowski drove up, followed closely by Amy and Kevin. Rosemary went to meet them.

Kevin rushed forward to her. "Rosemary. I was with Amy

when Ramirez's call came. Thought I'd better come see what happened." His eyes were troubled.

Rosemary shivered in the chilly air. "It could hardly be worse. I'm glad you're here. Amy, it looks like the passions in the budget committee, or somewhere, are real indeed."

Nathan Eames's shrill voice carried over to where they stood. "You have to understand, Detective. This is all part of a pattern! I'm convinced that Mason's death was connected in some way to Blanche Werner's. If you would just consider how she was handling the college, and who might be protecting her! You have to get to the bottom of this! Sanderson can't afford another of these horrors."

"Where is he?" Amy pushed through the tight huddle of men. "Oh, God!" She dropped down, balanced awkwardly on her toes. She pulled the shroud from his face. "Oh, poor Phil!"

Kevin leaned over. "He was always so confident. Thought he was invincible."

"Oh, Phil. What happened to you?" Amy Standish, oblivious of the group on the dock, reached out to touch his cheek.

"Here, Amy." Kevin put a hand on her arm. "Detective Ramirez, don't you think we might go inside for your questions? Might be possible to think straighter."

Ramirez nodded and set off for the boathouse. The little group followed obediently. When Chip had pulled out folding chairs enough for them all, Ramirez motioned them to the circle.

"We have here, I believe, all the principal officers of the college and, as it happens, two faculty members." He nodded at Kevin and Chip. "Now, we must assume Mr. Mason was murdered. There was a weight attached to his left leg. It was only by a freakish accident that his body was discovered at this time. It was not meant to be found. There is a murderer at large. Perhaps someone who acted at random. But more likely an individual connected with the college and almost surely still present in the community. The president is correct—we must move quickly. Now I need you to tell me if there is anything that you know of that might help us in this search."

Nathan Eames was accustomed to speaking first. "Well, Detective, as I was saying on the dock, I think you ought to consider Blanche's death, first of all. Is there anyone who might have held Mason responsible for her deterioration"—his voice dropped—"or have wanted to protect her reputation, even now? It's common knowledge that Phil Mason considered Blanche an adversary, and he didn't stop thinking so after she died."

"Was the enmity that deep? Do you agree?" Ramirez asked his question collectively.

Amy began, "I just don't know. I do know, however, that Phil was a great man for riding hobby horses. He was utterly reckless in that regard. He didn't care—I don't think he even *noticed*—if he offended someone in the process, or if his conclusions, in human terms, were outrageous. He was just plain tone-deaf to human relationships. And I think Blanche knew that. But whether anybody who cared about her would have . . . well, I just don't know."

"I'm not sure there is a direct connection to Blanche."

Kevin spoke carefully. "Phil did, as you may know, cause a great brouhaha in the budget committee meeting last Friday. He aroused tempers on all sides. But it's hard to think . . ."

"What were the issues last Friday?" Ramirez prodded.

Rosemary volunteered wearily, "Three, really. Whether expenditures were really well controlled by the late treasurer, or whether she had favorite projects that she supported without disclosing them. Whether the college was investing its money properly. And finally, whether the college's traditional governance structure should be allowed to stand. Phil was claiming there was insufficient supervision of resources by the administration and the trustees, and he called for something of a coup by the faculty budget committee. He proposed they should take over all resource allocation."

"He certainly wasn't shy," Ramirez commented without irony.

"He never hesitated to take an argument to its farthest conclusions," Kevin added.

"Mr. Zukowski, I understand Phil Mason got some documentation from you. What was it?"

"Well, he took all the treasurer's backup files, both for the expenditure side of the budget and for the investments. Frankly, I didn't have time to look them all over. And he downloaded the investment files onto his own computer."

"That's a lot of information," the detective commented.

"More than Miss Werner would have given out. But Dean Standish wanted—"

"Now, Pete," Eames interrupted. "You were wrong to give away all those documents without checking first with me." The president's mantle of office was fully in place again. "The college is going to go on in a manner as nearly normal as we can achieve. And now while we're all together, and the police are here as well, I think it is important to agree on how we shall proceed over the next couple of days." He paused to be sure that he had the group's attention.

"First of all, this is not like Blanche's death: the press will be here in numbers. The public relations office, with my supervision, will contain them as best we can. Second, we will all have to help the police as much as we can." He went on, "The students will be very much upset, and responding to them will be the responsibility of each of us. But above all, we must concentrate on carrying on the normal life of the college. I intend myself to carry on. Some of you may know that I am personally hosting the visit to the campus by one of Sanderson's most generous donors tomorrow night. I ask all of you to help turn the community's attention away from these terrible tragedies."

He must truly think he's being presidential, Rosemary thought to herself not for the first time, as she watched him stride away, head held high.

"Rosemary!" Kevin stopped by her side as they started for the door of the boathouse.

"Oh, Kevin!" Her face was drawn and lined. "When I saw that body in the water . . . oh, God!" She stopped, utterly still.

"I know," he said gently. "Petra told me how your husband died." He put his arm around her shoulders in a half-embrace.

"I'm all right." She paused. "It's poor Phil I'm thinking about. And Claus. Have you seen him? Do you know how he is?"

"I was with him yesterday. He's very angry right now. At himself, for never acknowledging his relationship to Blanche, so that now he has no status to mourn her publicly and no say in how she is memorialized. And he's angry at the police and the college, even a little at you. He believes there's more to the circumstances of Blanche's death than he's been told; that others know and refuse to tell him. He's certain that someone killed her. There's no place in his life for solace yet."

"What's he going to do?" Rosemary asked.

"Get on with his work, and all that goes with it. Keep himself to himself. Watch and wait. And find the murderer." Kevin's voice was grim.

"By himself? He can't!" Rosemary was horrified. "Kevin, do you think Nat was right? Could this murder have been revenge for Blanche?"

"Why would it be? Do you really think Phil was somehow involved in Blanche's death?" He spoke slowly, measuring possibilities with his words.

"I can't conceive of Phil having anything whatsoever to do with it."

Rosemary waited, and Kevin went on, "And if it was revenge not for her death but for her *reputation*—" He stopped and stood looking out at the river. "No. It just doesn't parse. Claus was furious at Phil. But he was angry at an insult, only at an insult. We're fractious, Rosemary, but we're not Montagues and Capulets. We don't kill over a dishonor. Not even dishonor done to the dead."

He resumed walking back to the car. "I think this murder must have happened for the same reason as Blanche's. Both of them were, after all, privy to the same financial information."

"That's what I think myself," returned Rosemary. She took a deep breath. "Somewhere in the financial records there's information that's worth killing for."

19

"May I catch you before you fly somewhere?" Raphael Ramirez stood at the door of Rosemary's office.

"Of course you can. But I have a group of students coming over tonight. All the ones I know who are most deeply affected by Phil Mason's death. And if the grapevine on campus is really effective, others whom I don't know. I was just going home to prepare a supper for them and grab a bite myself before they arrive. Would you like to join me?"

"Thank you."

As they made their way across the chapel lawn, he said,

"Dean Stubbs, I am so sorry that by bizarre fortune it was you who found Phil Mason's body. Are you all right?"

"You're kind to ask, but yes. I'm afraid the same can't be said for the students."

"Professor Mason was extremely popular with them, I believe?" the detective asked.

"Yes," Rosemary assented. "By all accounts he was meticulous with them, writing volumes on their term papers, spending hours counseling them. And it seemed like dozens were doing honors theses under his direction."

Arriving a few minutes later at her house, they moved on into the kitchen, where the detective took up a post by the window. He watched her at the cutting board preparing vegetables for a ratatouille.

"When did you arrive at the marina this morning?"

"Five-fifteen."

"Did you notice anything out of the ordinary?"

"It was pitch black. And I'd never been there before. When the sun did come up on the river, it seemed perfectly idyllic." Rosemary sighed.

"What did you yourself know of Phil Mason?"

"I'd had several encounters with him, actually. Twice in committee meetings. And twice just out on the street, when he stopped me to talk or, more specifically, to argue."

"How bitter were the arguments on Friday morning?"

"Bad enough. Phil had accused Blanche of colluding with Claus Henderson to purchase—secretly—an expensive piece of equipment, and Claus became very angry indeed."

"So I've heard. Was anyone else angry?"

Rosemary paused, knife in midair. "Amy Standish, amazingly, was not. She's a woman with a lot of self-control, and she's smart. The others were mostly embarrassed. Fortunately, Gertrude Bleeker wasn't there. It was a special meeting, and she hadn't caught wind of it, I suppose."

"Why do you say that?"

"Because Gertrude seems extremely protective of trustee prerogatives, and because she seems to throw her rather considerable weight around on less provocation than Phil gave that morning."

"What had provoked her?" Ramirez was paying close attention to Rosemary's answers.

"On Tuesday, Phil had claimed that a faculty committee should control resources. Gertrude told him in no uncertain terms that budget and finance belonged to the trustees."

"And?"

"He seemed to ignore her," Rosemary said, trying to remember the contretemps. "Amy Standish cut them both off, as I recall. She seemed very anxious to halt the meeting."

"Do you have any reason to think that Gertrude Bleeker was actively developing political opposition to Mason after that meeting?" Ramirez pressed on.

"Well, it's plausible, I suppose. But, no, I didn't encounter it. Ouch!" Rosemary wiped away a speck of hot olive oil that had spurted up to her throat from the pan of onions she had on the stove.

"What is your impression of Claus Henderson?"

She looked at Ramirez sharply. "I don't think he's a murderer."

"You're taking a lot of shortcuts there. Start at the beginning. What do you take to have been his relationship to Blanche?"

"Well, I'm sure you know it already. They were lovers."

"Had they separated recently?"

"That I simply do not know."

"Would he have had any reason to have been jealous of her, or angry with her on another score?"

"None that I— Excuse me." She was interrupted by the ringing of the phone. "Hello." There was a pause. "Yes." Another pause and then a vehement reply from Rosemary. "No, no, I'm *not* going to comment. I'm sorry. I have nothing to say."

Returning to the stove, she said, "The press! That's the fifteenth call I've had today. That one from Reuters. The AP stringer and the local reporters followed me around the campus this afternoon. I had a devil of a time to get rid of them without disgracing myself or my office in the process."

"Yes. They are all over the station as well. And the television cameras. I'm afraid we'll make the evening news tonight, and not just in New England." His voice was grave.

"It's going to be absolutely rotten for the students. And the president and Ross Easterly are probably beside themselves."

"Dean Stubbs . . ." Ramirez left his post by the window and rescued the onions on the stove from burning. As he adjusted the heat under the pan, he watched her take a charred pepper from the brown paper bag in which it was resting and burn her fingers on it as she tried to pull off the peel. "Let me do that."

She watched with admiration as he took the pepper, deftly quartered it, flicked the peel and seeds from each section, and lined them all neatly along the edge of the cutting board.

"Any other pro sports you've mastered?"

"Well, I can conduct an orchestra."

"You can *what?*" Rosemary was caught by surprise.

"Conduct an orchestra." For the first time she saw his eyes light up and a smile transform his face.

"Where do you do that?"

"You have the tense wrong. It's where *did* I do such a thing. Only once professionally, as it were. In Worcester. The Choral Arts Society was putting on a production of *Peter Grimes* with the local orchestra. I was allowed to understudy the conductor, and on the second night he couldn't perform."

"Murder or mayhem on your part?"

"I didn't break his wrist, if that's what you are thinking." He smiled at her. "He caught the proverbial cold. I think he really just wanted to give me the chance."

"Was that your last foray into opera?"

"Formally, yes. But do not ever get into trouble on a Saturday afternoon. I won't hear the phone until the opera's over." His voice was mock-solemn.

"What makes you think I'm going to get into trouble?"

"Because you're holding back information from me. And that almost surely is dangerous."

She laid down the eggplant she was peeling and looked at him, puzzled. "What do you mean?"

"You haven't told me yet all that you know about Claus Henderson. About any contact you may have had with him."

"What makes you think that is important?"

"Because, Miss Stubbs, the contents of Blanche Werner's handbag were found in his car. And because among his botanical extracts there was a very large vial of digitalis. And because his pocket calendar was among the books in your study on the morning after the attack on you."

"Oh, Lord. I don't believe it!" She sank into a chair by the kitchen table and covered her eyes with her hands. "I just can't believe it. You're *sure*?"

"It has his name in it. And we've checked the handwriting. It is his, I'm afraid." The detective took no pleasure in what he had revealed.

"It must have been a plant. Somebody must want you to think that Claus Henderson was in my office."

"That may be the case. But the other evidence, even though it is circumstantial, is significant. It means that I very much need you to tell me what you know about him." He came and sat at the table, looking sympathetically at her, and then shifting his gaze to the window. "Nothing you're likely to say can make things any worse for him. Perhaps it may even help."

"There's not much to tell, really. The day after Blanche's death, Claus met me outside the library after the trustee committee meeting. I went off with him to a laboratory in the greenhouse, and he asked me about finding her. I told him about the body and about your statement that she would have been dead before entering the water. That's all. Nothing about the digitalis. He—well, he kind of went berserk. He grabbed my shoulders and insisted I give him more information."

"What happened then?"

"Kevin Oxley came in and Claus just collapsed into grief." She paused. "You see, he *couldn't* have harmed her. He loved Blanche. He's mad with grief over her death. Surely you can see that. He was furious with me for a moment because I was associated with the fact that she was dead. But that was gone as fast as it came. I just *can't* think he would have come after me." She rose again and turned back reluctantly to the kitchen counter. She went on, "One of the troubles with grief is that it's so wrenching, so disorienting. It makes people seem what they aren't, even to themselves sometimes." For a moment Rosemary was overwhelmed by images of Blanche and of Claus, overlaid by those of her own first happy hours at Sanderson last winter.

"Dean Stubbs," said Ramirez gently, picking up a knife and setting to work on some brightly colored summer squashes, "when you are thinking about danger to yourself or to others, remember that there have been two deaths. It is possible that there could be two separate killers."

Rosemary declined to take up his course of thought. Instead she asked, "Will you join me in a bite to eat before the students arrive?"

He graciously inclined his head, and they worked together quickly to put the ratatouille into a very hot oven, defrost a baguette, and prepare a salad. She handed him a bottle of Nuit-Saint-Georges, and he uncorked it deftly.

Rosemary set two balloon glasses on the kitchen table. "You don't mind if we just perch here, do you? It hardly seems supper enough to move into the dining room." She wondered if his formality, which he had dropped so easily as they worked together, would return to make the meal constrained. But he leaned back in his chair, long fingers tilting his glass of Burgundy, watching the late-afternoon sun play through it.

Rosemary decided to take advantage of the thaw in his manner. "How did a first-class detective become an opera buff?"

"You can feed me, but don't flatter me!" he retorted with a smile. "Well, I could tell you that I'm a secret Plácido Domingo, merely lacking four inches in height and a profile to bring them to their knees in the dress circle. But that would not be true. Opera, listening to opera, is a family tradition. My grandfather came up from the Island, from Puerto Rico, in the twenties to work in one of the cigar factories in Tampa. It's careful work, preparing the wrapper leaf and rolling the tobacco in it with just the right degree of pressure so that it burns evenly. It takes a lot of concentration. So the rule in the factory was that everybody had to be silent. And each day one of the workers would be selected to read to everybody else."

"What did they read?"

"Newspapers, novels, poetry. Everybody voted on what kinds of things they wanted for the week."

"And where does the opera come in?"

"In the afternoon, instead of listening to a reader, they could play music on an old phonograph they had there on the factory floor. My grandfather remembers that most often they chose to play arias from the great operas. It was a habit he brought home to my father. And now I believe it is in my family's genes."

"And how did you come to combine police work with such a peaceful love as opera?"

He flashed her another smile, managing to raise an eyebrow at the same time. "Don't forget. There is hardly a peaceful opera written in the whole of the nineteenth century. *Tosca* makes police files look tame." He swirled the wine in his glass. "I went to college on a scholarship—partly because I'd studied music and performed so much in school, I suppose. And I did go on with it there. But I was young and wanted to save the world, of course. And what my world in lower Manhattan needed saving from most was crime."

"Then how did you get here? There couldn't be any place farther from New York City."

"You are right. But Metford offered me a quick promotion and a chance to run a department without a lot of, shall I say, long and weary dances on the way up. It is the experience I need to go back to the city someday and take a position that may make a difference to the people still living in that world."

"Is living up here what you expected?"

"I have learned a great deal here. I've liked rural life much more than I expected. There have been some difficult cases." Suddenly his demeanor changed. "But nothing like this. To speak frankly, I'm worried about what is happening here at the college. It is still a dangerous situation and, I fear, a long way from resolved." He got up from the table and restlessly paced around the kitchen.

"Look at that." He pointed out the window over the sink, where he had a wedge-shaped view of Cullen Street. A white van was drawing up to the curb and preparing to park. "I'm afraid Reuters was not your last call from the press. That looks like the same truck from Channel 38 that was at my office earlier."

"They must have heard that some of the students would be gathering here. Well, they'll have to get their interviews outside, because I'm *not* going to let them inside the door."

A long peal of the doorbell announced that the students had not overlooked her invitation.

Rosemary was taken aback by the sudden glare of klieg light on the porch steps. Three students hovered by the door, torn between coming in and waiting to hear the reporter's questions to Leslie, whom he had followed up the steps.

"I hear you actually discovered Professor Mason's body? With your oar?"

"Please. I'm sorry. Dean Stubbs is expecting me, and I—" Rosemary ushered Leslie in the door and shut it firmly. Within a few minutes most of the crew had joined them, along with the regulars from the chapel and a number of students whom Rosemary had not met before.

"It's been that way all day." Leslie's voice faltered slightly as she ran her fingers through her hair. The group that had gathered around her broke up and migrated into the living room.

Rosemary caught snatches of the conversation.

"Mr. Mason was always so smart about everything. I mean, he knew everything about finance! And he asked such great questions in class. He really made you think."

"He knew so much about Sanderson, too. Everybody always used to say *he* ought to be the dean. He always knew what you should do to make things fair."

"Well, he *was* a great teacher. But you know he really didn't approve of the crew. Coach Barbour said it was Professor Mason along with Ms. Werner who was responsible for taking away our national competition," Martha said reluctantly.

"Where is Coach Barbour, anyway? He said he'd be here."

"Oh, he will—he's always late. I bet he's down at the boathouse checking the rigging and doing more repairs. He's always there," Martha answered.

"Tell us something about Coach Barbour. Where did he row?" Raphael Ramirez's question wove smoothly into the general conversation, leaving no trace of intrusion.

"Oh, he was at school at Middlesex. He rowed stroke in the varsity there for three years. And they won the school championship each year!"

"And at college?"

"He went to Wesleyan. It's always a big deal when we meet their women on the river. He always wants us to be at our best then."

"Was that another championship eight?"

"Absolutely. Every year he was there. The year he graduated he made the national men's eight. And they were headed for the Olympics, but—"

Martha spoke up, eager to continue the story. "That was 1980, and Coach Barbour says that the U.S. boycotted the Olympics that year, so they didn't get to go. I can't remember why."

"That's because you chemists never read any history! That was the year Jimmy Carter was President, and he was determined to take an international initiative on human rights." Cheryl was serious again, lecturing Martha on international relations. "So, because the Olympics were in Russia, he boycotted them to bring pressure on the U.S.S.R. about its military intervention in Afghanistan. Only it never did any good. The only thing that happened was that Coach never got to go to his Olympics, and neither did any of the other athletes."

"Your coach must be a truly outstanding oarsman. Sanderson has been lucky to keep him from Penn or Harvard, or somewhere like that." Ramirez just floated the inquiry above the surface of the talk.

"Oh, he did go away on leave to Penn in the first semester of my freshman year." It was Martha again who responded. "He was filling in for their head coach or something. But he came back. We were afraid he wouldn't."

"Here he is now!" The oarswomen crowded around Chip as he came into the room, their thoughts taken momentarily even from the tragedy that so preoccupied them.

That's part of his secret, anyway, Rosemary said to herself. Whatever his expertise, the man is a real Pied Piper. She went to the other side of the room, to talk with students who were untouched by arguments about funding the crew.

Here her work began again, as the students gave way to their shock at Phil Mason's grotesque death. Sitting together in the comparative calm of Rosemary's home and under her careful attention, the young women felt their horror settling to become what it truly was: grief at the loss of a caring teacher and friend. The shrill top note of hysteria that had been so apparent on campus during the day evaporated.

The group stayed late. Ramirez stayed on, too, observing, occasionally asking a question but never intruding. He left as the last student started down the porch steps.

"Thank you, Rose—" he corrected himself, "Dean Stubbs. Perhaps I overstayed my welcome? But it was illuminating, and if it is possible to say in such circumstances, it was a great pleasure."

20

The engraved pasteboard invitation had nagged Rosemary from its position in the center of her living-room mantel ever since she'd received it. The evening was to honor the donor who had given the largest gift the college had ever received. Rosemary bet herself the guest list had been handpicked by Nat Eames, who had vowed even at the scene of Phil Mason's death that this particular show would go on. She didn't want to spend another evening talking about the deaths of Blanche and Phil, and she didn't want to listen to another of Eames's joking references to her former career. She kept thinking how nice it would be to stay home and invite Kevin for dinner. It's black tie too, she grumbled to herself, bound to be full of pretentious people talking too loudly.

But she couldn't turn down her first invitation to dinner at the president's house. With a shock she realized that he had a wife and family she knew nothing about, just as she knew next to nothing about the trustees and major donors who would certainly be there. With luck it would be one of those formal affairs that ended promptly at ten-thirty.

Reluctantly she dragged a wool cocktail suit from her closet, gray to match her somber mood. As an afterthought, she added the double strand of pearls that had been Jim's last present to her. Looking crossly at herself in the hall mirror on her way out the door, she suddenly laughed at her own gloomy face and set forth for the president's house, determined to enjoy the party.

On the same side of the street as the chapel, just opposite the library, the college's official residence was set back from the road, protected from any possible traffic flows on Cullen Street by a broadly sweeping drive. Odd, thought Rosemary as she walked between the twin pillars that marked the start of the drive, that I've never even been curious about its other inhabitants, though goodness knows I've thought a lot about Nat Eames and that strange conversation about Blanche.

Several cars drove past her as she hugged the curb. They discharged their passengers with that absolute punctuality usually reserved for ecclesiastical gatherings. Doesn't make any difference whether it's a bishop or a college president, thought Rosemary wryly, the only vestige of authority that's really left to them is the power to draw in all the invited multitudes at the stroke of the appointed hour.

The door opened to her knock as if on a spring. It was held wide by the hand of a plump, henlike woman with bright brown eyes. She enveloped Rosemary immediately in the warmth of her welcome. "You're the new chaplain! I saw you at Convocation and thought you were marvelous. The last chaplain we had, you know, could never stop praying. It used to plague Nathan so. Always wore out the audience before Nat had a chance to begin. So tiresome. But not you! You're young. And female, too. That's something, you know."

"Patti! Have you already confided all the household

secrets to the chaplain? But who better?" Nathan Eames put a hand on his wife's shoulder and greeted Rosemary with a smile of conspiratorial, if slightly official, welcome. "Rosemary, I'm glad to have the opportunity to introduce you to some of the more important friends of the college, as well as faculty in the sciences whom you might not know." His voice lowered slightly. "I've set a strict rule for the evening: no talk about our tragedies. This is a night to celebrate the future of the college. Now let's see, we'll start on the drawing room before the door summons me again."

"Don't let him saddle you with all the old bores," Patti twittered nervously. "After all, someone as young and pretty as you should be having some fun!"

Eames ignored his wife's remark and guided Rosemary among the knots of people still in the ample foyer, veering off to a long drawing room on the right. Rosemary was struck by its lovely proportions. A high ceiling set off by molding in the Greek key pattern gave a luxurious expanse of wall on which to hang the treasures, or near treasures, from the college's collections.

When Rosemary remarked on the singular effect of the array, Eames chuckled. "Mostly forgeries, I suspect—otherwise the museum director would never let us hang them here. Except for the Prendergast—that was in a bequest particularly for the house.

"Now let's see, whom do you know here? Here's someone you should meet! Dick Devises, one of our trustees, a native of Metford, now president of one of the operating companies at Pratt & Whitney."

Rosemary met the firm handshake of a man in his sixties whose shrewd black eyes had her summed up in an instant.

"I read in the paper that Sanderson had acquired a CFO for the chapel. Damned smart, Nat. Not everybody who can pray over your budget."

"Don't be snide, Richard! You industry types may be making pilgrimages up here soon to see what she can do for you."

"Incantations aren't something that I've mastered yet anyway!" Rosemary was laughing with them. "I have my hands full with the ordinary problems of twenty-year-olds."

"I see some new arrivals to greet. Dick, would you introduce Rosemary around?"

"If I must. Though without the assignment, I'd have been sure to back her into a corner to see what a nice accountant like her is doing in a college pulpit."

"Ah, but would I have told you?" Rosemary smiled at him.

"Probably not. And there are hundreds of good conversations to be had in this room. Come meet another Sanderson old-timer, Powell Simonsen. Years ago he was editor of the *Globe*. Looks like he has that young geologist on the ropes."

As they crossed the room, Rosemary heard a harsh voice to her left say, "Phil Mason?" She looked quickly over toward the corner and saw Gertrude Bleeker surrounded by a mixed group of faculty and strangers. Over the rising din of cocktail talk, she could just catch Gertrude's strident tones.

"Of *course* it was a terrible *way* to go. But he brought it on himself. He was trying to steal the college's whole power of the purse! As if *he* were president and chairman of the board!"

Rosemary heard no more as she turned to acknowledge the cheerful intensity of a small man of uncertain age whose features were sharpened by the concentration of myopia. He had been engaged in a rapid exchange of talk with a diffident young professor.

"Ah, Ms. Stubbs. I've heard about you. I'm Powell Simonsen. Daniel Sondheim here and I have just been discussing glacial formations in this part of the world. Would you believe that with all this geological history right in the valley, Dan and his students are off in search of a hot new activity?"

"Pretty hot at that. Vulcanology is a subject we pay a lot of attention to." Dan Sondheim wasn't intimidated by the investigative habit of the older man. A gentle politeness had held him in check until the conversation opened naturally for him. Now, however, it was he who leaned into the group, face intent, hands gesturing, as he explained the unique opportunity offered by active volcanoes to give data about the central core of the earth.

"Here in New England, science has never had any trouble with religion—or biology for that matter. None of this Scopes business." Simonsen looked puckishly at Rosemary, giving away the fact that he made needling his stock in trade.

"I always suspected that was a problem that began in the

newspapers, anyway, rather than the pulpits," Rosemary replied.

"Good for you! Quite up to Sanderson style." Powell Simonsen's laugh had the effect of catching his bow tie on his Adam's apple so that it danced smartly while his shoulders shook. The whole comic effect was clearly an advantage for one who, despite his retirement, was still driven almost entirely by the need to know.

"Powell, there you are! I've been looking all over for you!"

Simonsen turned to greet a blond woman slightly shorter than Rosemary who had joined the group close to his right side. Her short black cashmere dress had sleeves to the wrists and a deep décolletage. Rosemary was struck by her exquisite complexion and her eyes, deep blue and bright with energy.

"Louise! What a treat—usually I only see you at those dreadful business lunches in Boston where you know what everybody is going to say months in advance. I'd forgotten you had a Metford connection." Simonsen beamed at her.

"I do since I joined the Commonwealth Bank. That was over two years ago, Powell." She looked at him reproachfully.

"Oh, yes. Of course! I knew they had the college's accounts. Here, let me introduce you to Rosemary Stubbs, chaplain; Dan Sondheim, geologist; and Dick Devises, trustee. Louise Middleman, banker extraordinaire. She sorted out the computer systems for Colonial. And now that she's gone on to Commonwealth, we're all expecting to see their quarterly reports with starbursts around the profit figures."

Louise caught the tone of his bantering flattery perfectly and tossed the conversation elsewhere. "Well, of course we'll have profits to report, but nothing like the astronomical earnings of the Anglo-American media empire owned by Mr. Stuart over there." She nodded toward a fair-haired man of medium height whose thick neck and strong shoulders strained at his well-cut dinner jacket and whose voice had the resonance and authority of someone accustomed to being listened to.

From the attention being paid to Richard Stuart by Nat Eames, Rosemary did not need confirmation that he was the major donor named on the party invitation.

"You do know him, Dick, don't you?" Louise asked. "Then you can introduce me. Forgive us, won't you?" She smiled brilliantly at Rosemary. "I've heard so much about him. And the people who *control* the media are always fascinating, don't you think?"

Before Rosemary had a chance to reply, Louise was embracing both the president and Richard Stuart in a smile designed to make hearts race. She's not starstruck for a minute, thought Rosemary, but she's ambitious as hell. I've seen plenty of that kind of charm—in both men and women. But it's odd that Nat seems as susceptible to it as Richard Stuart. Maybe power soaks up flattery even in the academic world. She suddenly realized that Powell Simonsen and his geologist friend had melted away, and she was borne down upon by what looked to be a delegation of Sanderson alumnae.

She was right, and for the next few minutes it was impossible for her to avoid rehearsing the personal tragedies of the last weeks. There were exclamations of sorrow at Blanche's death from the older graduates in the group, many of whom had known her, and troubled murmurs about how bad all this news was about a much-loved professor. To Rosemary's relief, the sign was given that the guests should go in to dinner.

She found Dick Devises waiting for her. "I'm going to take your arm, my dear Dean Stubbs. Or, to be exactly proper, offer you mine. Despite Nat's prohibition, I'm going to try to wring some news about these bizarre murders from you while we hover over the salad dressing. I gather you were there, as it were."

Rosemary didn't have time to reply before they were interrupted by Amy Standish, who made a secondary hostess, effective as ever in moving a crowd and cutting individual members out for special duty. "There you are at last, Rosemary! The president sent me to find you. He's put you and Dick at the head table. You'll be here, in the dining room," she explained with a gesture dismissing the library and the foyer, where, magically, smaller tables had sprung up to fill the square space. "You'll find your card on the far side, about a third of the way down the table." After so instructing her charges, the dean was off in pursuit of others to fill the long table, which even at its full extension hardly crowded the generous proportions of the dining room.

In Amy's wake, Dick Devises debonairly steered Rosemary along. At the far end of the room, a wide bow window was filled with flowers. On either side of it French doors opened into porticoes designed to accommodate the daytime entertaining demands of the college. Elegance was in every proportion, but the spare lines of the room avoided any hint of ostentation. The white walls displayed only two paintings. One was a vigorous Len Pearce from which a paddle wheeler steamed, flags flying, seemingly straight into the dinner party. Over the sideboard an enormous oil depicted a three-masted schooner sailing over rough waters, crested by foam that caught the reflection of a cloud-torn sunset. Rosemary, struck by the simplicity of it all, stopped a little way from the crowd at the buffet table.

"One does tend to think there should be a buoy on the table, just to make sure the paddle wheeler misses us!" Beryl Pettit, whom Rosemary remembered from the faculty budget committee, gave a collegial nod from her to the paintings.

As the party assembled at the table with plates from the buffet, Rosemary found herself at three removes from Nathan Eames, who had Gertrude Bleeker, in a rather plain navy silk dress, on his right. On his left he had the trustee Madge Grant, who captured the decorum of the evening with her stunning trouser suit of chocolate brown threaded with the least hint of gold. One doesn't need the double C on the buttons to know it's Chanel, Rosemary said to herself.

Rosemary found herself seated just opposite the guest of honor, a determined Louise on his right. Dick Devises began a series of *sotto voce* questions to Rosemary about the two murders. She answered him absentmindedly while she took in the rest of the table. She could see Patti Eames, her face wreathed in smiles, chattering animatedly, while seated on her left, Amy was clearly doing some of the heavy pulling in conversation directed at two prosperous-looking alumnae. Rosemary was relieved to have Dick Devises between herself and Madge, a man clearly chosen to be relied upon to entertain celebrities, whereas Madge made a career of seizing the center of attention. It was Devises who began the conversation.

"Richard! It's good to have you back in these parts. You're such a media mogul now, and since you've moved your head office to London we scarcely see you."

"I'm not here as much as I'd like, Dick. But tonight's dinner is proof that you can come home again." Richard Stuart had mastered the art of polite distancing.

"Your gift is going to bring the world to Sanderson—and to Metford, Richard!" Nat Eames had found the exact moment for a combined thank-you and compliment, and he followed it immediately with a toast to a gift that would create a center for international studies with an endowed faculty chair, a building to house classrooms, and a media center. "With the plans just drawn, I'm already the envy of my colleagues among the New England college presidents! And it's not often that Williams and Amherst *both* admit to being outdone."

"Well, neither one *would* admit it, if the other had done it." Richard Stuart again tried to deflect the effusive praise directed at him.

Louise, sensing his desire not to speak about his own generosity, engaged Richard with another of her brilliant smiles. "What do you think the future of newsprint will be with all this competition from online and other media sources? I've heard people say that within five years local papers will have taken enormous market share from the big dailies."

He responded as enthusiastically as she had calculated, and within moments an animated conversation between the two of them left the rest of the table behind. Rosemary stole a look at the president. He knows exactly what Louise is doing, and he admires her, she observed. Louise is so perfect . . . I wonder if he's a little bit jealous? She hadn't time to speculate, for Gertrude Bleeker reentered the conversation and brought Rosemary in with her.

'Isn't it bizarre, Dean Stubbs, that you should have discovered *both* the bodies of our colleagues? What on earth should we make of that?"

"Nothing at all," responded Rosemary, struggling not to take offense at her question or at her nuance. "Unless you want to say I've had extraordinarily ill fortune. Finding Blanche's body was not an experience I wanted to repeat." She looked over at Eames to see if he would curb Gertrude's open defiance of his rule for the evening.

"Well. I think there's another coincidence that is even more significant." Gertrude Bleeker plowed on as if supremely indifferent to the customs of the occasion. "Nat, surely you see that both of those people were trying to take the direction of the college away from you—and from *us*. It really is extraordinary. Blanche was just having things her own way without asking permission from anyone. And Phil Mason! Well, if he'd won power to control the budget for a faculty committee, it would have been a coup d'état! Surely you saw that."

"I saw nothing of the kind, Gertrude," answered Eames in a voice that kept a perfect low pitch. "On arguments of 'sovereignty,' as it were, Phil was always given to high rhetoric. He merely wanted some specific victories. That's all he ever really aimed for."

"Nat," she insisted, "you can't just smooth this one away. Even if Phil only wanted a few 'specific victories,' as you put it, with the things he'd already wrung out of the trustees, such as the faculty budget committee itself, it would have added up to the same coup!" Gertrude leaned close to the president.

"Nonsense, Gertrude. This is normal college governance. You *negotiate* resources at a college. What matters is not the process but the outcome: a balanced budget and an increase in the college's resources. Now what I worry about"—he raised his voice slightly, and Dick Devises paused in his conversation with Madge long enough to listen in—"is that someone connected to Blanche may have killed Phil out of revenge. The police have got to find that out. We can't risk another tragedy around here."

"Then you think," Dick intervened, "that someone *inside* the college killed Phil?"

"I don't presume to think about conclusions, Dick. I am only worried about safety. I want the police to accelerate their investigations. I understand you, Rosemary, were subject to a minor attack?"

"Yes, but I don't think it was important," Rosemary hastened to say as the group around Eames turned toward her with concern. "It was a simple break-in at my office, probably some vagrant looking for the collection money."

"Well, you can't be too careful," Nat observed. "I don't want any more of that happening to you, or to anyone else."

Richard Stuart picked up the seriousness of the conversation adjacent to him and turned to Rosemary. "Not only did you find the victims, but you have been counseling the students through all this tragedy. How are they taking it?"

"As you might expect," she replied. "They are grieving. Those who had been Phil's students have been deeply affected. But even those who didn't have him for a teacher have been caught up by a kind of hysteria of grief and fear."

"What's been your most difficult problem in dealing with them?" he continued.

She paused a moment. "If you'll allow me to be undiplomatic, I'd have to say the news coverage and the reporters who've been all over the campus."

"I'm sorry," he said quietly. Rosemary had the sense that he meant it.

"I think we should talk about something else," Madge Grant cut in firmly. She was right, and everyone turned to other conversations, which carried them through dessert. As the Eameses stood up and invited their guests into the drawing room for coffee, Rosemary could see Louise, who was already clinging to Richard Stuart's arm, reach out and pull Eames into their conversation. Now *that's* success, she thought, but in another world from mine. She turned and saw Amy alone by her end of the table.

"It looks gorgeous out on that terrace, Amy. Do the Eameses ever entertain out there at night?"

"Not much," Amy answered. "There must be a million breeding mosquitoes down by the river, and they just love to feast on people. But it's probably safe for the two of us to poke our heads out." She opened one of the French doors, and they made their escape from official bonhomie to the stillness outdoors.

When they returned inside, Rosemary found that the party had dissolved with a speed reserved for official functions. All that remained was the flotsam of coffee cups beached on the various tables scattered around the room for that purpose. A clatter of dishes behind the large sliding doors that now closed off the dining room indicated that the kitchen crew had moved in on schedule. In the foyer, Rosemary could just see the president, cornered by Dick Devises and Powell Simonsen along with Louise Middleman, all deep in conversation. She drew back to the French door so as not to disturb them.

"Dean Stubbs!" Patti Eames was alone at the back of the hallway. "Imagine finding you by yourself! My husband is saying goodbye to everyone. It takes so long, you know. Everybody has some business to take up with Nathan, and they do go on at the door. It makes for a longer line than the one coming in. And then sometimes it gets so late."

"I'm sure he works quite long hours."

"Really, you have no idea, Dean Stubbs. Nobody does. I worry so much about him. That he might have a heart attack or something from all the stress."

Thinking to comfort her, Rosemary wanted to point out that Eames seemed to flourish on his current schedule, but Patti Eames, wrought to a high pitch by her nervous distraction, didn't stop.

"I don't know what I'd do without him. Nathan has been everything to me and to the children. Of course, he travels so much now. But he can't help that. And we understand, really we do. You see, we've been married now for thirty years, even though the children are so young. You know, I had to work to put Nat through graduate school, and then there were all those years when he wasn't earning very much. Nathan likes everything to be just right, nothing skimped, you know, so we didn't have children until we could afford them. But then he became a dean at Iona. And ever since we've been at Sanderson, it's been *so* much easier.

"But in the last few months, with all this fighting about the budget and things, the faculty making trouble, it's been so *hard* on him. Just when he has a big chance to get just the position he's been wanting for so long! I *wish* all these complications would just go away and let him—"

"Patti! What are you boring Dean Stubbs about?" The president stopped his wife in midstream.

Rosemary assured him quickly, "Not at all, President Eames. In fact, Mrs. Eames was just keeping me company while I waited to say good night and thank you to you."

She made her brief farewell, leaving Eames to speak his disapproval to his wife alone.

So Nathan Eames is looking for a big new job, Rosemary
thought as she strolled down the drive, and his wife is
something of a brake on his ambitions. Now there's a familiar academic story. She worked to put him through school,
but now he's ready to fly higher than she'd ever imagined.
I'm not sure I'll like the dénouement.

21

A full moon robbed the night of darkness and threw a
long shadow beside Rosemary as she walked home.
Overhead the sky was a tinny blue, most of its stars obliter-
ated by the sheen; only at the edges, just above the tree line,
was there a rim dark enough for punch holes of starlight.
The half-light was welcome to Rosemary, and the rising
breeze seemed almost playful as it lifted her hair and
brought an occasional leaf swirling across her path. The outlines of the college, its trees throwing long shadows, its windows alight for midweek studies, had an aura of delicacy
lost in the hubbub of its daytime life.

It would be very beautiful indeed if it *were* really peaceful, she thought. Her thoughts began to dance among the
desperate possibilities surrounding Phil Mason's death. She
swerved from naming any possible killer among those she

knew. And yet she could not stop herself from worrying each supposition. As she mounted the front steps slowly, her mind still scrambling for some perch among the facts, she heard the telephone ring. She ran for the door and caught the receiver at the last possible moment.

"Rosemary, it's Amy. When I got home from Nat's, I found a message that Claus was arrested earlier this evening."

"Good God, Amy. Does the president know?"

"I'm sure he does by now. It was Penelope Wharton who called me. Apparently the police tried to reach him through his office while he was tied up at the party."

"What about Kevin? And Petra?"

"I've told Petra," said Amy. "But I couldn't reach Kevin."

"Amy, what if I try to find Kevin? I might just drive out there to his house."

With Amy's grateful acquiescence, Rosemary hung up and reached for her car keys. It would be a relief to do something, if only to escape from the claustrophobic shuttle of her own thoughts.

Eerie shadows of trees both dead and alive danced in front of her car as she drove out of town into the foothills where Kevin lived. The moon was a godsend on barely familiar country roads, and she was relieved to find the rise and then sharp dip into Kevin's valley without getting lost. The lights in the house and the barn on the other side of the roadway guided her the last hundred yards, and she was just considering which way to turn when the barn lights switched off and she saw Kevin stride out and head for the house.

"Kevin!"

"Rosemary?" He extended a hand to her.

"Have you heard from Claus recently?"

"Not since yesterday. Why?"

When she had told him Amy's news, he closed his lips in a tight line and set off without comment for the house. He lost no time in phoning the police station, but he wasn't able to get through to Detective Ramirez. Hardly a word was spoken between Rosemary and Kevin as they headed out for Claus's office to see what they could find there.

"You know the roads, so you drive. It's faster." Rosemary tossed him her keys, and they careered down the hills, arriving at the lower quadrangle in minutes. There were lights throughout the biology building and in Claus's greenhouse office as well. The shades were drawn, but they could see a number of silhouettes thrown up against them.

Inside they discovered several students, all talking at once. On the worktable was scattered a cache of photographs; Tara was bent over them. As Rosemary entered with Kevin, she looked up, her face troubled.

"Oh, Mr. Oxley, Dean Stubbs! The police have just been here. That awful detective and two other men. They've taken Mr. Henderson with them! They took some of his files, too. Only they left these." She gestured to the tabletop. The photographs were of a laughing couple, arms linked, at the beach, in evening dress headed for the opera, happily smiling for the photographer in a Parisian restaurant. There was a dazzling studio portrait of the woman, a younger and peaceful Blanche Werner. In several snapshots she appeared in a series of estate gardens, sometimes alone, sometimes with a carefree and affectionate Claus Henderson. With the photographs were the usual mementos of lovers—a few handwritten notes, a menu or two, postcards of favorite places.

Tara looked beseechingly at Rosemary. "What do they mean?" She clenched and unclenched her hands, her jaw set, fighting against emotion.

Rosemary blinked her eyes and shook her head to dispel the mist of tears gathering at having seen the achingly sad collection. "I think they mean Professor Henderson and Ms. Werner were lovers, very happy, devoted lovers, over some years. I think we do have to show them to Detective Ramirez."

"I'm glad I've seen them, Tara," Kevin said gently. "I'm happy to know that Blanche and Claus were once so joyful together. You can understand better why he's been so sad."

Some of the tension went out of Tara's shoulders, but she was still watchful. "Will these pictures harm him?"

"I don't think so," Kevin said quietly. "It makes it very clear there was much more between them than just an affair."

Tara suddenly wept, inconsolable grief breaking through all her efforts at self-control. "But why did they hide it?"

"An open relationship—even marriage—wasn't in the cards for them," Kevin explained. "You know Professor Henderson is already married. His wife has been ill for a number of years and is now in a special institution for patients with Alzheimer's disease."

Weight seemed to slide from Tara's shoulders.

"When did the police come? Were you here?" Rosemary pulled Tara's attention from the personal tragedy spread before them.

"I was in the cell tissue laboratory next door, working on my research. Professor Henderson usually comes in there to check the lab setups for the next day, so I knew I could catch him there with some questions."

"We'd come in, too," said Sootie. "Everybody knows where to find him in the evening, and it's so much easier than office hours. Then the police came and asked him to go into the office with them. And we could hear them talking for a while. Professor Henderson sounded very angry. And then they all left, the detective with Professor Henderson, and the other two carrying a bunch of manila folders. Professor Henderson was so upset. It was horrible."

"You don't think they could actually believe he would kill Professor Mason, do you?" Tara asked.

"Anyone who knows Professor Henderson would know that's impossible, Tara." Kevin left no room for doubt.

"And what about Ms. Werner, Mr. Oxley?" Sootie broke in.

"Does anyone know how she died? You don't think they'd accuse him of killing her?"

"Sootie, I know that's unthinkable. And perhaps these photographs will prove it is. But the police think differently from us. They focus on the externals. Who had an opportunity to harm someone, who might have gained from it, all those sorts of things."

"So you have to refute them by externals too?"

"That may be the case."

Rosemary spoke gently but decisively. "Look, all of you. Mr. Oxley and I will try to track down Detective Ramirez and find Mr. Henderson tonight. We'll take the photos with us. I promise we'll let you know in the morning what happens. Sooner if there's real news."

It wasn't long before Rosemary and Kevin were seated in the detective's office at the station, the photos spread before them.

"These are very revealing. . . . Yes . . . it's clear what the relationship was." Ramirez paused and then turned to Kevin.

"Do you have any idea what could have soured this affair?"

"Soured it? You mean in the face of all these signs of affection, you still want to suggest that he could have killed her?"

"Unfortunately, it's the most frequent pattern we see."

"Well, in this case you'd have to be crazy to hunt that line! Claus Henderson was as devoted to Blanche on the day she died as he had ever been." Kevin moved opposite Ramirez at the oversized desk and leaned toward him.

"Do you have reason to know that—at first hand?" Ramirez challenged him evenly.

"Any fool has reason to know that! Look how distraught the man is! He's numb with grief," Kevin shot back.

"There's more than one reason for grief."

"Good God. Stop and think! Henderson had no reason

to kill this woman. Even if they'd had a battle royal, he wasn't married to her—and she wasn't the kind to go off with someone else! These photographs are the best evidence that he's not the killer!"

"Professor Oxley, it's an Arcadian picture you paint. A decade of devotion, no restraints, no regrets. But I'm afraid I still must consider Professor Henderson among the possible murderers, indeed, perhaps the probable murderer." Ramirez spoke distinctly, looking first at Kevin and then at Rosemary.

"You can't have anything but circumstantial evidence. You sure as hell don't have a motive." Kevin turned away in exasperation, then confronted the detective again. "If I can't prove the love affair was still on, you don't have a snowball's chance of proving it was off! And where does that leave you? Not one step closer to a case."

"And if you are right, and Claus Henderson had any reason to think Phil Mason had harmed Blanche Werner, even by attacking her reputation, then . . ." Ramirez paused.

"Dammit! Don't you pay any attention to a man's character? His reputation?"

"On a college campus, almost no one can be *imagined* to be a killer, Professor Oxley. And yet we have had two murders at Sanderson within two weeks. One has to begin to consider the impossible. I'm sorry, but it is our responsibility." Ramirez got up to dismiss them, standing with shoulders hunched as he held the door, his face very pale in the fluorescent light, his eyes tired.

"Will Claus be free to leave shortly?" asked Rosemary.

"We haven't finished questioning him," answered Ramirez.

"And when you have?"

"He may be able to leave—for the time being."

Kevin paced awkwardly around the dingy little office, almost entirely taken up by its desk and the two straight chairs Ramirez had brought in for them.

"Then I'll wait for him."

"As you like." Ramirez looked inquiringly at Rosemary.

"There's no reason for you to stay, Rosemary," said Kevin, interpreting the glance. "I'll give you a lift home and then come back, if you don't mind my keeping your car for the night."

She nodded briefly. "There's no use both of us waiting. And Claus might think I was intruding anyway."

They didn't speak again until the car started up the long hill back to the college's end of town.

Kevin broke the silence. "I know I overreacted to Ramirez, but it's outrageous. Claus has been wounded and now he's being goaded, and he's completely helpless!"

Rosemary was silent for a while as they drove up the hill from the town center to the college, then, breaking into her own thoughts, she said, "It's not just the digitalis, Kevin. Detective Ramirez told me last night that Claus's pocket diary was found among the papers in my office the night of the break-in. And some of the contents of Blanche's handbag were in his car."

"Rosemary, it's too much. Those things have to have been planted. *Nobody* who actually committed a crime would be stupid enough to create a trail like that."

"That's just what I told Detective Ramirez last night. But obviously I didn't convince him." She sighed deeply.

Kevin hit the steering wheel with the flat of his hand. "So that brings us back to the original question. If Claus couldn't have killed Blanche, who did?"

"You know the people here better than I, Kevin. Whom can you even imagine?"

"Chip Barbour?" The name seemed to be a question he was posing to himself.

"You know"—he gave her his first smile of the night— "Olympic gold can make people crazy. *I* know. It's got a thousand karats, and somehow looking at it straight on, it's more blinding than the sun."

"Is there really Olympic hope on the Sanderson varsity eight?"

"Chip certainly thinks so. Leslie. The number four. And the stroke. Any one of them has a shot at the Olympic eight—if they have a powerful season this year."

"So Chip, as their coach, has reason to murder? To keep them in competition?" Rosemary was doubtful.

"Perhaps. But so do the students." Kevin slowed the car as he spoke.

"Now *that* is unthinkable!" Rosemary protested.

"Unlikely, yes. But unthinkable, no. They're adults, and we're talking about the Olympics, maybe even gold if they listen to their coach."

Rosemary was unconvinced. "What about Gertrude Bleeker?" she offered. "My uncle knew her family. He told me she was a thwarted Olympian herself . . . and she's certainly poured millions of dollars into athletics at Sanderson."

Kevin continued, "And she is close to Chip. He and Nat seem to be the only people who can get along with her." He stopped the car in front of the chaplain's house. "Rosemary, here we are. I'm going to see you safe inside." His face was grim. "Then I'm going back to the police station. To see what I can do for Claus."

2 2

Rosemary and Fannie were headed out for a run the next morning when Tara and Sootie intercepted them at the front of the chapel. Catching Fannie up in her arms, Tara swung her around in a circle. As she turned back to Rosemary, she said with excitement, "We've solved it!"

When they were settled back at Rosemary's in the living room, Sootie began. "Tara and I were talking most of last night about Professor Henderson, what a wonderful teacher he is, and how awful it is for him to be under suspicion like this. Then we talked about the photographs, and Tara said how much they upset her."

Rosemary smiled quizzically at Tara, who picked up the thread. "Sootie and I were thinking about what Mr. Oxley said about external evidence." Tara grabbed the arms of her chair. "You know that student who was misting things in the cool-temperature greenhouse, when you went by last night?"

"Yes. She was still there when we left after eleven o'clock."

"That's right. She's always there. Her name's Eileen Fraser. She's a real nut about plants. She even likes to do her papers in the greenhouse. She has a key to go in and out, because it's part of her work-study job to mist the plants on weekends. And I know she keeps a little logbook of when she's been at the greenhouse and what she's done there, because she showed it to me once."

Sootie broke in. "She must have been there on the night Ms. Werner was killed! She would have seen Professor Henderson in his office. He always comes in about eight o'clock and works, sometimes to midnight. We thought she'd be able to prove to Detective Ramirez that Professor Henderson couldn't possibly have hurt Ms. Werner. He must have been in his office the whole time! We're going to find Eileen and ask her to check her book. Then we can show it to the detective."

They both jumped up to go.

"Wait a minute! You're going to find Eileen now?" Rosemary asked.

"We're sure she'll be in the greenhouse."

Rosemary held up a hand. "*If* she does have her notebook, either I or Mr. Oxley will take you down to the police station."

"Okay!" they called as they headed off, straight across the campus.

Rosemary lost no time in getting Kevin on the phone.

"You're kidding!" he said. "To think that neither of us nor the police thought about an alibi. It just goes to show—"

"Let's just hope Eileen was there that night, and that she did see Claus," Rosemary reminded him.

"Claus is still at the station. I waited there until five this morning, but then I went home to feed the animals. I never did see him or Ramirez again."

"What a hideous ordeal for Claus!" Rosemary half-muttered. "Not much fun for you either."

"Never mind. Look, I'll get in your car and meet those students at the greenhouse right now. I'd like the satisfaction of seeing them deliver the evidence to Ramirez myself."

"Okay. Keep me posted." Rosemary put down the receiver and decided not to go for a run after all. Instead, she made a quick change and headed for her office.

She was still thinking of Tara and Sootie when she sat down at her desk. She shook her head, smiled broadly, and thought how wonderful it would be if their initiative could spare Claus. And then she reminded herself that even if the danger to Claus was eliminated, there was still a threat of violence everywhere.

She reached across her desk for the finance committee reports Amy Standish had sent, determined to search once more for anything that might speak of another motive, another interest in Blanche Werner's death.

She had cleared away her notes on both the early church and on routine chaplaincy matters to make room for the stack of spreadsheets. She'd been working for several hours without interruption when a projectile landed under her nose. Her keys. Startled, she looked up to see Kevin standing in her doorway, his face wreathed in smiles.

"That's done it! Not even Ramirez could keep him any longer when there was both a witness *and* a written record to say that he was in his office until one a.m. the night Blanche was killed. Claus is getting his car right now, and he's going to run me up to my place for mine. And tonight, ma'am, I'm going to take you out to dinner for a celebration! No arguments." As she started to speak, he held up his hand. "There'll be enough to talk about then." He turned, still smiling broadly, and was gone.

Rosemary's next interruption was not nearly so welcome. Gertrude Bleeker pushed open the door without ceremony. She walked to the desk and peered over Rosemary's shoulder. "'Income statement, Second Quarter 1998,'" she read. "What do you think you're doing?" she asked abruptly. "Still combing through Sanderson's financial statements?"

Rosemary hastily closed her file around the spreadsheets before swiveling her chair around to take in her visitor's full gaze.

Gertrude looked down at her for a long moment, then turned abruptly and strode across the room to the bookcases opposite Rosemary's desk. She began to jab at the book spines one by one, sending them against the shelves, each with a sharp thud.

"It'll make a fascinating sermon," she said sarcastically and then whirled around to face Rosemary. As she did so, the light from the doorway caught her shoulders, and Rosemary was struck by her impressive frame and the athletic power that seemed always to be held in suspension in her person. This morning, however, that power seemed raw, as though it were about to fly away from the precarious control in which it was held.

"I'm just helping Peter Zukowski, Gertrude. He's gotten stuck on some fund balances." Rosemary was aware of the lie and aware, too, of possible danger in advertising too much that she was deeply involved in exploring the college's finances.

"Humph. Looks like meddling to me." Gertrude abruptly changed the subject. "You went out to watch the crew this week. What did you think of them?"

Rosemary spoke truthfully. "I thought they were breathtaking. I've never seen anything more beautiful than those shells flying in the early light. The power and precision of those rowers is astonishing."

"Exactly. And if you had an asset like that, what would you do with it?"

"I'd use it, of course. That crew will bring attention to the college that has to be valuable. But I suppose it's naive to think that it could counteract the damage all this murder coverage has done."

"Perhaps not." Gertrude had picked up a small chessman, an ivory bishop from a medieval set, a present from Warren Walters on his niece's ordination. She rolled it into the center of her palm and closed her hand around it, squeezing until her knuckles turned white. "But it would help with recruitment. And most important, it would guarantee that we live up to our commitments to these women!"

"Is there really so much money involved in intercollegiate rowing? Surely there would be some individual donors ready to help. Have you spoken to Nat?" Rosemary tried to appeal to reason.

"Dammit!" Gertrude flung the little bishop down on Rosemary's desk and it shattered into three pieces. Rosemary rose in a fury, only to see Gertrude even more agitated. She had turned and walked back to the bookshelf with her shoulders drawn up, weight tipped forward onto the balls of her feet. "I *did* speak to Nat Eames. I've spoken to him several times—and I've just come from his office trying to see him again. Of course I'll pay for the crew."

"And he's refused? *Why?*" Rosemary held hard on her own temper and forced herself to concentrate on Gertrude's words.

"Because, he says, it's the *principle*. He's cutting out all travel to national and regional championships this year, and he's not going to make an exception for crew."

"And he thinks that will balance the budget?" Rosemary couldn't understand it.

"No. He thinks it will make a great show of his firmness in balancing the budget." Gertrude's tone rose. "And do you want to know *why* he has to balance the budget? So publicly? " she almost shouted at Rosemary.

"It's self-evident, I suppose." Rosemary was on her feet,

facing her visitor. "Fiscal responsibility is his job as chief executive."

"Don't be a *child,* Dean Stubbs! You know colleges like this one have reserves. And they have donors like me who help on the important things. Nat could easily flow some other monies to this line if he weren't so dead set on making a record for himself."

"What do you mean?"

Gertrude turned again. Her full agitation showed as she clenched and reclenched her fists, her mouth working strangely. "Do you want to know why Nathan Eames is so bloody fixated on 'fiscal responsibility'?" She didn't wait for an answer. "Because Nathan Eames thinks he has a chance to be the next president of Yale University, that's why!"

Rosemary looked at her in amazement. Slowly, she recalled the odd snippet of conversation she'd had with Eames's wife, Patti, at the dinner party. Just when he has a big chance, Patti had said. "Of course," she whispered to herself.

"You bet!" Gertrude was walking even faster now. "Melanie Storey told me this morning that she'd had a call from one of the members of the Yale Corporation. All very hush-hush, you know. Wanting to know all about Nat. Wanting to know particularly how he handles budgets and whether he could eliminate a deficit!"

"I don't know what to say."

"Well, I could supply some words for you!"

"Are you sure that Melanie said it was Nat?"

"Of course I am! I haven't lost my marbles yet! Nat is a finalist for the Yale job. And he's kept his ambitions from everyone at Sanderson!"

Rosemary spoke slowly. "The other night, after the dinner at the president's house, Mrs. Eames found me in the dining room and blurted out something about this being Nat's 'big chance' now."

Gertrude was triumphant. "You see! What did *she* say about it?"

"Nothing. He came into the room just at that moment and was very angry to find us talking together."

"Oh, he was, was he? So Nat doesn't want anybody to know about Yale?"

"Apparently not."

"Don't you see what this means, Rosemary?"

"Well, I can see his ambition, and I think I can understand it," Rosemary answered neutrally.

"No, that's not what I mean! It means that Blanche had *nothing to do with* the budget cuts this summer!" Gertrude's voice was rising again. "She was acting under Nat's orders. Working to get him his new job without even knowing it! Suffering the anger from me and Chip, and even Phil Mason! Absorbing everything . . . as she always did. It wasn't her fault at all."

"What you say may be true, Gertrude. But it won't change anything now. Except maybe the way people remember Blanche. You can help remedy that—but not if you wear yourself out this way."

Gertrude wheeled on her. "We are not dealing with

predestination here! There are some things I certainly *can* change." She headed for the door.

"Wait a minute, Gertrude!"

Gertrude paused at the doorway and then turned back to Rosemary.

"What are you going to do?"

"I'm going to confront Nat with the facts about his own ambitions. And tell him that I'll expose his specious budget-cutting before the Yale Corporation has made up its mind! They'll have me to deal with before they make Nathan Eames president of Yale University." She turned to go.

"Gertrude." Rosemary went to the door, catching her by the arm. "Don't do this. There's enough trouble already."

"Don't be ridiculous. Nat wants to be a hero among the fiscal conservatives and do it under klieg lights. Well, I'm just going to be sure he pays for his laurels." With that she turned and was off.

Rosemary stood looking after her until she slammed the outside door, then walked heavily back to her desk. She reached for the telephone and dialed the police station. The operator put her through to Detective Ramirez. When he answered, she wondered for a moment why she had called.

"Detective, I'm sorry to have bothered you, but—"

"Not at all," his precise voice cut in. "I should have called you myself to tell you that your friend Mr. Henderson has been released on the strength of the student's testimony."

"Yes. I've heard. And I am glad. I'm sure that was a painful episode for you as well as for him."

"You are good to say so," he responded.

"But I called for a different reason. Gertrude Bleeker has just left my office. She's on her way to confront President Eames and accuse him of using Blanche Werner to further his own interests." She paused. "Gertrude was very upset. In fact, she was so irrational I thought you ought to be informed, though I don't know which one might need protection."

"Don't worry, I'll protect them both. And thank you for calling."

Before she put back the receiver she dialed Amy's number.

"Amy, it's Rosemary. You know, don't you, that the police have released Claus? It looks as though he's cleared of any suspicion about Blanche's death."

"Yes, I did. He called this morning. But Claus is still worried that they might arrest him anytime for Phil Mason's murder."

"That's what I've called about. I've been going over the committee materials you sent to see if there's any other possible motive, a purely financial one, that would clearly eliminate Claus. But I can't see a thing from these documents. Could you possibly have those files that Phil Mason was working on downloaded into my computer?"

"It can be done, Rosemary, but are you sure that you want it done? Suppose there's something in them that led to Phil's death?" Amy's voice was worried.

"Suppose there is? Somebody has to find it."

"But the police have already taken a copy of everything."

"The police may be looking for only one thing. I'm not trying to build a case, only to see the facts. I'd really like to give it a try, Amy."

"All right, Rosemary. I'll call Kurt Young, head of our computer services, and ask him to transfer them himself. And not to let anyone else in the college know that he's done it. Kurt is the closest thing to an apolitical human I've ever seen. If anyone on this campus is absolutely above suspicion, I should think it would be Kurt. But don't you go telling anybody you have those files."

Within an hour, Rosemary was able to call up the files Kurt Young had entered into her computer. She sat chewing on a stray lock of hair, frowning at the cash flow records in front of her. As she worked, she docketed the average interest recorded for each weekly period against the rates published by the bank for the same dates.

She thought aloud softly. "Somewhere there's a gap. I keep losing about twenty basis points, sometimes fifty . . . but I don't see how. All the money transferred by the college seems to get to the bank all right, and clearly nothing stood in the way of the college pulling all that money to meet bills . . . and Sanderson seems regularly to have swept its cash account, especially on long weekends. It would put the money into a mutual fund then for better rates. So they were on top of cash management.

"Still, I wonder why the interest the college received on those funds at the bank seems to have been lower than one would expect. It would be odd for the bank to give Sanderson an unfavorable rate. I would have thought the college would have been one of its best customers. If anything, it should have received a higher rate."

She switched off the computer. I just can't see what's wrong, she thought.

She had no idea how long she sat there, making no progress. She was brought sharply back by the ringing phone.

"Oh, Corolla, hello." She reassured the caller, "No, this is an okay time to talk. I was just distracted by matters here, that's all." In recent days Rosemary had dreaded talking to old friends because the preliminary exchanges about life at the college always seemed to take a macabre turn. The national media had made Sanderson a household name, and there was no avoiding at least a cursory discussion of the murders. But her Yale classmate Corolla Winnants didn't even pause at the bait. She was distracted in her own turn by a crisis on a purely academic scale.

"Look, Rosemary, I'm stuck. You know the big symposium we're having this week in Washington at the National Cathedral on women in the clergy? I'm in charge of the Thursday schedule. And Lucinda Walker, who's supposed to comment on the main paper, just called me. She can't come. I've used everybody else I know somewhere on the program. Do you think you could possibly come down and do a fifteen-minute comment? I could fax you the paper."

"Oh, Corolla, I don't know how I can—"

"Don't say no, Rosemary! You don't have to do any more preparation than you could do on the plane. And if you stay over, I'll take you out to dinner on Friday night. Just the two of us, to somewhere where they'll never suspect we're clergy! And we can talk. It's been ages since I've seen you and—" She stopped to catch her breath.

"Okay, Corolla. Hold it!"

"Does that mean you'll come?"

"No, it just means that—well, why not?" Rosemary paused, wondering why, indeed, not. Wouldn't some distance put the Sanderson problems in perspective and give her a chance to think about those wretched financial statements from another angle? "I'll have to cancel a dinner here tonight if I'm going to get an early flight from Hartford tomorrow. You're sure I can be back here on Friday?"

"Sure I am. Look, Rosemary, I'd be so grateful—"

"I know, Corolla. I'm happy to do it. And besides, I have a sneaking suspicion you've just done me a favor. I need to get out of this place for twenty-four hours and think!"

23

The taxi ride through the morning traffic to the National Cathedral was unexpectedly restful. Rosemary was surprised by the relief she felt at escaping from the tensions and anxiety of Metford. The program for the day stretched before her luxuriously. A whole day devoted to women in the ministry, something she'd had precious little chance to reflect on during the last few weeks in Metford. Perhaps away from the campus she could work through her growing suspicions about Sanderson's finances and the growing dread she felt that Blanche must have known the origin of the problems. She would slip off for a good dinner somewhere where the noise level wasn't high, and if she couldn't think, at least she could enjoy some uninterrupted quiet.

The cathedral loomed solidly ahead as the taxi sped along the highway beside the Potomac, while the city's great monuments passed by across the river. Corolla, now on the cathedral staff, would have organized the day thoughtfully, no doubt, inviting women clergy from all denominations, and leaders of the Catholic movement for women's ordination. Rosemary thought irritably, I hope we don't have to listen to too much talk about the Great Goddess. It's an androgynous godhead we need, not an endless fuss about why so much of the creation has two biological sexes. Oh, well, I can always doze off.

Her mind sped back to the problem that kept intruding on the forefront of her consciousness. Sanderson's accounting procedures were meticulous in every respect. Blanche had known her stuff. The endowment performance was more or less as it should be, in the mid-to-high range of nonprofit investers. But, as Phil Mason had said, there should be income beyond that. Why had Blanche left the cash management with Commonwealth Bank? She *must* have been too savvy to accept that level of performance. It was a mystery. Mason had apparently cottoned on to it. And by boasting about it, could he have brought on his own death? Rosemary shivered suddenly in the warm sun-drenched taxi. If she found the answer, what might happen to her?

She came out of her reverie to find the cab driver gazing curiously at her, as they sat at the curb outside the cathedral.

The crowd inside carried Rosemary back to her divinity school days. They were all there—the celebrators, the thinkers, the healers, the mystics. Women draped in colorful scarves and hung with heavy pre-Columbian jewelry. Women in conservative gray who exuded a quiet inner force. Women with their hair pulled back in severe chignons, women with wildly flowing locks in every shade from red to silver, wearing prints that evoked tribal cultures. The collective energy positively crackled in the vast nave of the cathedral.

Rosemary dutifully took her badge and settled down to read the program. Good. There was a section on celebration and ritual as the basis of community; then her session on campus ministries; and the inevitable section on gender and language. The afternoon was to be devoted to Biblical studies and the history of primitive Christianity, finishing up with three women prominent in the ministry of their respective churches reflecting upon their experiences and offering practical advice.

The expected speakers made up a Who's Who of women concerned with female spirituality. Rosemary was so engrossed in running down the list of names that she jumped like a nervous yearling when Corolla Winnants touched her on the shoulder.

"Rosemary! How did you get by me? I've been watching for you to arrive! Are you all set to comment on that paper for the session on campus ministry?"

"You bet! I got the fax, and I've given it what thought I could under the circumstances. You'll make some excuses for me, won't you, in the introductions?"

"Of course. And besides, you're new to the job."

"And what a job!"

"Oh! I forgot all about *Sanderson*! Well, you don't need to go into all that."

"Don't worry, I won't! And I won't take any questions on it, either." Suddenly Rosemary's face was caught up in a frown. "The press don't know I'm here, do they?"

Corolla laughed. "The press don't know any of us are here! Despite our best efforts to alert them. This is definitely not the year of women clergy! Old hat, I'm afraid." Corolla looked as though she might start a disquisition on the media and women's issues, but then a frantic hand from across the aisle summoned her.

Rosemary sank into the bliss of anonymity and prepared to concentrate on the program. The sub-dean of the cathedral, a lonely male figure in somber clerical black, began to call the conference to order, trying to appear jolly and, at the same time, apologetic for the history of misogyny in the church. Concluding from the expressions of the assembled crowd that he was not succeeding at either task, he quickly called on Corolla to take over and positively hurried away.

The session on ritual and community got off to a shaky start because the first speaker was too enraged by the history of women's exclusion from ritual roles to move on to the main point. The second speaker, a nun in a well-cut navy suit, was riveting. In summing up she made it clear that in its ritual life the Christian Church had been unable to exclude the female principle, which kept reappearing in the cult of the Virgin, the cult of great female saints, and in popular images of Jesus as mother. In fact, it was impossible to build coherent communities without recognizing both principles in worship, something that most male hierarchies in the past had always been obliged, despite themselves, to do. It was true that the figure of the Virgin, and the female saints, stood for profound symbols about human experience, even if expressed as sentimental male projections about idealized females. But the ordination of women and their role in Biblical exegesis would soon change that.

The buzz of conversation at the coffee break was lively. Rosemary and Corolla Winnants were enthusiastic, but the remainder of their small group by the coffee urns wanted to pigeonhole the last speaker. Was she essentialist? Where would she fit lesbian spirituality into her model of a community of ritual? Wasn't she giving in to patriarchy?

The next session was something of a comedown from such exalted themes. Rosemary, thinking of Tara and Leslie, her breakfast study group which was to start next week, and the violence stalking the Sanderson campus, found it hard to concentrate. All the talk of young adult psychology, modern norms for sexuality, and social responsibility seemed so far from her event-packed weeks at Sanderson. Her work was pastoral, to be sure, but the same forces of evil and redemption that threatened the rest of humanity seemed to be swirling around her young charges. She was too distracted to come up with some conventional boilerplate. When her turn came, she spoke from the heart.

"I think the work of a campus minister is not to surround the young with tolerant understanding for developmental crises. Certainly the chaplain shouldn't be too preoccupied with the sexual life of the students. Most seem to be able to understand all too well what is exploitive and immoral in human affairs. I think we have to open up what real spiritual concerns are to young people, who are pressured to be totally secular in their approach to life, and guide them in how to use their minds as well as their emotions to think about those spiritual concerns.

"I'm a little biased in my view of the job because there have been two deaths on my campus during the short time I've been there, and the students have faced squarely into the pain of their circumstances. They have been as 'adult' as any of us, and their spiritual concerns are quintessentially human."

As Rosemary sat down to stunned silence, she thought, Why did I say that? I just told Corolla that I wouldn't talk about the murders, and now I've opened myself up to all sorts of questions. Then, looking around her, she recollected herself. No, they won't press me, she thought. They really are my colleagues. There's none of that *curiositas* here that Bernard of Clairvaux talks about—the itch to pry or to chew information just for the savor of it. These women have imagination—they'll know what it's like.

She was interrupted in her own reflections by the chair of the session, who was calling on her to reply to a query that apparently had been raised about her presentation. Embarrassed, she turned to the questioner, reoriented herself, and entered a dialogue on the effects of early trauma on college-age women. When the session ended, she withdrew, surprisingly exhausted.

She found Corolla and explained, "I think I'm going to pull out early. It's a shame, I know. I'd like to hear the afternoon papers, but I just can't concentrate." She left the room and, coming out into the lobby, went downstairs to the phone. A quick call to the Sulgrave, the corresponding club to her own in New York, assured her of a room that she could use for the afternoon and overnight too, if she chose.

Rosemary hailed a cab and set out for the gracious old mansion just off Dupont Circle, with the wrought-iron canopy that always signaled a refuge to her, no matter how rushed her visit to the city. The doorman greeted her with half-remembered familiarity as she hurried into the severe but gracious entrance hall.

This is the only place in the world where peach walls could actually convey a sense of restraint, she thought, as the seconds became minutes while the formalities of being a guest were dealt with. She laughed with pleasure when the doors of the best third-floor room were thrown open. The big oval room made the most of its English chintzes in rose and pale gray. The garden magazines on the circular table seemed to guarantee an orderly world.

This is where I need to be, Rosemary told herself. I'll

take a short nap, and then review those cash flow statements once more . . . and maybe something will occur to me at dinner.

When she awoke it was nearly six o'clock, and she was ravenous. The financials can wait, she thought. She slipped back into the same silk-and-wool dress with the pleated skirt she'd worn during the day and doubled a strand of pearls at her neck to make it more formal. Then she brushed her hair straight back from her forehead and let it fall. A touch of lipstick and powder and she was ready to set off across Dupont Circle and up Massachusetts Avenue at a more energetic walk than she'd mustered for days. When the headwaiter ushered her to a small table by the wall in the Jockey Club's expansive dining room, she slipped in by its red checkered cloth with a sense of anticipation. A double Scotch was just what she needed to approach the menu, and soon she found herself in amiable conversation with the waiter, who'd been a fixture there for years.

"I can't believe you're still serving soft-shell crabs in a month that has an *r* in its name! Doesn't everybody know that crabs are off season in those months? They've got to be frozen!"

"Well, to speak of things that are out of season, you might want to try the asparagus vinaigrette. It is excellent before the chateaubriand."

Rosemary assented and set aside her Scotch, which she knew she'd been gulping too hungrily. Now, let me just go over Sanderson's financial records in my mind, she thought. The endowment returns are fine. The monthly reports at the college tally with the investment manager's. Every item in the general ledger is as it should be. All the backup material is there. The only thing at all out of the ordinary is that the cash management is poor. The Commonwealth Bank always seems to be paying Sanderson less than the best going rate. Twenty basis points here, fifty there can add up to a lot over time. But there's no overt reason to query that. What I can't understand is why such a savvy woman as Blanche Werner accepted such shabby treatment from the bank. I'd expect her to have given them hell for such lousy returns.

Rosemary leaned back against her chair, her eyes half-closed in concentration. If I wanted to siphon money off a college endowment and still leave the books squeaky-clean, how would I do it?

The waiter hovered anxiously.

"Is there anything the matter with the asparagus, madame?"

She looked guiltily at her food, which just a few moments before she'd been so anxious to get. "Oh, I didn't even realize you had served it!" She picked up her fork in deference to the waiter's concern, and then, her concentration broken, glanced idly around the room.

Her eye was caught by the headwaiter's fussing over a striking blond woman and her escort, whose hand at the small of her back seemed more than just attentive. Although their backs were to her, she was sure they were familiar. As they slid into a corner banquette in the farthest section of the room, Rosemary froze. It was Nat Eames, bending over the woman she'd met at his party honoring Richard Stuart, the major donor. The woman from Commonwealth Bank—Louise Middleman. A natural vivacity, heightened by an obvious intimacy with her escort and the room's soft light, seemed to shimmer from her—catching her diamond earrings and the diamond tremblant pin on her lapel.

With a start, Rosemary realized that she was staring at them. She shivered. I've got to get out of here and back to Sanderson. They mustn't see me, she thought frantically as she rose from her table and headed for the lobby.

24

The cab drew up in front of the new U.S. Airways terminal at National Airport and Rosemary climbed out, awkward in her anxiety to catch the plane. She took care of the cabbie, grabbed her briefcase, and slipped through one of the glass doors as another passenger stepped out. Once inside, she checked her watch and made straight for the pay phone.

"Detective Ramirez? It's Rosemary Stubbs. I'm at the airport in Washington and heading home, but I have an idea that I'd like to work on right away. . . . Yes. . . . I have the financial schedules Phil Mason was studying, but I wonder if your people have anything more. Especially with regard to the cash management? Kurt Young at the college has my access codes. Do you think you could have the information downloaded to my computer this evening? I should be back by eleven. Have you been in touch with the bank auditors from Commonwealth, Sanderson's bank? I know it's unusual, but if I could see this year's records from the bank and, best of all, the records for the last three years, I think I can find what Phil Mason must have suspected. If you have any printed records, could you just leave them in my office? You have a key, right?"

She paused, breathless, and listened to his response. "No. I can't say anymore—I'm running for my plane now. Thanks." She hung up the phone and looked at her watch.

She took the escalator down to the gate, jumping two steps at a time, and cut, unseeing, past the purveyors of chocolate chip cookies, hot dogs, and clam chowder that dotted the inside wall of the huge, open port-of-call. At an outright run, she formed up to be the last straggler in line as ground personnel prepared to close the gate on the last flight to Hartford. Her sigh of relief was only partly for the plane ride assured; there was also the reassurance of knowing that there could be no pursuit on another jet that night. Did they see me? She worried. Am I crazy to read anything into that conjunction? Fear and self-doubt teetered in her mind as the flight droned its way northward.

When she arrived at Hartford, she spun her car out of the airport and headed north, falling only half-consciously into ancient habits of speeding well past the limits and right against the edge of the unsafe. When once she looked down to see the speedometer, it read 85. She shrugged and thought that tonight, if stopped, at least she would have a story worth telling the police. But she reached Metford untouched by traffic patrol and slowed to speeds acceptable to habitation. She passed by her house and drew up outside the chapel addition.

Once in her office, the door carefully locked behind her, she found that Ramirez had been as good as his word. She brought up on her computer screen the files with the bank's records detailing Sanderson's daily deposit and money market accounts, including one with the paperwork for the college's three-month CDs purchased since January 1. She printed them out as fast as she could and started to work on them, checking them off, as she knew others had done, against Blanche Werner's records. Nothing notable. Then she opened the file with records of the overnight depository accounts and was struck anew by the large amounts of cash that had come into these accounts, been parked overnight or perhaps for two or three days, and then moved on to money market accounts or other short-term investments. Painstakingly, she checked each day's subsequent interest, which was credited always at the announced bank interest but then shown to Sanderson at a slight difference. Frantically Rosemary searched the bank records to see where those monetary trace elements might have gone.

"Detective Ramirez!" Rosemary's voice was taut with excitement as she reached him by phone. "I think I've got it. In fact, I'm sure I have. I want to show what I've found to the people you've had working on the financials and run through it with all of you, to get your take. Are they still at your office? Can you get them there? . . . I know it's late, but

. . . I'll just pack these disks up and be right down to the station. . . . I'm leaving right now. I'll be there in fifteen minutes."

Rosemary folded the college spreadsheets and slipped them into her shoulder bag. Then she unloaded the disk currently in her computer and added it to her bag. It was only then that she glanced up at the clock tucked into the top shelf of the bookcase opposite.

Three in the morning, she noted with surprise. I had no idea it was so late. The poor guys from the DA's office will hate me. Well, I think we're done now.

She stepped out with determination, checking briefly on both sides to see if the hallway was empty. Then she hurried to the car at the curb right in front of the chapel. Her keys were already in hand as she slipped behind the wheel, and she was on the empty street in an instant.

Didn't realize how nervous I was till I got on the road, she thought ruefully to herself. Now it's just a straight shot down the— What the—!

There was a crash, and her car leaped forward crazily. She flew forward against the wheel and was knocked breathless with pain.

Crack! The car was hit again, and this time instead of lurching forward, it tilted on impact and skidded to the left. Rosemary clutched the wheel in an instinctive effort to keep the vehicle upright, and found herself turning onto a side street.

What is this? Wait. This is South Street, the boundary of the college. I've got to get back. This isn't the way to—

Then she looked up in her rearview mirror and saw coming around the corner behind her a car with no head-lights on, heading straight for her.

"Oh my God!" Rosemary cried. She leaned over the wheel and floored the accelerator. Her car sped on so that the impact of the other vehicle behind simply grazed it, making it shimmy under her as she fought to keep it on the road. "How am I going to—" She felt the bumper of the car behind thump repeatedly against her own. He's trying to lock them, she thought. We'll flip over. I've got to brake.

She wrenched the wheel to the right, pulling the car vio-lently to the side of the road. Her assailant shot past and braked suddenly, but even as she craned her neck, Rose-mary could not make out the person inside. A gully that opened past the right shoulder of the road forced her to forget her attacker for a moment and throw her full weight to the left. As her car careered across the road it was struck broadside again and spun out of control.

The moment of spin seemed to go on forever to Rose-mary, as every green light on the dash leered at her while the roadway and then the trees joined a surreal dance past her windshield. The descent off the road to the left had all the quality of a roller-coaster ride, and it was with a shock of unreality that she felt the car shudder to a halt in the midst of a dense roadside thicket.

The car had tipped heavily to the passenger side. Rose-mary turned to gain leverage on the driver's side door han-dle and then fell back against the seat.

"I can't, I can't do it," she panted, as she reached uselessly for the fire in her rib cage. She lay back, still, and then she heard the roar and scrape of the other car, turning in the roadway above. Once more she threw herself up and outward against the door. It yielded, and she scrambled out, plunging straight into the bushes. For a moment she thrashed wildly forward, mad to escape the figure who she knew would be right behind her. Then she stopped. Her thoughts raced. It's the South Road. That means the lake is straight ahead, through these woods, and the last place I want to be found is by the lake. If I can circle back and run parallel to the road, isn't the security office along this way? Not far past the woods.

She turned and made her way on a diagonal, back in the direction of the road, stumbling in the dark, heightening her own fear each time a branch snapped under her weight. She felt a surge of relief as the bushes thinned and a gentle slope brought her to a broad expanse of macadam. Oh, God, if it might just be the security office. No, it's something else. I've never been here before. But there's a light.

Rosemary stepped out on the blacktop, suddenly aware of the sulfur glow of the streetlights the college used in all its parking lots. In a panic she realized that in the light she was a ready target, and she broke into a run. She made for the only door she could make out. It was a garage roller of unusual height. In hope of some wild long shot she ran her hands along the frame, searching for an electric switch that might open it. As her hand found the button she heard a footstep reach the tarmac from the woods.

Rosemary plunged inside, too panicked to look for another switch that might close the door. In the dim light she looked around, hoping to find protective cover or some sign of a worker who might offer safety. There was no one. Her feet sounded on the concrete flooring of a vast area, its gray walls and floor offering not even a corner to hide behind. Ahead a pair of bent pipes seemed to promise an economy stairway, and she ran blindly for them.

She found herself on a circular stair that led down into a great sunken theater, the stair opening onto a concrete catwalk around four huge cylinders that rested on a level four feet below. The heat was intense, and a living, roaring noise overwhelmed her.

"It's the boiler room for the whole college!" Rosemary gasped. She ran forward along the catwalk, but there was no way out except up the stairs she'd come down. She leaned over the railing and peered between the furnaces, then drew back in horror when she saw that they burned with their doors open, the great flames jumping red and black against the circular walls that held them.

Rosemary heard an even-paced tread descending the stairs behind her. She whipped around and came face to face with Nathan Eames. He said nothing, his expression intent, eyes blazing at her. She found herself backing up as he approached, but then, hesitating, she stood her ground, knowing there was no retreat. He was only yards away when she crouched and in a wild gamble grabbed the bars of the catwalk and swung over the side. Singed by the heat that rose all around her, she hit the floor and ran down the narrow aisle between two of the great furnaces. She could hear nothing but the fire, but over her shoulder she saw the form of Eames as he jumped down after her.

She turned the corner at the end of the furnace and started up the next aisle, only to see him already partway down, facing her. Without any sense of herself, she let out a shuddering scream and turned to run again.

"Rosemary!"

The cry reached her even over the fire, and she thought she heard the sound of running feet on the catwalk above. She turned to see Detective Ramirez plunge off the concrete margin and leap for Eames's back.

He caught the larger man off balance, and the two of them fell to the floor. Ramirez seized Eames by the hair and swung for his face with his fist. But Eames rolled away, knocking Ramirez down close to the furnace. Rosemary cried out in terror as she saw the open furnace door just above Ramirez's head.

He pulled himself up on all fours as Eames jumped for him, then with a rising thrust of shoulders and head, he caught Eames before he landed. Eames's body was knocked against the furnace, striking it headfirst. Rosemary watched in horror as it fell limp and then rolled into the flames.

25

Rosemary leaned against the wall outside the building, shaking uncontrollably. Even her efforts to hug herself, arms tight around her chest, didn't help. The crowd of medics and police moved by her, a trancelike procession of figures. Inside she saw Detective Ramirez moving among them. As they gradually departed, Ramirez came out to her and leaned against the wall beside her.

"You're still determined not to see a doctor?"

"He never touched me," she responded.

With an effort, he straightened up to his usual erect bearing and held out a hand. "Come, then. Let me take you home."

"No!" Her answer came out close to a sob. "I can't just go home as if nothing's happened. He was going to kill me. And now he's dead. I can't take it in. I need to walk for a while."

"Then I'll walk with you." He touched her elbow as though nothing could be more normal than a stroll, and, still shaking, she settled her stride to his. They began the climb up the hill.

As they walked past the police wreckers busy removing her car, she gazed at it. "How did you know where to find me?" she asked the detective in a low voice.

"I wanted to stop you from driving anywhere alone when you called. But you were in too much of a hurry. I was afraid someone would find a way to attack you, so I went directly to your office. Of course, you weren't there. I started searching the side streets. Fortunately, South Street was the first one I tried."

She stopped and turned to him. "Detective Ramirez, you saved my life. It seems so banal just to say 'thank you.'"

His smile wiped the lines of tiredness from his face, and she noticed absentmindedly the striking clear brown of his eyes. "I have a first name, you know. It is Raphael."

"Raphael!" she said, smiling in return. "*Raphael*. It did take an archangel tonight." She gave another involuntary shiver. "I've never believed in evil as something in itself, but tonight I saw it. Nat's face!"

He stopped and turned to her, his hands on her shoulders. "Yes. I saw it too. And Rosemary, life wouldn't have been worth living if I hadn't gotten to you in time."

"But Raphael, you did. And I'll never forget it."

They were both silent for a moment, and then he asked, "Can you tell me now why you called me?"

The first light of dawn was just beginning to dim the streetlights. Rosemary walked on for a few more paces. "I found a pattern of shortfalls in the interest the college was receiving on its cash deposits at Commonwealth Bank. Sanderson didn't have a fixed rate of return—it floated with overnight bank rates. But the monies it received didn't tally with the bank's own records of its daily rates. Blanche had downloaded those onto her own computer. She must have figured it out and gone to the president. His first misstep after her death was not to destroy those records. So Phil Mason found them, and then *I* found them.

"Then, in the bank's records that *you* got for me, I discovered another account listed. It caught my eye, because the deposits into it replicated exactly the missing income that should have been going into the Sanderson account. I guessed it had to be the vehicle for siphoning off a part of the interest—the overnight float—automatically each night. And there were occasional large withdrawals from it."

"And did you know it was Eames?"

Rosemary admitted, "I just had a hunch, that's all, when I called you from the airport. I'd flown to Washington at the last minute to help out a friend at a conference. And, again on an impulse, I stopped in at the Jockey Club for an early supper before heading back here. Nat came into the dining room with a very glamorous woman whom I'd met just a few days ago at a dinner at the president's house, Louise Middleman. She works for Commonwealth Bank, in charge of their computer systems. They were seated at a very intimate table for two. It was very clear that those two were much more than just friends. It dawned on me right there what might be going on. I ran out of there like a madwoman, hoping they hadn't seen me."

Ramirez listened attentively. "And that's when you knew it had to be him, working with her to divert the money?"

"Well, I didn't *know* rationally. I just had an overwhelming feeling that suddenly everything fit together. And then I panicked. I didn't want them to know that I'd seen them together. I caught what I thought was the last plane north to Hartford. I thought I was safe."

"Eames must have chartered a plane to fly back up here, and he could have flown into Keene," Ramirez interjected.

They walked on, mostly in silence, turning off Cullen Street through the campus and around the lake. As they were coming up toward the formal garden, shafts of sunlight caught the tallest Michaelmas daisies in a bright glow.

"You have a lot of work to do today," she said suddenly. "And so do I."

He nodded.

"I'd like to call on Patti Eames as soon as possible after you've seen her," Rosemary went on. "What will you tell her?"

"She's been informed of his death already. I will only tell her today that we are investigating his possible role in the other two deaths. That will be true."

"All right. And will that be your statement to the public? How much do they have to know about the way he died?"

"He fell into the furnace. That much will be public already."

"I guess it is," Rosemary said. "I think I just saw that ubiquitous white van from Channel 38 heading up Cullen Street now. We'd probably better begin our rounds, since the world's already started its own. I'll ask Amy's office to take messages for me if you need to reach me." She stopped walking and looked at the detective. "Raphael, I owe my life to you. And you've taught me a lot in the bargain."

"You're an apt pupil, Rosemary," he said, smiling as she turned toward home. Then he caught her hand. "An odd thing happens when you save someone's life. That someone becomes very important to you. . . ." He let go of her hand and was gone in the opposite direction before Rosemary could reply.

2 6

Rosemary could barely walk for fatigue by the time she made her way home late that afternoon. She grabbed the rail beside the front steps of her house and prepared for a welcome from an ebullient Fannie. She'd spent the day at her office dealing with an ever-increasing stream of students and faculty. After the news flashed around the campus the rumor mill had gone into high gear, until Amy called an all-campus meeting to share the barest facts about the president's death.

Melanie Storey, breathless from having made a rushed flight up from New York City, had announced that Amy had been appointed acting president and that Kevin would serve as acting dean. After the meeting broke up, Rosemary had spent a heartrending hour with a distraught Patti Eames, helping communicate the news to Eames's family and participating with very ambiguous feelings in the plans for Eames's funeral. She was enormously relieved that she had been able to arrange for the Episcopal bishop of Vermont to preside.

At three o'clock, Raphael had phoned to tell her Louise

Middleman was in custody and ready to be a cooperative witness, but somehow Rosemary hadn't been able to feel any triumph about the accuracy of her detective work. The time spent with Patti Eames had moved her from elation at still being alive to a deepening sense of tragedy.

Melanie and Amy were due at her house in a half hour to hear a full account of the previous night's events. Rosemary didn't want to talk about it anymore, and she hoped Raphael would be there to help with the unraveling of the whole awful story.

She went mechanically about preparations for their arrival, stopping occasionally to apologize to Fannie for a day of neglect. Mercifully the arrival of the furniture from her New York apartment meant that it was possible to sit on chairs in the living room, although they were set about at random as the movers had left them. As she was looking for teacups, she heard a sharp tap at the kitchen door. She opened it wide for Kevin and, behind him, Claus, his arms full of anemones, Michaelmas daisies, and deep purple barberry. He laid them in the sink and turned to face her.

"Rosemary, you've released me from hell. Not knowing who killed Blanche drove me mad. I owe you my heartfelt thanks."

"I've been thinking of Blanche all day, Claus," Rosemary said gently. "She loved this place, and she died for it. I asked her once if colleges that suffered fraud ought to survive. She said she knew they could be mended and productive again. Now we've got to keep faith with her and make sure Sanderson recovers."

A long moment passed before Claus spoke. "Blanche was right. She was bound and determined to bring you here." He paused. "She must have had some inkling of how much we'd need you."

Kevin saved them all from their emotions. "It looks like you're expecting someone, Rosemary. Can we help?"

"It's Amy and Melanie Storey. Why don't you stay? Raphael will come if he can get away, and he'll fill in the gaps of what we know about Blanche and Phil. And you certainly can help. Wash these teacups while I freshen up. And, please, after everyone goes, take Fannie for a run. I'm bushed."

By the time she came back downstairs they had arranged the furniture in the living room, located and washed her good tea things from New York, and set Claus's vibrant fall bouquet in front of the fireplace.

As Amy and Melanie came in the door, Kevin announced that he was in charge of tea. Rosemary flashed him a grateful smile and sank into a comfortable chair. A few minutes later, Raphael arrived, walking more slowly than usual. As he settled into a chair and accepted a cup of tea, it was clear, however, that his usual calm had returned. He shot a glance at Rosemary that carried an unspoken question: was she all right? Rosemary nodded back and sat up straighter.

Melanie brought them to their task. "I'm still in shock," she announced. "Why would Nat kill Blanche? What could make him do such a violent, terrible thing?"

Ramirez's voice was gentle but authoritative. "Yes, Mrs. Storey. He did kill her. She was on the verge of unmasking his long career of embezzlement, just at the point when he had the chance of major career advancement. She had stumbled on the evidence that someone was skimming off major sums from the earnings of the overnight float on Sanderson's cash at Commonwealth Bank. Once she had gotten that far, President Eames knew she would soon discern him. He couldn't stop her from discovering his plot.

"So he must have met her shortly after the Athletics Department members had left her office. Presumably he made a date to meet her somewhere on the campus, perhaps even near the new athletic building. When they were together, he must have attacked her very suddenly with a hypodermic filled with digitalis. There were no signs of a struggle. And when she was dead, he carried her body to the new pool and dropped it in."

Claus, who hadn't been able to sit through this recitation, turned now from pacing by the mantel. "Why? *Why?*" he insisted.

"Because Blanche had discovered evidence that part of the interest on funds deposited as overnight cash in the College's bank were systematically being siphoned off. She must have kept him posted on her investigations, and he had to silence her before she reported her findings to the trustees, who were due on campus the following day."

"Then Nat was an embezzler?" Claus alone seemed prepared to accept that conclusion.

"Yes. He had been stealing the college's money for two years," Raphael confirmed.

Melanie sat bolt upright to protest, her teacup rattling as she set it down. "That flies in the face of everything I knew about Nat! I've worked with him for years. He was brilliant. He didn't need to steal anything."

Ramirez tried to let her down gently. "I think Rosemary can answer that question better than I."

Rosemary took the cue. "He was having a passionate affair with that stunning young woman who works at Commonwealth Bank, Louise Middleman. Do you remember the diamonds she was wearing at Nat's dinner last week? She had expensive tastes. She was the kind of elegant woman Patti Eames never could be, and he'd fallen for her in a big way."

"But it seems so unlike Nat! He was always so fastidious, so perfectly fitted to every occasion. . . . Somehow I can't think of him losing his head so badly that he'd steal to keep his mistress in the lap of luxury."

Amy shook her head. "I can, Melanie. He and Patti Eames had been in different worlds, socially and intellectually, for years. You know how often that happens when couples marry in graduate school, as they did. Nat was always so very disciplined. He never let himself show feelings that weren't perfectly appropriate to the setting—and the audience. I imagine that if anyone, or anything, ever got under that carapace of control, he would have no resources left at all for self-restraint. And Louise Middleman did."

"Rosemary," Kevin put in, "how did you spot their affair? I must have seen them together a dozen times, and I never noticed anything."

"It was pure accident, Kevin, although I had noticed something of the effect she had on him—and other men—

at his dinner for Richard Stuart. After that, well—do you remember I was supposed to have dinner with you . . . was it just last night, or the night before?"

"I certainly do!"

"Well, you know I went to Washington to help Corolla Winnants with her conference instead." She looked over at him. "I saw them together in town; it was . . . only too clear."

"So it was a case of prima facie evidence?" Kevin gave her a wry look.

"Well, I knew by that time that someone was skimming off some of Sanderson's earnings on its overnight cash, and suddenly there was Nat with Louise, who was in charge of the information systems governing depository accounts at Commonwealth. She had the means to do it for Nat."

"So that put it all together for you?" Kevin pressed her.

"It just told me where to look. I caught the last plane home, and I called Raphael from the airport to ask if he'd share with me the bank records that the DA's men had been reviewing. In them, I found a series of entries for an anonymous account that tallied exactly with the daily shortfalls in Sanderson's cash return."

"So Middleman set up the account. Who drew out of it?" Kevin asked, turning to Ramirez."

"President Eames made the withdrawals, by wire, to an account he had offshore," Ramirez responded.

"What about Middleman? Has she admitted her part?"

"Fully," Ramirez responded. "When she realized the scheme had been penetrated and the president was dead, she couldn't tell us about it quickly enough. She and her lawyers have a plea bargain in mind."

Melanie was still puzzled. "If the real problem was embezzlement, what was all this ruckus about balancing the budget at the expense of so many of the college's programs? I could understand if Gertrude had wrung the necks of both Blanche and Phil. But not Nat. What did he gain from that but trouble?"

Rosemary took a deep breath before explaining the rest of the puzzle. "He had a lot to gain. Remember telling Gertrude about your call from the Yale search committee? Well, Gertrude confronted me with it, and she was threatening to expose Nat's intentions to the trustees. He was running hard for that office. It would have paid a great deal more than Sanderson—in salary and in prestige. He could just leave Sanderson behind and no one would have been the wiser. And it might have been a career move to put him in a league that would persuade Louise to marry him. But he was convinced that to get the Yale presidency, he would have to establish that he had been a tough financial manager here at Sanderson, one who could stand up to faculty and to staff as well as students."

Rosemary paused and continued more slowly, "Of course, what he really did was to intensify the pressure on Blanche so that she began to scrutinize every detail of Sanderson's finances."

"And Phil?" asked Amy. "Did he just stumble on an unlucky discovery in those reams of financial records?"

"We will never really know," Raphael answered. "We can only surmise that Professor Mason must have had some suspicions that were close to the mark and that he took them to the president."

"How did Phil die?" Amy's sadness was written over her face.

"He was struck from behind on the left side of the head with such force that the blow broke his neck. He was dead before his body was thrown in the river," the detective said.

"How did Nat think he could get away with it?" Claus paced between the window and the fireplace.

"By framing you, Professor Henderson!" Ramirez responded grimly.

"Yes, I know. But that seems so childish! You police would have been sure to see through it eventually."

"You flatter me, Professor! If it hadn't been for the students and their testimony about your whereabouts, I might have been tempted to call this case closed." His voice was solemn. "We're not infallible, you know."

Claus persisted. "But the evidence was so clearly trumped up. The digitalis used and then left at the front of the cupboard. Blanche's things in my car—I never lock my car; anyone could have put them there at any time. . . ."

"But Nat was being very clever, Claus, about suggesting some private entanglement in Blanche's life and in exaggerating the contretemps between you and Phil. He had several of us on the board fairly convinced that you had a double motive. It was very dangerous for you," Melanie pointed out.

"I am afraid she is right, Professor Henderson," the detective agreed in a soft voice, almost to himself. "Your own life was at risk, and Rosemary nearly lost hers just a few hours ago." The shrill persistent sound of his cell phone broke the mood. The detective answered it, listened briefly, shut it off, and stood up to go. "What broke the chain was Rosemary, but she was very nearly the next victim. She and you are all part of that unspoken alliance that hauls society back onto a civilized path when it spins out of control." His energy had returned. He smiled at them all as he moved toward the door.

Rosemary walked out with him while a buzz of conversation erupted behind them. "When will you want a statement from me?" she asked.

"Tomorrow morning will be time enough. Rest well tonight." He held both her hands a second and seemed about to speak, but his cell phone sounded again and he was gone.

"Rosemary!" Kevin called from the hallway behind her. "It was Nat who attacked you in your office that night, wasn't it?"

"Yes, it must have been," she answered slowly, her mind on Eames's face as he had closed in on her in the steam plant.

"And it was my fault!" Amy broke in as Kevin and Rosemary came back into the living room. "I called Nat the morning after you came to my office to go through the budget. And I told him about your suggestion that we look into our cash management. That the figures didn't seem to make sense. My God, Rosemary. You *could* have been killed."

"Yes," Rosemary agreed, her concentration slipping away, her hands beginning to shake.

Kevin was beside her at once, holding her hands, ordering Amy to fetch her a stiff drink of Scotch from the kitchen.

Rosemary took a large gulp, but it didn't help. She felt old and empty with the picture of a weeping Patti Eames in her mind. She covered her face with her hands, and then it was Nat's face that she saw again.

The room was very still, except for the quiet sounds Kevin made as he held Rosemary and gently stroked her hair, while she gradually became calmer.

Melanie and Amy were the first to stir and then depart, heading for dinner at the Metford Inn and a session of planning for what remained of the semester. Claus gave Rosemary a hug and left with a wave at Kevin and a pat for Fannie, whose pacings before the front door and excited whimpers announced her expectation of a run.

Kevin got Fannie's message. "I'll take her out, Rosemary. We won't be long. And don't move till we get back."

Rosemary woke a half hour later to find Kevin perched on the arm of the chair she'd dozed in, a satisfied Fannie at her feet. I'm glad to be alive, she thought. It *is* a great gift. I mustn't waste it. She smiled up at Kevin.

He smiled back. "I'm going to stay here tonight, Rosemary. Fannie will need a run in the morning. And you— you need someone to remind you that it's good to be alive—for one night at least."